BEDLAM ACADEMY

FAE ACADEMIA

BOOK ONE

KATHY HAAN

This is a work of fiction. Names, characters, places, and incidents either are the product of the author's imagination or are used fictitiously. Any resemblance to actual persons, living or dead, events, or locales is entirely coincidental.

Copyright © 2022 by Kathy Haan

All rights reserved.

No part of this book may be reproduced in any form or by any electronic or mechanical means, including information storage and retrieval systems, without written permission from the author, except for the use of brief quotations in a book review. For more information, email kathy@idyllicpursuit.com.

ISBN 979-8-9855077-8-2 (eBook)

ISBN 979-8-9855077-6-8 (paperback)

ISBN 978-1-960256-17-1 (hardback)

First edition December 2022

Book cover design, artwork, and map by Leo Burk and Kathy Haan

Edited by Fervent Ink

Published by Thousand Lives Press

*To those Shell Rock guys who helped mend my broken heart one fine summer.
I'm sure my readers thank you immensely.*

INTRODUCTION

Bedlam Academy is the first book in the Fae Academia series. It is a spin-off of the **Bedlam Moon Trilogy**. You don't have to read the first trilogy to understand this book, but you might appreciate some of the backstory. The first trilogy follows Lana and her paramours, whereas Fae Academia follows their children at a magical university. More members of Rose's group of lovers join in future books in this series.

You can find a list of triggers at kathyhaan.com/triggers.

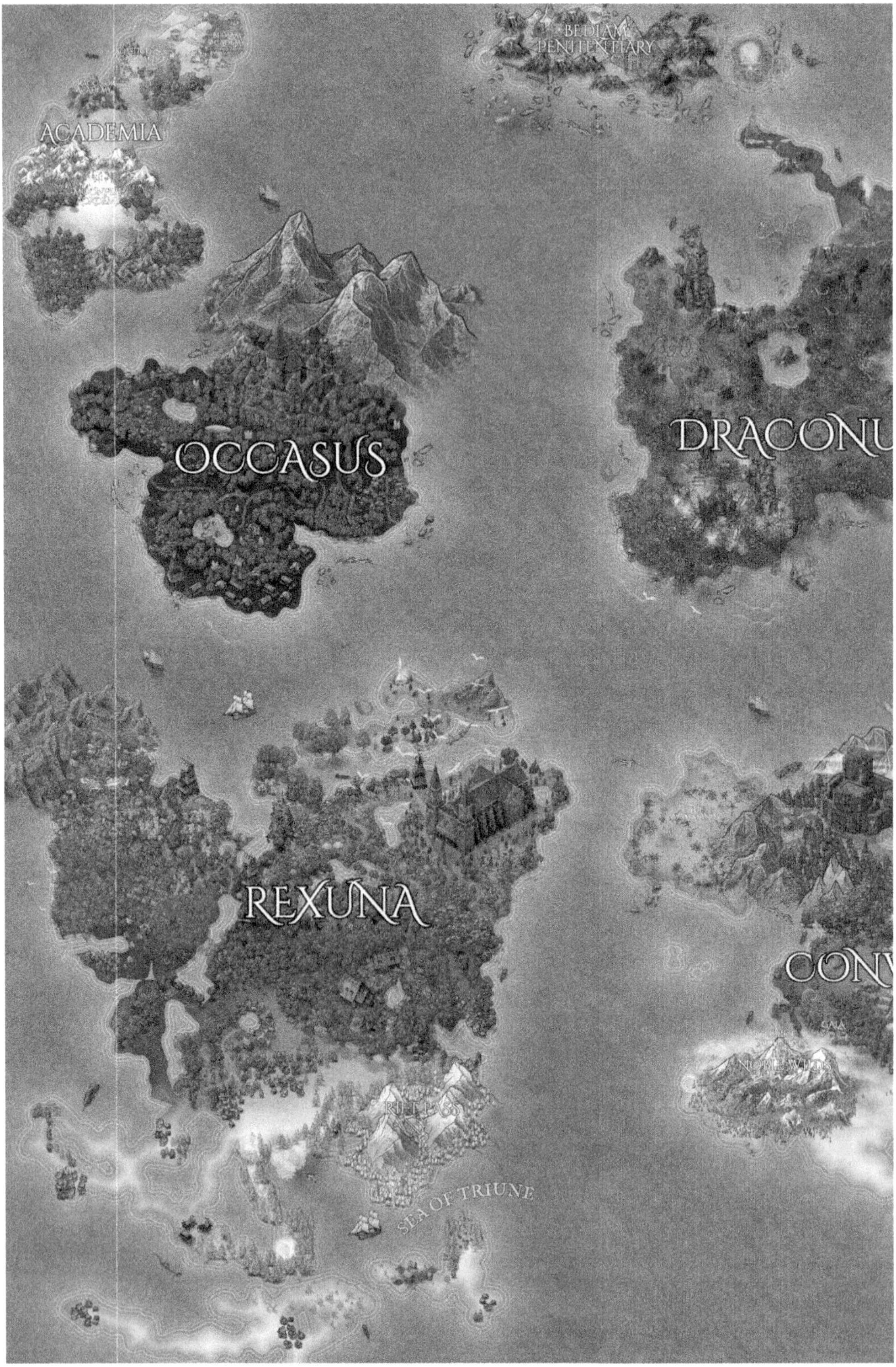
BEDLAM PENITENTIARY
ACADEMIA
OCCASUS
DRACONU
REXUNA
CONV
SEA OF TRIUNE

LUPORIA
UM
TRISTIQUE ISLANDS
SUNDAHLIA
PARALLEL ABYSS
TRULAN ISLES
VECTUS
N
W
E
S
BEDLAM

PROLOGUE

ROSE

In the depths of the forest, high atop a sun-drenched mountain, time spins out of control as two hearts collide. Or at least, that's what it feels like as Mekhi and I sit in the warm August sun, desperate to slow it down.

My family took Mekhi in a year ago, and we've since grown closer by the day. But now these little moments together are slipping away, like sands through an hourglass. When our carefree childhood gives way to adulthood, can this—whatever it is between us—survive the transition?

We talk about everything and nothing, always coming back to that single question: what will happen to us once college starts? We don't have an answer, but I feel like something's shifted in our relationship—something neither of us is quite ready to let go of.

The grass tickles my bare feet and I lean back, allowing his arm to slip around my shoulders. Tucked in his embrace, I try to memorize everything: the smell of his scent, the way our hearts seem to sync when near, and the feel of his callouses against my smooth, fae hands. He'd wanted to heal them, along with the scar across his chest, and as a witch, he could. But I like the reminder of our differences; how opposites can come together so perfectly. Like the dimple that only appears on his right cheek, so at odds with the other side, but as a whole, he wouldn't be the same without it.

Having spent the summer exercising with Bennett—my twin brother—and me, Mekhi has grown far from the scrawny street kid we'd met at the market a year ago. He's now a confident, well-built guy. His hazel eyes have a new kind of strength, as though they'd seen more than his years should've allowed. He hasn't forgotten his past, though; he still wears the same puka shell necklace he had when we first met him.

My fingers trail over the strand of coarse shells, and his throat bobs as he swallows. My acute fae hearing picks up an uptick in his heart rate, and I raise my eyes to meet his gaze. Time seems to stand still; all of existence beyond the two of us fades away as he takes my chin in his hand and draws me in until our lips meet.

My eyes close, and I lean into it. The kiss is gentle, sweet, and everything I expected my first to be, though my heart threatens to leap out of my chest. Just a kiss, but it tastes like everything. It's a promise of something more—something that can exist beyond college. We linger, neither one of us wanting to end it, but when the sound of a bird cawing overhead breaks our trance, Mekhi pulls away, a half-smile on his lips as he takes in the blue glow of my skin. My cheeks heat, having been caught. Luna fae only glow when in pain, healing someone, under the moon, or when aroused.

"I can't believe I wasted the entire summer being too chicken to do that." His lopsided grin undoes me. His lips are full and perfect, and I long to trace them with my finger.

"Neither can I, though my dads might've had something to do with it." While they love Mekhi like a son, there's a reason they put him in a room on the opposite end of the house from mine. They're protective of me.

My thumb grazes the stubble on his jaw.

"No regrets, though, yeah?" he asks softly, his voice a rumble in his chest, and his rich tone coaxing me closer, encouraging me to meet his kiss.

I can't help but smile. "No regrets."

He leans in close, his hair falling forward. Soft brown locks frame his handsome face, and his eyes are a deep, warm hazel. Flecks of emerald, gold, and umber glitter in his irises, as though the stars wanted to put on a show, plucked them from the sky, and sealed them in his gaze. "I don't want to let you go," he whispers against my lips.

"So don't."

Mekhi shakes his head, leaning back. "You don't understand. You and I, we can make this work. I don't want to leave without you being mine."

"What are you saying?"

"Be my girlfriend, Rose."

I pull away, my heart pounding and dizzy from the moment. "Mekhi, I—"

"Think about it." He cuts me off, and his expression changes from hope to understanding. He takes my hands in his, squeezing them gently. "I know you need time to explore your options and decide what you want. But you need to know you're the only one I want to be with."

My vocal cords fail to respond, so I nod, my eyes on his. His fingers are tender as they touch my neck and gently sweep the loose strand of hair away from my face, tucking it behind my ear. His touch sends a shiver down my spine, and my heart soars at his words, but a part of me still pictures the miles that will come between us. I reach up to cup his face in my hands, feeling his warmth against my palms as his gaze intensifies. I take a deep breath, then let it out slowly before speaking.

"It's not just the distance I'm worried about. What if they come for you, too, just because you're my boyfriend?" The thought paralyzes me with fear and the only thing grounding me is the sweet scent of his cologne mixed with the earthy smell of the grass beneath me.

"They'd come for me just by my proximity to your family. I'm no more at risk as your boyfriend than I've been sleeping under your family's roof the last year." He cups my face. "You think a little thing like a severed head on castle steps *thousands* of miles away will scare me? They don't even know where we live, Rose."

True. All the letters and boxes come to our family via courier with no return address, all delivered to the main castle on Convectus, where we only stay when entertaining various leaders between the realms. The rest of the time, we're on Rexuna, high in the mountains at our family home, and only our personal guards know about it. With this latest string of threats that vow to kidnap and murder the high prince and princess of the fae—that's Bennett and me—they haven't let us leave the mountain.

It took all summer for Bennett and me to convince our parents to let us go to college to further our craft and make alliances with other families. He and I aren't one to let fear stop us. We both want a real college experience where we don't have to live under the thumb of the crown, and where we can be our own person. They'd only agreed after we made several concessions.

One: no one can know we're really prince and princess. This means we only use the Drake name on official paperwork. Otherwise, our friends will know us as Rose and Bennett Ankida.

Two: we can't attend the same university, so should the threats escalate, they can't get us both at once. One of us will rule Bedlam someday, and spreading the risk is a smart move either way.

Three: we'll let our parents know of anything that might be perceived as a threat as soon as we can.

Four: we won't be reckless with our magic. This one is going to be a little more difficult to navigate because we've both used magic far more powerful than most students will use in their lifetimes. That's what happens when you help your parents fight a war.

Five: we won't lose sight of who matters most. Yes, our realm is important, as are our people in it, but family is everything. We'd raze villages—and have done—to keep each other safe.

"I want to be your girlfriend, but I meant what I said."

"About you wanting to be just like your mom?" His eyes soften.

"Yeah." A smile twitches at the corner of my mouth. "Please don't take this the wrong way."

"You know me better than that."

"I have too much love to give." I wince, trying to phrase this with as much tact and diplomacy as I can. "To only give it to one person."

Back when we thought we'd all be attending the same university, being with him just made sense. We spent just about every waking moment together. He's part of the family, and he knows me—even the ugliest parts I keep hidden from those closest to me. But now that I'll attend Bedlam Academy without him and Bennett? I'm more conflicted than ever.

Surrounded by so much family, I've *never* been alone. The thought of a long-distance relationship, where I must steal time to talk or text, let alone visit, makes me feel like a caged bird—something I vowed never to do. Does this make me selfish and co-dependent? Yeah, it probably does.

"I can't promise you forever, Mekhi, but I can promise you right now." A tingle of magic stirs between us. A fae promise can't be broken.

Unless I want to die, anyway.

"Would you feel any better about us if I agreed to share you?" His lips twitch, as if he's trying to keep a straight face.

My eyes widen. "You'd share me?" The first time I mentioned wanting multiple mates, he'd shut that down quick, and that was before we even talked about dating.

He shrugs his shoulders. "You'll have to get used to the distance between us, but you don't have to be alone. If you make a few friends—"

"Boyfriends."

He sighs. "Boyfriends, then. I can live with that if it makes you happy. We'll make our own rules, just not the usual ones."

"I won't share you. You understand that, right? I'd sooner claw a girl's eyes out." We *did* already establish I'm selfish.

He smirks. "While I'd love to see that, be honest with yourself. You're more likely to lob off her head than claw her eyes out."

"Glad we're in agreement, then." I grin.

His hand slips around my neck and up into my hair. I draw in a breath and tilt my head back, wanting to make sure we understand each other.

"So ... we're official then?"

"Yeah, we're official."

With a final kiss and an embrace, Mekhi sends me off with a silent promise: no matter what the future brings, this summer was our own special kind of magic.

CHAPTER ONE

ROSE

Perhaps coming here was a mistake. Technically, I've only been alive a couple of years, and my life's already been in danger several times—and that's when I've been under the direct protection of my royal and powerful family. What happens if the shit hits the fan, and I can't keep myself safe?

But then I often find myself in precarious situations. Usually it's self-induced—and more than preventable. The risk of sudden death or the danger of being late has never stopped me from choosing adventure first. Or second.

Until it did.

I give myself a shake and a wry grin. This isn't the time to dwell on the past. I've got a brand-new chapter of mistakes to make.

In black wedge sandals, my feet slap against the rain-dappled pavement as I race across the deserted campus of Bedlam Academy, doing my best to avoid standing water. It's not even a quarter past yet and the place is dead. I know I'm not the only one who had to do last-minute registration, but you'd think there would be at least a few stragglers. Tears gather in my eyes, and I gulp in air, willing myself not to cry. It's not like me to be so emotional, but everything has changed.

Rounding the corner, as the wind rushes in and blows my chocolate-brown hair into my face, a fae yanks the door open to Drake Auditorium. I curse, stumbling to a stop when he flashes me a toothy grin. Dark lashes frame his sea foam-green eyes, their every shift cataloging the view in front of him like a serpent. He gives me a slow, languid survey of my sandaled feet, then up my bare, tanned legs, pausing on the khaki shorts sitting just above my knees. Then they dart to the deep V of my loose blouse, trail up my neck, settling on the rapid pulse below my ear, before landing on my own set of deep pools of blue.

His pupils dilate as he parks himself in the doorway, blocking it. A black band t-shirt strains across the lean muscles of his chest, his broad shoulders wedged against the teak wood like a barricade. An arrogant smirk plays on his lips as I shift my feet.

He's enjoying this.

"Excuse me." I bristle, trying to push past him.

He doesn't move. A thick mop of raven hair falls into his face, and he pushes it back with one hand, his steely gaze fixing on me. "Not so fast." His voice is like honey and fae wine, lazily rolling off his tongue like sweetened words meant to trap and manipulate. "What's the hurry?"

I cross my arms and pin him with a glare. "I'm late for orientation."

"So am I," he shrugs, not moving an inch. "But that doesn't mean we can't have a little fun first." Once again, his eyes trail down my body, making me feel exposed.

"What's the matter with you?" I narrow my eyes and cock my head. "All that metal poisoning your brain?"

His tongue toys with the snake bite piercing in his lip, and grins. "Nah, I'm just a fan of playing with my food."

I level him with a stare while I shift foot to foot. When it's clear I'm not entertaining his advances, he moves out of the way, and I slink into the auditorium, my heart thundering in my chest.

Who was that guy? I glance back, but he's already gone, melting into the darkness of a stairwell leading to the balcony.

A few heads turn my way as I duck into a maroon leather seat near the back. The auditorium is large, though only a hundred or so students mill around. The room smells of dozens of different perfumes and cologne, old books, and strong coffee. Everyone settles into their seats when the lights dim. At the podium, a woman with long, gray hair speaks, her sing-song voice carrying through the space.

The wrinkles marring her strawberry skin display her non-fae status: she's a witch. This professor could live forever if she wanted and might already; perhaps she performed the immortality ritual later in life. Professor Blush if I recall the faculty roster correctly. She teaches herb magic.

Pride shines on her face as she lectures. "I never thought I'd see this." Her gaze flits over the audience of students and faculty. "So many witches and fae, together in one room. It's a historic moment. As you know, witches from other realms can't enter Bedlam without their grimoire and Ebbswick key, and they must wait for a Bedlam Moon to use the portal. We'll therefore be welcoming several new students later in the term."

Professor Blush smiles and her eyes glisten as the melody in her voice switches up a gear. "There's one reason why so many fae births have been happening lately…" A sudden sense of foreboding washes over me and I sit up straighter in my seat, eyeing the exit as she drones on. "And that's because our two worlds are merging. All thanks to High King Finian and High Queen Lana Drake being united with one another as a soul-bonded pair and restoring Luna magic. The very magic that runs through your veins." Her hands raise, and her fingertips turn from strawberry-colored to a glowing, deep green. "This power imbues you with your fae abilities. *Our entire realm.* It's the same magic that makes it possible for a witch to do this—" A ball of light forms in her hand and she tosses it into the air. The orb explodes in a shower of sparks, and the audience gasps as each particle erupts into another cascade of color and light. Her eyes go searching through the crowd, and panic seizes my chest. "And somewhere, one of their very own children sits among us."

A squeak escapes me before I can stop it. All eyes swivel towards me and the blood rushing to my cheeks feels like a brand. For the love of the gods, didn't she get the memo that they're not to even discuss it amongst themselves who I am in case they're overheard? Let alone to the whole student body?

I've slid out of my seat and am halfway to the door before I realize what I've done. A smile curls my lips as I spin around, taking in the student body. They're glancing at each other, none the wiser that I've used magic to cloak myself. It's one of the first things my twin brother and I learned as children, so we could play pranks on our dads.

A prickle of awareness has the hairs on the back of my neck standing on end, and I turn to find the owner of the stare boring into me. She leans against the wall, arms crossed over her chest. Shock-white hair falls over one shoulder in a long, sleek bob, the pitch of her skin flawless. Almond-shaped silver eyes gleam under the fluorescent light showing the exit sign above her head. She wears skintight black leather pants and a matching halter top, and there's a sword strapped to her back. Her lips are blood-red, and they tilt up in a smirk. She's easily the most badass looking fae I've ever seen. Considering my bloodline, that's saying a lot.

"I know who you are," she mouths, before disappearing in a puff of silvery vapor, all evidence gone in a blink.

Terror strikes me to the core, freezing my blood and numbing my mind. How could she know me? And why had I seen recognition in her eyes? Panic spreads like a plague as I realize where I might've encountered her before. I'm almost certain she looks just like a girl that used to live near us on Earth in Australia. The chances of it are next to nothing, though.

I don't stick around to find out.

It took Bennett and me months to perfect cloaking, and we both know quite a bit of magic. The problem is first-year students aren't supposed to use magic outside the classroom or pitch. It's a rule that's strictly enforced at all academies in Bedlam.

I climb the steps two at a time, my feet light on the tile as I sneak out. Should I stay to listen to the rest of what Professor Blush has to say?

Yes.

Will I? No.

I want my family to be safe, and I won't put myself in added danger by being outed at college as the princess. Singling me out in front of the entire school will only lead to trouble. Besides the inherent danger in doing so, I want a real college experience before duty and the crown rule the rest of my days.

I step out into the balmy air and lean against the brick wall, sinking down until reaching the damp grass. Power swells within me as I run my hands across their prickly ends, watching in awe as the dew melts away, leaving nothing but clean blades of grass behind. I'll never tire of magic—especially something like this, making it easy to dry my clothes or hair in seconds.

The sun peeks over the horizon, chasing away the last of the clouds. I was supposed to have gotten my room assignment yesterday, so I could've been all moved in last night and up early for orientation, but that would have involved tearing myself away from my family and Mekhi even sooner, and I just couldn't bring myself to do that.

Slipping my phone out of my pocket, I pull up the screenshot I'd taken of my official class schedule:

STUDENT: Rose Drake
ORDER: Luna
MAJOR: Inter-realm Studies
MINOR: Astrology

Period 1: Herbology 101
Instructor: Professor Blush
Location: The greenhouse

Period 2: Elemental Magic 101
Instructor: Professor Rowan
Location: North Woods

Period 3: Combat Training 101
Instructor: Coach Thorn

Location: Arena

Period 4: Lunch
Location: Cafeteria inside the commons

Period 5: Free

Period 6: Free

Period 7: Fae History 101
Instructor: Professor McColt
Location: Windmill Lighthouse

Period 8: Dark Arts 101 (BEGINS SEP. 16)
Instructor: Professor Shadows
Location: Witches Woods (East of sand dunes)

Hour 22: Astronomy 101 [BEGINS JAN. 1]
Instructor: Professor Pyxis
Location: Bell Tower Observatory

A bead of sweat trickles down my back. Yes, I have my list of classes, but I've had no communication sent through about my room assignment, nor about where they have my trunk of clothes I sent ahead.

My attention catches on hour twenty-two. They must mean 22:00. Makes sense for a class requiring stars. It starts so late during the school year on account of the Bedlam Moon, which doesn't make it easy to see anything other than our moons, as it washes the sky red for weeks. Conditions are best January through June, just before the next cycle.

I might ask to switch my eight a.m. class for one of my later free periods, especially if I'm going to be up late for class every night once the semester is underway. Although, having three free hours midday might come in handy. It'll give me time to explore and figure out where I fit in at the academy.

I can be more than just the princess everyone caters to. More than Bennett's twin, and the sister who got him killed. Zero expectations of who I'm supposed to be, and maybe I can learn who I really am. All without the weight of my mistakes preceding me, and no amount of privilege or consequence can tell people how to treat me.

A bell tolls, the sound ringing through the air and jolting me from my thoughts. Excitement bubbles in my chest, and I crack a smile. I stuff my phone back in my pocket and stand, rubbing the back of my khakis to dry them with my Luna magic. Time to go find out where I'm supposed to be.

Students pour out of the double doors to the auditorium, some in groups and others alone. A few give me funny looks, like they might be able to place me if they only had the time to look longer—a result of the glamor they've only ever seen me with in public. It causes the brain confusion and leaves a vague sense of déjà vu—but most ignore me. Though I've been seen in public occasionally, I *always* wear a glamor in the fae realm. Strictly for security purposes. Until today. No one knows this is what the real princess looks like.

On Earth, I spent most of my time on my family's compounds in Australia and Chile, and very little time anywhere else to be recognized. Such is the life of a princess of both the high fae and the vampire court.

Glancing down at the crinkled campus map from a brochure, I make my way towards the large glass building towering over the center of campus.

The greenhouse.

DAMP AIR and the smell of dirt fill my lungs as I step into the greenhouse, the moist atmosphere not all that different from the jungle-like setting of the academy, though the loamy concentration of scents invades my nostrils. Rows and rows of plants, trees, and shrubs line the room, reaching up to the glass ceiling seven stories above. The morning sun shines through, casting a warm, dappled glow on the room.

A small group of students gather around a tan table in the back, and I make my way over.

"Is this Herbology?" I ask a girl with bright-pink hair and near-translucent white skin. One side of her head is shaved, while the other hangs long, nearly to her waist. Stud after stud punctures her ears, and when she blinks, her pupils take on a feline-like quality.

She nods and points to an empty seat next to her. "Yeah, have a seat. Prof is usually right on time." Her accent has a lilt to it I can't quite place.

I slide into the chair in the back row, pulling my leather notebook out of my bag just as the woman in question clears her throat. The teacher, Professor Blush, is a short woman, so at odds with most on campus. But that's not the most unsettling thing. Fae all hover around seven feet, though females are a little shorter, whereas witches are in a variety of human-like sizes. What's most unusual is how Professor Blush got here so fast from where she just spoke on stage. I wasn't aware witches could sift—or teleport—and she got here from the stage really fast.

Peculiar.

Though only minutes have passed since the assembly she presided over, Professor Blush has changed clothes already. Instead of the black business suit she wore at the podium, she now wears a flowy green dress with actual flowers and live butterflies flapping about. On her desk sits a small potted plant. When her eyes catch on me, they widen, and a smile breaks out on her face. She was part of the welcoming committee at Convectus Castle when I got my acceptance into the school. Not many faculty even know what I look like.

I give her an imperceptible shake of my head, my brows drawing together in a pleading expression. The last thing I need is for her to out me. Thankfully, she seems to understand and simply nods before turning her attention back to the rest of the class.

"Welcome, students!" she beams, and her butterflies take flight, flitting about the room and into the treetops soaring high above the class. "My name is Professor Blush, and I'll be your herbology teacher this year. For those of you who don't know, herbology is the study of plants and their magical properties."

Pretty sure we all know, lady.

She goes on to explain the basics of the class, but I tune her out, letting my mind wander. I should be paying attention, but I can't focus. Mekhi keeps popping into my head. I'm crazy about him, but am I being unfair?

As though he knows I'm thinking of him, my heart catches in my chest when my pocket buzzes with a notification. I discretely pull out my phone.

> Miss you. I'm glad I asked you to be my girlfriend before you left. Why didn't we do this sooner?

A smile breaks out on my face, and I thumb a response while keeping my eyes pinned on the professor. I glance down to ensure I haven't misspelled anything before hitting send.

> I miss you too. Wish you were here with me. We didn't do this sooner because my dads probably would've spent the summer gleefully burying bits and pieces of your body across Bedlam.

"This." Professor Blush holds up a plant with a spindly root and bushy top. Coming from its roots is a melodic song that resonates in my bones and soothes me, as though it were lulling me with a lullaby. "Is called a Sea Serenade, and if you can learn to tap into its magical properties, it can bring comfort and relaxation to whoever has it in their care."

My eyes wander around the room, now lit up with a cozy kind of hum. A fond smile curves my face. Mom would love a plant like this. Especially with a baby on the way.

"But it can also be used for odious purposes. When combined with a second plant—such as a Sanguine Crocus—it can suppress magic and block spellcasting." Professor Blush's voice is careful and sobering.

My head snaps up. Block spellcasting? That doesn't sound like something people should be doing, especially not with something that can cause so much trouble.

To the rest of class, the professor shows off other plants with dual purposes, though none with as much potential for harm. She pairs us off to work with a partner, and I get saddled with a timid fae named Prim. She speaks in fast, quiet tones, though she's wicked smart the way she's already memorized each part of the plant and how you can manipulate them to work together with other, complementary cuttings. Next to us is Snake Bite Guy and a hot-blond fae who are both so loud, it sets Prim on edge, and we have to work hard to ignore their antics. *Are they trying to draw attention to themselves?*

Class ends and I've just stepped out the door when my phone buzzes with a notification that Mekhi laughed at my last text. I reread his first text to me and make to click it off when the loud blond guy from class appears in my peripheral vision. Tucking my phone into my back pocket, I pause my walking to turn towards him.

"Hey." He grins. "I'm Deakan. I don't think I've seen you around before. Are you new this year?"

"I'm in a 101 class, aren't I?" I raise a brow. Cheesy pickup lines won't work on me, even if he is beautiful.

"I'm a second year. There are even fourth years in 101. Your classes depend on your order, and herbology isn't high on my order's priority list." Deakan's smile widens as he moves closer to let someone pass us on the sidewalk.

"Oh, sorry." I wince and chuckle.

The edges of his mouth curl up into an irresistible smile, his deep dimples appearing and disappearing with each twitch. His gleaming white teeth sparkle in the light, and despite my apprehension, I find myself feeling almost giddy in his presence. "How about I show you around campus? What's your next class? I'm free next hour." He's tall and muscular with shaggy blond hair, with skin the color of sand—a lot like the surfer boys back in Australia.

Deakan and I are in each other's orbit, so engrossed with each other, I've hardly noticed how close he is to me until his hand comes to tuck a curl behind my ear and he leans in, almost as if to kiss me. I'm about to pull back when he veers for my ear, instead. Heat flushes my cheeks, equal parts relieved, embarrassed, and disappointed he wasn't going in for a kiss.

He smells fresh, like sea salt and lemon. "Say cheese." His breath fans against my ear.

"Huh?" I pull back, but not before a flash of light blinds me.

Snake Bite Guy, who had been standing behind Deakan unnoticed this entire time, slips away with a snicker and I'm left to blink away the blindness in my eyes.

Dread settles in my stomach as I reach for my back pocket, only to find my phone missing. I panic and whirl around, eyes wide and searching, until I see Snake Bite Guy's fingers flying across my touchscreen.

He shares a mischievous smirk with me. "So damn photogenic, aren't you?"

"Give that back," I stalk towards him.

Deakan has got his elbow on Snake Bite Guy's shoulder, inspecting the picture. "Definitely going to keep this one. Thanks, man."

Panic grips me as I lunge for my phone. "You can't share that with anyone!" The last thing I need is my face plastered all over social media. There's a reason I don't have it, and if people find out who I am...

No. He won't do this because I won't let him.

Snake Bite Guy holds my phone over his head, backing away as I try to spring for it. He tosses it in the air for me to catch, and I fumble with it but manage to snatch it back before he can say anything. Before I know what I've done, I've conjured a ball of water in my hand and blasted him in the face with it. His eyes widen in surprise, and he takes a step back, sputtering.

Didn't expect that out of a first year?

I ignore the way the rest of the students have gone silent as the two assholes bolt, and I take chase. My phone buzzes in my pocket, a repeating pattern that picks up again as soon as it's done. but I ignore it, continuing to chase the guys. I won't let them share the picture with anyone.

"Might want to get that," Deakan shouts from just ahead of me.

Snake Bite Guy chuckles. "Or don't."

My lungs heave and my thighs burn as I sprint after them, but they're fast. Way faster than I am. They dart through the dense jungle on the Western edge of campus, and I follow, not caring that my bare legs are getting scratched up by the branches and spiked leaves. *Witches Woods*. It's less of a forest, and more of a jungle. The venom in the leaves can make one feel disoriented. And that's not even considering the creepy crawlies that call it home.

I no longer hear their footfalls, but I push forward anyway, fueled by anger. I'm about to give up and turn back when I stumble upon a trail of silver water droplets. Bending down, I touch one and it sizzles against my skin.

"Ouch." I yank my hand back, clutching it to my chest.

I glance around, trying to find the source of the weird water, when a movement in the woods catches my eye. I'm about to head towards it when a shout rings from behind me.

"Stop right there!"

I whirl around to see a woman with onyx hair pulled tight into a bun, glaring at me. Just under her creamy white skin sits a pattern of millions of ice blue snowflakes.

Dean Frost.

Not her real name, of course, but what they call her. Dean Blossom Fallgren is her proper title. I open my mouth to explain, but she cuts me off, her voice clipped through her sapphire, frost-speckled lips.

"In my office. Now."

I follow her because I have no idea where her office is yet, and because I'm still in shock. Though she's smaller in both stature and frame, she somehow manages to give off an air of authority that makes me want to cower. I hardly recall crossing the academy grounds and to the main castle on the South end of campus, but the next thing I know, I'm sitting in a plush chair across from her oversized mahogany desk. Though the woman is petite, and her desk, large, it still makes her feel so imposing.

"Rose, I'm sure you're aware of the strict rules we have here at Bedlam Academy." Her voice is like ice, and I can feel the cold emanating from her body. A clean, cold scent fills the room as glittering crystals stretch from where she sits, growing with her anger.

"Y-yes, Dean." My teeth chatter and I wrap my arms around myself, trying to warm up.

"Then you know that using your magic outside of class is strictly forbidden for first years." She pauses and I nod, my throat too frozen to speak. "I'm sure you also know that if you break one of our rules, there are consequences, even if you are a princess." Though I tower over her in my seat, she manages to look down at me, making me feel much smaller.

"Yes, Dean," I croak out. I don't bother telling her what happened with the assholes who stole my phone because one, I'm not a snitch, and two, it changes nothing.

"Good." Her cold eyes pierce through me, and I fight the urge to squirm under her gaze. "Then you understand why I'll need a meeting to discuss expectations and your behavior at this school. It's a privilege to be here, and if you want to continue as a student, you must adhere to the rules."

My shoulders sag, not out of defeat, but out of relief. I thought she'd get my parents involved or suspend me for a month. Is this what it's like being an adult? *I* answer for my actions, and not my parents?

"Now go to your dorm and change into something more appropriate for class." She tilts her chin up, eyeing my summer-like outfit with distaste. I'm used to Australian heat, but I can't handle the humidity of this part of Academia. The thick jungle and sand dunes surrounding campus blocks out most of the sea breeze that would otherwise help it cool down.

I worry my lip. "I haven't been given my dorm assignment yet."

She levels me with a look that says she doesn't believe me. "Then go to the office and get it," she clips.

I want to point out that it's my first day, but I don't dare speak out of turn again. It's everyone's first day. I should've gotten my room yesterday like everyone else. "Yes, Dean Fallgren."

I MANAGE to find my way to the office just down the hall from Dean Frosts', and the line is shorter than I expect. Once I reach the front, I'm about to give my name to the older witch at the desk when someone bumps into me from behind.

"Sorry," a voice mutters, and I turn to find a girl with long curly hair apologizing profusely.

My wide eyes catalog her small frame, high cheekbones, and delicate features. Her nose twitches with uncertainty, and her warm, chestnut-colored eyes dart around the room like a frightened animal. On her shoulder is a large black canvas bag overfilled with ... *are those boxes of cereal?* I scrunch my brows. A first-year student, if I had to guess from the way she carries herself. Like Professor Blush, her skin has a rosy tint to it. Though, I don't peg her as a witch. Definitely fae. She's too pretty not to be.

"No problem," I blurt, before she can start apologizing again. When the clerk at the front desk asks for my name, I tell her what I'm there to obtain. I approach her and whisper my name, then recoil in surprise as she jumps up from her chair and falls to her knees. Why do they always do that? I wish we could've used my alias instead of my proper title on official paperwork.

"M-my princess!" she sputters, her face ruddy, eyes wide.

"Oh, no, no, no. Please don't do that," I beg, casting glances behind me to make sure no one else is catching the spectacle she's putting on. Terror floods my veins, and a small bit of relief enters me when I see it's just the pretty, mousy brown-haired girl and the receptionist left.

"Of course, my princess. Forgive me." She scrambles to her feet and shoves a piece of paper into my hand. "This is your room assignment.

Would you like me to show you to your room?" She starts to come around the desk, ready to show me.

"Thank you." I smile at her. "Not necessary. Have a good day."

I'm about to leave when the girl who bumped into me clears her throat. "A-excuse me, princess?"

I raise an eyebrow at her and wince internally. She seems pretty harmless, but I can't have her calling me that. "Call me Rose. Not Princess Rose, or Princess, or anything else that might out me. Okay?"

Her eyes begin to well and I put a hand on her forearm. "Please. No one else can know who I am. Can I trust you to do that?"

She nods. "I'm sorry," she looks down at her feet. "Rose?" She fidgets with the straps of her bag, not meeting my gaze.

"Yes?"

"Can you show me how you did that spell? The one where you made yourself disappear in the auditorium?"

I blink at her, surprised. "You saw that?"

The girl nods again and I take a closer look at her. There's a desperate look in her eyes, one that sets me a little on edge.

"Please, princess. I-I need to know how to do that spell."

"Why?" I can't shake the feeling that there's more to this girl than meets the eye.

"I-I just do. Please." She drops to her knees, her bag thudding to the ground. "I'm begging you."

"Okay, okay," I glance around to make sure no one else sees the fuss she's making. "Gods," I help her to her feet, and she grabs her bag, clutching it to her chest. "Let's go somewhere more private."

I take her to a neighboring vacant classroom and enchant the door so no one can listen in.

"You're not going to use this for anything nefarious, are you?" I study her, and the girl shakes her head, a horrified expression on her face.

"N-no, of course not. I just want to learn the spell. I'm a mouse order with serious anxiety. Sometimes ... I shift to hide, but I keep getting stepped on. If I'm invisible, I won't need to shift to hide." She rubs her side, as though she'd recently been stepped on.

My shoulders soften and I sigh before positioning myself in front of her. Poor thing. "I've got to get to class, so you're going to need to practice this on your own, but I'll teach you the basics. Think of your magic as a blanket." I hold out my hands, imagining my magic as a warm, fuzzy shawl, like the one my Aunt Maeve made me. "You want to wrap the blanket around you, like so." I wrap the cloak around myself, snuggling it close. "And then you want to visualize yourself becoming ... invisible." I almost let out a giggle at how stupid it is.

I close my eyes and imagine myself disappearing. Opening my eyes, the woman gapes in my direction, and I uncover my cloak.

"That's it?" she squeaks. A lock of her mousy-brown hair falls into her face, and she shoves it back. She has the most adorable freckles.

"Pretty much." I shrug. "It takes a lot of practice to get it perfect, but that's the gist of it."

"Okay, I'll try." She takes a deep breath and wraps her arms around herself.

"Good luck." I start to leave, but her voice stops me.

"Rose?"

I turn back to her. "Yes?"

"Thank you. You don't know how much this means to me."

I give her a small smile. "What's your name?"

"Penelope."

"Well, Penelope, you're welcome. I hope you can master the spell."

With that, I pull my phone out to check the time. My heart seizes in my chest at the enormous number of notifications I have. Thirteen missed calls and twenty-seven text messages. Many from Mekhi, and the rest are from my twin brother, Bennett.

My fingers tremble as I locate Mekhi's contact info and hit dial, panic rising in my throat.

Has there been another threat?

He answers on the first ring.

"What's wrong?" I demand. "Are you ok?"

"I'm fine." His voice is tight. "I just ... I need to know why."

"Why what?" My mind races, trying to pinpoint what could possibly be wrong.

He's quiet for a long time. So long, I have to check the call is still connected. "Mekhi?"

"Really, Rose?" His voice breaks. "I thought you were better than this."

"I'm sorry, I don't know what you're talking about." My voice is small.

"You know exactly what I'm talking about." Mekhi's anger is clear, but it's the underlying heartbreak that cuts me the deepest.

A tear tracks down my cheek, and Penelope reaches out a tentative hand to pat my arm. I shake my head to clear it and focus on Mekhi again.

"Mek—"

Click.

I stare at my phone, stunned. He hung up on me? Bennett's name flashes on my screen a second later, and I answer it with unsteady hands.

"What the hell is wrong with you?" he shouts, and I flinch. I've never heard him so pissed off.

"I don't know what you're talking about," I whisper, my throat clogged with emotion.

"I'm your twin!" he hollers. "You don't get to lie to me, remember? *We don't do that to each other.*"

I'm ugly crying by the time he's done speaking, and Bennett sighs loudly. "I'm sorry, I didn't mean to yell. Just ... please tell me what's going on."

Taking a shaky breath, I try to compose myself. "I don't know what you're talking about, Bennett. I swear it."

"Mekhi called me in a panic an hour ago, saying you texted him a picture of you hanging all over some dude, and how you've found better options now that you're at college and don't need him anymore. He was hysterical, and I had to calm him down before he sifted over there to steal you away."

My stomach drops and my heart shatters. "I would never," I whimper. "These assholes snatched my phone right out of my hand and sent that. You have to believe me."

"Rose ... you were almost kissing some guy. Hours after making things official with Mekhi," he accuses.

My shaky hands pull open my text messages, and I suck in a clipped breath when I see the picture. Deakan's hand is on my cheek, and he's leaned in like he's about to kiss me. And it definitely looks like I'm into it, even though I remember how I was about to pull away.

"It's not what it looks like."

"You need to fix this, Rose. Mekhi is our best friend, and I won't let you hurt him like this."

The call ends, and I'm left staring at my phone in horror. Mekhi ... I would never upset him on purpose. He must know that. Sure, we've talked about me keeping my options open, provided he remains my boyfriend, but this is all new to us. I would never tell him I didn't need him anymore or start something without talking to him about it first.

I never make it to the rest of my classes that day. I'm too busy trying to get in touch with my boyfriend, but he ignores all my calls and texts. Knees to my chest on the floor of the empty classroom, I've sat here, near catatonic between crying spells. Penelope had left and came back with hot tea for me, but I barely taste it. I'm too busy wallowing in my own misery. I know Mekhi sees my calls, because after a while, they go straight to voicemail. He's shut off his phone.

Penelope was kind enough to let the office know I'm sick, so at least I won't get in trouble about my classes. Instead, I make my way to my dorm. It's on the North end of campus, a large, white building with clay tile shingles. There's a wide porch that wraps around the entire building, where trunk after trunk of student's things pile high. Vines climb the pillars, their ropes dotted with giant, tropical flowers. Insects buzz around them, collecting pollen. I collapse onto one of the wooden rocking chairs with a sigh while I pull the dorm assignment paper out of my pocket.

Room four-zero-two.

I heave myself up and trudge inside, squinting in the dim light. The maroon carpeted hallway is long, with ornate wooden doors leading off to the sides. A stairway curves to my right, and I climb them until I reach the fourth floor, wall sconces casting a flickering glow every few feet. My fingers trail along the little nicks and defects in the wood half-way down the wall, using magic to fix the imperfections. Though it's daylight, all the drapes are closed, so not a lot of light reaches inside, but I can still see the wear on the building.

I find room four-zero-two easily enough. The room numbers suggest there are hundreds of rooms to the dorm, but there are only ten per floor. Our campus has one-hundred-forty students in total. The larger numbers near the stairwell, and I must pass several doors to reach my room at the end of the hallway. Pausing in front of the door, I focus my eyes on the round device just over the threshold. It scans my irises and the lock clicks. I push the door open and slide in, sighing in relief at finding my trunk at the foot of one bed. The room is more spacious than I'd anticipated, and there's even a small bathroom, complete with a shower and tub, though it's an open concept with just a privacy screen. My thumb rubs over the sensor to turn it on, but the glass remains sheer. Great, it's broken. I haven't figured out how to repair electronics with magic yet. There's a small alcove with a working door to the toilet, though.

The walls are a powder blue, and the furniture is all cream colored with gilded accents. Actually, upon further inspection with a scrape of a nail, white paint flecks off the furniture, revealing solid gold underneath, too. Buttery yellow drapes cover the floor-to-ceiling windows, and I can see a sliver of the courtyard below when I peek behind them.

The room is wide enough that each side has a bay window complete with built in bench seats, and when I glance out the one opposite my bed, I see the back of the enormous white lighthouse with a view of the crystal blue sea beyond it. In front of the window is a giant padlocked chest, all manner of jewels encrusted in its lid. Carved on the top is the name "Cavë."

Humph. Dragon order?

I spin back around, taking in the room as a whole. It's not home, but it's nice. And it'll do for my first year. Let's just hope my roommate is easy to get along with.

Dropping myself to the bed, I sigh before propping my hands

behind my head to get a good look at the place. The room is more cozy than opulent on account of the paint covering most of the gold, save the smattering of treasure lying about, but still ... understated regal. *Fit for a princess.* No doubt my parents are behind the nice room. Even the bedding, with soft golds and blues, match the rest of the décor.

I pull my phone out of my pocket and run my thumb over the picture of me with my sister, Novaleigh, on my lock screen. My heart squeezes painfully that I'll miss most of her maturing. Fae take eighteen to twenty-four months to go from infant to full maturity, where physiologically, we're about twenty-five human years. This means the fae students here—me included—are chronologically only two to six years of age, and the witches are actually eighteen years or more, depending on when they get their key to the fae realm, since they age like humans do.

Setting my phone on the nightstand, I turn over and tuck my hands under my pillow. The scent of pine and musk fills my senses. I inhale, the fragrance permeating the air. It has a soothing effect on me. I've eaten nothing today, but have no appetite, so I decide to sleep through supper after slipping into my pajamas and scrubbing my face and teeth.

I'll try again tomorrow.

CHAPTER TWO

ROSE

A scream peels from my throat, and I thrash wildly, fighting against my attacker. I'm trapped, suffocating. I can't breathe. *They've come for me. No no no.*

Fighting with every scrap of fear in me, I shriek as I tear into him. A deep masculine voice shouts when I dig my claws into him, and I chomp down on the thick flesh of his arm, metallic blood coating my tongue. My body glows blue from inflicting pain on my intruder. He curses and pulls away, holding me at arm's length just as someone flicks on the light.

"What the hell are you doing in my room?" he roars, eyes narrowed in anger as he grips his wound. Blood spills between his fingers, dripping onto the floor.

I blink, trying to clear the sleep from my eyes as I scramble away from him. "What are you doing in *my* room?" I shout back, heart thundering in my chest.

His brown hair is tousled, falling across his forehead into his cobalt eyes. His eyes, flecked with yellow and green and the perpetual smirk of a man who knows the right answer, are half-lidded as he glares at me. He's shirtless, and I can see the tan rippling muscles of his chest and stomach. The color is from a life lived in the sun, covering a body that is strong with the work of muscle and sinew and energy. A puckered scar decorated by a black tattoo of some kind of bird sits near his hipbone, and I tear my eyes away before they can wander lower.

"I'm Jax Cavë," he says, as if that explains everything. "Why are you in my bed?" He seems to think for a moment when I stare at him, dumbfounded. "Not that I mind, I mean. You can stay." His mouth tips up in a smirk.

I swing my legs out of bed, backing away until I hit the wall. "This is my room," I say slowly, enunciating each word. "I'm Rose. And you're not welcome here. Four-zero-two," I punctuate while waving my arms. "My. Room."

He cocks his head to the side, studying me for a moment before he seems to remember something. "Oh, shit," he says, running a hand through his hair, seeming to forget it's got blood all over it. The scene is a little macabre. "*You're* my roommate? I thought the trunk said Drake Rose?"

Glancing at the trunk, I curse. I only used my real name on my trunk, so they'd know where to put my stuff. Rose Ankida is obscure enough to not mean anything to most people here but affords me some semblance of protection as it's a prominent surname for vampires. I cross my arms and scowl. It's too late to lie. "That's my last name. First name Rose. But if you tell anyone, trust that I will kill you."

"*The* Rose Drake? As in High King Finian Drake is your father?"

"One of them," I mutter, feeling my cheeks flush. I don't know why I'm embarrassed, but I am. Even before I matured, I always said I'd be just like Mom—with a small army of mates by my side.

"Huh." He looks me up and down, and I have to fight the urge to squirm under his scrutiny. "You don't look like a princess."

What the hell is that supposed to mean? "And you don't look like you have enough brain cells to form two sentences, yet here you are, stringing them together."

A chuckle comes from the doorway, and I finally tear my attention away from my roommate to find *Deakan* leaning in the frame, arms crossed. "Someone's feisty," he says, a grin playing on his lips.

That makes three people who know who I am. Fuck. Fuck. Fuck.

"What the hell are you doing here?" I storm over to the door and shove him out, slamming it in his face.

"Hey!" He protests, his fists pounding on the wood, but I ignore him, throwing the lock and planting my back against the door.

"Pack your shit," I say, voice trembling. "I'm not sharing a room with either of you. And don't you dare tell anyone who I am, or you won't just be dealing with my wrath, got it?"

"What, you don't like guys in your room?" The amusement in Jax's voice is clear. "Besides, Deakan isn't rooming with us. He's one of my best friends. His room is next door."

"Fine, whatever." I wave my hand dismissively. "I don't care who rooms with who. Just get your stuff and get out."

"I was here first, Princess," his voice drips with derision. "You can leave." He gestures wildly. "In fact, feel free."

"You can't just tell me to leave my own room!" I screech. "And don't call me that!"

"I just did." He shrugs his shoulders. "Look, I get that you're used to people doing whatever you want, but that doesn't work here. You're not the only fae at this school, and you're certainly not the only one with a roommate."

"Fine," I grit out through clenched teeth. "I'll leave. But I'm going to talk to the Dean about this!"

Lifting a dark eyebrow, he pulls out his phone and glances at it before crossing his arms against his chest. "Good luck with that."

My eyes dip to his thick biceps, then dart back up to meet his stare. "Why?"

"It's almost midnight."

"This is ridiculous," I mutter, turning away from him and stalking over to the other bed. I yank the covers back and crawl in, burying my face in the pillow to let out a scream. "Who the hell decided it was okay to give me a male roommate?"

A deep rumble of laughter reaches me from across the room,

burrowing under my skin and pooling low in my belly. "Get some sleep, Princess. You're going to need it." Amusement coats his voice, and I tuck the blankets tighter over my head.

～

JAX

The High King and Queen don't parade their children in public, so I wasn't sure what to expect when I found out that their daughter, Princess Rose, had come to Bedlam Academy. We'd all heard during orientation she was here, but no one knows who she is, and I got the impression it had been a slip-up from Professor Blush.

When Dean Fallgren made me give her a fae promise to keep an eye on my roommate and report their whereabouts, she made it sound like whoever I was rooming with was trouble. I'd only agreed when the dean promised to room me next to Kieran and Deakan, and we'd have the nicest dorm rooms on campus, complete with lots of gold trim. The others don't care about that, but I do. It's in my nature to care, and my magic draws from it.

But I had no idea the princess was … stunning. Those huge doe eyes, tiny nose, and smooth skin? *And she's my roommate.* No wonder the dean wants me to keep an eye on her. It's a matter of realm importance she's kept safe. An unhealthy dose of male pride swells my chest, knowing I'm the one the dean trusted with this task.

Even over her grandson.

I chuckle but stifle it when Rose's sleeping form shifts across the room. Her breathing is heavy, so she's still asleep. It makes sense why the dean asked me to make a fae promise to report about Rose's movements and anything suspicious that happens to her. A royal living out in the world for the first time is a big deal.

I can make out her curves even through the loose t-shirt she wore to bed, and her legs go on for days. If she was wearing anything under that shirt, I couldn't tell. And the way her dark, silky hair cascades down her back …

Her side of the room brightens with an ethereal blue glow, and I stiffen when I see her silhouette against the light. I sit up in bed, transfixed by the sight of her, and approach her side of the room, the cool floor biting into my bare feet. My order runs warm, and we like it hot.

It's like she's made of stardust, and she looks so unsettled as she sleeps. I've never seen a Luna fae up close, save for the few seconds I accidentally landed on her in the dark. Soft whimpers escape her lips, and her brows furrow in her sleep. I want to reach out and smooth away the lines, but I don't dare. The shimmer of her skin reflects the light coming from the sliver of moons half bared in the sky.

Panic floods my veins when I see her nails gouging her palms as she sleeps, drops of glowing blood wicking away into the silky sheets, cerulean like watery bruises. The scent of her blood is cloyingly sweet, like the faintest traces of bracky blooms on a warm summer's night. I know better than to touch a sleeping fae, but I can't just sit here and watch her hurt herself.

When her whimpers turn to sobs, I can't take it anymore, her irregular heartbeat beating like a drum against my ears as though she were in fight or flight mode. "Rose." I sit on the edge of her bed and shake her shoulder gently. "Wake up."

Her eyes fly open, and she gasps when she sees me. The deep wells, glassy with tears, hold pain so fierce, it cleaves a fist around my chest. She pushes herself away and scoots to the other side of the bed, as far away from me as she can get. "What are you doing?" Her voice trembles.

"You were crying in your sleep. I wanted to make sure you were okay." I gesture towards the blood dripping from the half-moons her nails made in her palms. "You were hurting yourself."

Her gaze slides to her hands and she winces, curling them into fists to hide the evidence of her self-harm. "I'm fine," she says, though she's clearly distraught. "Just go back to bed."

"You're bleeding."

"So what?" she snaps. "I can heal myself."

I flinch at the venom in her voice. "Magic is forbidden for first years."

"I'm sure they won't care I'm healing my own injury."

"They'll know something happened," I point out. "And then they'll investigate." I don't tell her I'll have to tell the dean, too.

She stills. "They can tell when someone uses magic?" Alarm laces her voice.

"Dean Fallgren can." I run my finger along the stitching on her comforter. "She's a Tracker."

"What's a Tracker?"

I furrow my brows. She's the princess, and doesn't know what a tracker is? How sheltered do they keep them? "They're fae who can track down other fae by their magic signature. All ice fae have the ability because it taints the air they try to freeze." I'm almost certain the High King has this ability. Though they might call it something different on Rexuna where the royal family are mostly based. He probably uses the moons' beams to detect magic.

"Oh." She worries her lip, and it takes everything in me to not focus on it. "I can't control my magic regenerating. It just happens, and I usually only have nightmares when it does."

"What kind of nightmares?" I scoot closer to her. One way Luna fae refuel their magic is through pain. I hadn't realized doing it to herself could do that, too.

She swallows hard and looks away from me. "It doesn't matter."

"It clearly does, or you wouldn't have been crying and hurting yourself in your sleep."

"I said it doesn't matter!" she yells, standing up from the bed and backing away from me. "Just leave me alone."

"Rose," I reach out to her.

She flinches away from my touch and wraps her arms around herself. "I'm fine." Her voice shakes. She's *not* fine. "Just go back to bed."

"I'm not going to bed until you tell me what's wrong." I cross my arms over my chest.

She studies me for a moment. "Fine," she snaps. "I have nightmares about my twin brother dying. There, are you happy?"

"Well, that's alright. Your parents can just bring him back to life if that ever happens." The feathers from a fae's wing can regenerate the dead, and with the amount of power in their feathers, the high king and queen can permanently bring fae back to life. Others, like my order, need nearly every feather on their wings to revive someone for good, and often, we wouldn't have enough. My wings haven't even come in yet, and fae don't usually show them to anyone but their mates because our feathers are so coveted.

"He did die."

"Bennett ... died?" My stomach drops, feeling like I've been punched in the gut for prying. Why haven't we heard anything about it? There should've been an announcement, and a mandatory period of mourning.

"Yes, when we were kids." Her voice wavers. "But he was brought back by one of my dads."

My eyes widen and I run a hand through my hair. I knew the high king and queen were powerful, but I hadn't realized they could bring a *child* back to life. Adult fae can usually come back to life if they're revived with a feather in time. But when a fae child dies, it's *permanent*.

"I'm sorry," I whisper, not knowing what else to say.

We sit in silence for a few moments before she speaks again. "You don't have to stay up with me." The quiet hum of her voice fills the space between us. "I'll be fine."

"I don't mind." I shrug my shoulders. "It's not like I was sleeping, anyway." What I don't say is that her glow is so mesmerizing, I don't want to sleep, for fear I'll miss the beauty of it. "I'll keep the nightmares away."

She gives me a small smile, and I can't help but feel my own lips tug up in response. "Thank you," she whispers.

"Don't mention it." I wave her off.

We both settle back down on the bed, and I find myself scooting closer to her until our sides are pressed together. Neither of us speaks a word, but I find myself feeling more at peace than I have in a long time. Maybe there's something to this whole roommate thing after all.

ROSE

I jolt awake some time later, disoriented and confused. It takes me a few moments to remember where I am and what had happened. Slung across my waist is an arm, and I stiffen when I realize it belongs to my roommate. Its weight presses into me, his heat like a brand against my skin. The warm breath stirring the hair at my nape gives me goosebumps. Every inhale I take, it's like I'm consuming him. It's not entirely an unwelcome feeling.

I carefully peel his arm off me and make to slide out from under the covers, trying not to disturb him. I'm not sure what got into me last night, but I found myself opening to him in a way I never have with anyone other than Bennett and Mekhi. And now I'm feeling embarrassed and exposed, like he can see into my soul.

Just as I uncover myself, a groan escapes Jax's lips, and he tugs me against him. "Where are you going?" he mumbles, nuzzling into my neck. He carries a deep, masculine scent, and now, it's all over my sheets. There's something about it that soothes me.

I still, feeling my entire body flush at his touch. "Um ... I have a boyfriend," I croak, trying to keep my voice steady while avoiding the obvious feel of his morning wood. "I'm sorry if I gave you the wrong impression last night."

We'd done nothing other than talk, and sometime between two and three this morning, we both must've dozed off, the sound of a haunting voice crooning to a guitar through the window lulled us both to sleep. But still, waking up in his arms feels ... intimate, and guilt gnaws at me.

He lets out a low chuckle, and his lips move against the sensitive spot behind my ear. "Relax, princess," he purrs. "I won't try to steal your virtue. Or your heart."

I shiver at the rough, rumbling tone of his sleepy voice. "Okay," I breathe, trying to calm my racing heart.

"Besides," he continues, his hand coming to rest on my lower stomach and pulling me flush against him. "I fully intend on you giving it to me willingly. No theft required."

I whip around on him so fast my elbow lands in his gut with a whoosh of air. "You arrogant ass!" I hiss, pushing against his chest.

He grunts and doubles over, and I take the opportunity to scramble off the bed and put some distance between us. This is a dangerous man. Dangerous for my heart and my head.

"What the hell, Rose?" He wheezes, looking up at me with a pained expression.

"You can't just say things like that!" I shout, throwing my hands up in the air. "What part of *I have a boyfriend*, don't you understand?!" Sure, I can have more than one boyfriend, but I'm not jumping into bed with a stranger, especially not before okaying the guy with Mekhi.

After he recovers, his arm rests behind his head, and he levels me with a smug look. His mop of short curls falls across his brow, and my fingers itch to tangle in them. "I'm not interested in your boyfriend."

"Well, I'm not interested in *you*!" I fire back. Okay, so maybe parts of me are, but I don't know this man.

He raises an eyebrow and gives me a look that says he doesn't believe me. "Really?" he drawls. "Then why were you glowing half the morning? And isn't your mom the one with like ... a bajillion mates?"

I flush and look away, feeling exposed. I had forgotten about my Luna nature for a moment. "That means nothing," I mumble. "And it's seven. Seven mates." Plus one more who might join them, though things aren't official.

"Uh huh," he says, clearly not convinced. "If it means nothing, why were you so eager to get away from me this morning? Guilty conscience?"

"I told you; I have a boyfriend!" I throw my hands up in frustration. "What's so difficult to understand? I don't cheat!" Technically, not cheating, as Mekhi and I have already talked about this. But I want to tell him before I bring anyone into our relationship.

"Who said anything about cheating?" He looks bemused. "I'm just helping you regenerate your magic."

I fall to my knees and spin the combination on the lock on my trunk. I'm so aggravated, I take several tries at the combination to get it to click open. Sitting on top of my clothes is a picture frame with my family in it, from a couple of weeks ago when we visited the Earth realm. We're piled on the deck of our beachfront property in Australia. My mom, swollen with my little sister—Brianna, or Bee, or Bumble Bee—while my dads stare fondly at something she said. All seven of them.

Then there's my grandma and grandpa. My little sister, Novaleigh, has a frisbee in her hand just behind them.

A pang of agony crushes my chest as I run my finger over the two males sitting with their arms draped over my shoulder. Bennett and Mekhi lean affectionately against me. How hadn't I known how much Mekhi liked me back then?

Clutching the frame to my chest, I spear Jax with my glare. "You're just like your stupid little friends." I breathe. "Last night I thought you might be different, that you weren't a womanizing pig like the rest of them, but I was wrong."

I can feel his eyes on me as I reach for a pair of jeans. "What exactly did my friends do to you?" he asks, his voice tight.

"As if you don't know already!" I snatch my shirt off the bed and stomp towards the bathroom. "You probably put them up to it!"

I don't stick around to listen to what he has to say. Stepping behind the little partition, I slump against it and bury my head in my hands. My mind keeps coming back to his comment about my dads—there are a lot of them, and I always joked I'd have as many mates as Mom when I matured. Before I ever explore that route, I'll need to clear things up with Mekhi. Maybe inviting him and Bennett over for the day will help. It's Saturday, and the first full week of classes won't start until Monday.

JAX

"What are you doing here?" I step aside to let Deakan in. He's got his blond, wavy hair tucked behind his ears and he's only wearing low-slung board shorts. He brushes past me, checking my shoulder. Though he's tall, I've got a couple inches on him, and a good twenty pounds, too. He's still jacked, but I spent the summer training for Spar Games with my dad. He was a pro back in his university days.

"Is she here?" After a moment of scanning the room, he makes his way over to Rose's side.

I block him before he can start digging into her things. She's got her bra and underwear laying on top of her trunk so she can change when she gets done showering. It's a cute little pink number, and seeing his eyes zero in on them stirs something inside of me. "What did you do to her?"

He plops down onto her bed and buries his face into her pillow before flipping over and holding it out to me. "Why do I smell you on her pillow?"

Jealousy punches me in the chest. I don't know if it's because I slept in the same bed with her last night, or if it's just selfishness because I'm supposed to keep an eye on her, but I can't help thinking about the fierce possessiveness I feel toward her. "We slept together." I shrug. Not the way I'm implying, but we did sleep in the same bed last night.

His grip tightens on the pillow and his jaw clenches. "I saw her first, I get dibs."

"Dibs? On what?" I ask, bemused. I ignore the jealousy stirring in my gut.

"On her." He sits up. "You can have anyone you want, Jax. Why go after someone who's taken?"

"She's not taken by you, that's for sure," I point out. "She has a boyfriend back home."

He scoffs and stands up, stalking towards me. "So? That means nothing. You know as well as I do that relationships back home don't mean anything at university. She's from Earth. Haven't you ever watched a Hollywood movie? To them, college is a time for frat parties, red solo cups, and keg stands. And sex. Lots and lots of sex." I want to punch the wistful look off his face. "Do you think she's ever had sex?"

Doubt it. Luna fae can be wanton creatures, but she's been under the royal thumb her entire life. "Boyfriends mean something to her. She's different. And it's not like you've ever been in a relationship, so how would you know?" I shoot him a glare. He steps right into my personal space, our chests almost touching. "You're just going to get shut down, Deakan. Let her go."

"No," he growls, pushing me away. "She's mine." What has gotten into him? He and I have never so much as argued, and now he's getting all bent over a girl he just met?

Rose picks the worst possible time to come out of the bathroom. I hadn't noticed the shower shutting off, and though it isn't allowed, she had to have used magic to give herself some privacy. Otherwise, I can see right into the shower, thanks to that broken screen. She freezes when she sees us, her towel clutched to her chest. My attention dips to the swell of her breasts before I tear my gaze away. "What's going on?"

"Nothing." I try to usher Deakan to leave but he just plops down on her bed like he belongs there. "He was just leaving."

"No, I wasn't." His eyes never leave Rose.

Someone raps their knuckles against our door, and Rose and I glance at each other. "Expecting more company?" she hisses, clutching the towel tighter to her chest.

I shake my head and open the door to find a male witch with dark hair, tanned skin, and a white shell necklace at his throat. The crooked smile on his face falls when he sees me and steps back. "I thought this was Ro—" His eyes lock on Rose, and the blood drains from his face.

"Rose?" he whispers, as if he can't believe she's here with me, and he loses the shine in his gaze.

"Mekhi?" she squeaks, rushing to throw her arms around his neck. He stumbles back from the impact but manages to catch himself and crushes her to him. He's buff for a non-fae, and I can't help but size him up. Sure, he's attractive for a witch, but he'll never compare to us fae.

I inch back, giving them some privacy, but Mekhi's next words have me frozen in place. "What is a guy doing in your room?" he asks, his voice even. He's trying not to betray it, but I can hear the rising pulse at his neck.

"We're roommates," I say, gesturing between Rose and myself. I don't mention why the dean let us room together as male and female. That was part of the deal, although I was careful not to promise that part. "Are you her brother?" Instinctively, I know he's not, but I'm an asshole.

They part, and Mekhi puts a possessive arm around Rose. "I'm her boyfriend," he spits.

"Mekhi, this is Jax," Rose introduces us, her voice shaking, eyes finding me. Her brows raise in a way that tells me to behave. "He's *just* my roommate."

He doesn't bother giving me more than a cursory glance now before he takes in the rest of the room, though his posture has gone rigid. That's when he notices Deakan on Rose's bed.

"Who the hell is this?" he demands, advancing on Deakan.

Deakan stands up and meets him halfway, not looking the least bit intimidated. "Oh, don't be coy," he gives him a sly grin. "You got the picture she sent you, right?"

The witches' face turns red, and he shoves Deakan. In turn, Deakan shoves him back, and they start swinging at each other. I step in to try and break it up, but Mekhi throws a magic-fueled punch that catches me in the jaw and sends me flying. I hit the wall with a thud and slide to the ground, seeing stars. He's not as big as us fae, so it catches me by surprise. He must have some kind of training.

"What the hell, Mekhi?" Rose cries, trying to pull him off Deakan. "Stop it!"

"He was in your bed!" he shouts. "He's the dude who was all over you in that picture!"

Rose's hands clutch the witches' shirt, causing him to pause and lean into her. "It was just a stupid prank Deakan pulled with this other guy. Why they did it, I don't know, but you know I'd never cheat. There will be no one else without us agreeing to it, okay?" She searches his eyes and presses her lips to his. Ugly, green jealousy rises in my chest, and I clench my jaw.

He nods and backs off Deakan, who's nursing a bloody nose. I get to my feet, feeling a little shaky. I'm still processing the possibility she could want to have more than one boyfriend. It's not uncommon amongst royals to take on more than one mate, though there are special protocols in place. *I think.*

Could I share her?

The idea is foreign and a little scary, but the more I think about it, the more I realize I could if it made her happy. And if she's anything like her mother, she'll need more than one mate to keep her satisfied.

Who am I kidding? I want to yank her from his arms right now. It'd take a miracle for me to be able to share her with anyone else. Least of all a witch I don't even know.

I've got to get out of here. I'm losing my gods-damned mind.

I drag Deakan out of the room to give Rose and Mekhi privacy to deal with whatever mess Deakan and Kieran made between them. He isn't happy, but we head to his room next door.

Kieran is there, smoking mystic juice on his bed with the window cracked open, guitar poised next to him. It's like star dust, but instead of hallucinations, it induces a euphoric, dream-like state. Tattoos cover his arms, marring nearly every space with some kind of design. He even has some on his neck. But the giant one in cursive on his bare chest? The sight of it steals my breath, and I have to avert my eyes because even this one hurts me, too.

It's his parents' names, and their dates of death. His mom first, and not long after, his dad.

Kieran is an asshole, but we grew up together, and I know better than anyone how much he's hurting. He wasn't always this way. Before the war, he'd been a carefree, happy kid who'd do anything to help his friends. He's brilliant, but barely passes his classes now. And when he's not getting high, he's moody and pissed off, though I have a hard time blaming him. Anyone in his position would be broken.

Deakin and I both promised our parents we'd look out for him, even if we want to throttle Kieran half the time. The only time I see a glimpse of the old Kieran is when he's singing and playing the guitar. He's got a voice on him, deep and burdened, like the timber of a thousand storms, but it's a haunting, soothing sound. He sits in his room, lit only by the glow of his laptop, the cherry of his blunt, and a small lamp on his desk. He is hunched over his computer, and the light is too far from him to illuminate any more than his face. His t-shirt is crumpled and barely conceals his tattoos, all of them looking like pieces of art.

"Dude, you owe me," Deakan growls as he slams the door.

Kieran raises a pierced brow, taking a drag of his joint. Bloodshot eyes, paired with his green irises, give him a festive look, though I'm not going to spoil his mood any more by pointing it out.

"Your little prank got me punched in the face." Deakan points to his swollen nose.

"My prank?" Kieran laughs, unphased as he ends on a smoke-induced cough. "You're the one who wanted to ask her out!"

Deakan yanks a shirt from his drawer and presses it to his swollen nose.

"What happened with the girl?" Kieran blows out a stream of smoke.

I plop onto the burgundy leather couch and let out a sigh. "She's got a boyfriend." I scowl.

"We know. That's who she was texting in class." Kieran shrugs, taking another drag and closing his laptop.

"Yeah, well, he came over and found us in her room," Deakan gestures to the door. "He started swinging, so I did too. And he doesn't even know Jax fucked her."

Kieran whips his head to me. "You did what?"

"I didn't say that."

Deakan shoves my shoulder. "You said you slept with her!"

"Yeah, we slept together. In her bed. But we didn't fuck." My mood sours even more.

Why am I talking about her like she's just a piece of ass? Yeah, I wouldn't mind sleeping with her, but she's not someone you'd just pump and let go of.

Kieran shakes his head while Deakan looks like he can't decide if he wants to punch me or give me a hug.

"So, you didn't sleep with her? But you got your asses kicked?" Kieran laughs.

"Wait."

Our heads turn towards Deakan.

"What?" We ask in unison.

"You don't know who she is ... do you?" Deakan kicks his bare feet up to rest on the glass coffee table.

"Shut your mouth," I warn.

"Who is she?" Kieran's brow furrows.

"She's the princess," Deakan leans in conspiratorially. "Rose Drake."

"She doesn't want anyone to know!" I shove his shoulder.

"Did she tell you that?" Kieran laughs. "That looks nothing like her."

"You dumbass, they use a spell to cloak the children's true faces until maturity when they're in public or on the throne." I toss a throw pillow at Kieran, causing his joint to fall onto his chest and he shouts.

"I'm going to go ask her out." Deakan makes for the door, ready to head back over there, but I stop him.

"And get punched by her boyfriend again? To be honest, I'm surprised he didn't kill you for that."

"Neither of you can date her," Kieran says after a long moment of silence. A muscle tics in his jaw.

Deakan and I both bristle. "Why not?" we say in unison. We do that a lot. The three of us have been best friends since we were infants.

"Because she's royal and we're not," Kieran replies plainly. "It's forbidden."

"That's not true," I argue. "Her mother married a vampire. And I'm pretty sure the high queen also slept with one of the guard."

"She married the *King of the Vampires*, and that guard has *royal blood*," Kieran counters. "Look, I'm not going to sit here and argue with you about this," Kieran stands. "But I'm telling you, it's a bad idea. You're better off staying away from her."

"Her boyfriend isn't royal." Deakan points out.

"He's a witch who has earned their respect and approval. They took him in." Kieran spins to face us. "Which might as well be the same thing."

"How do you know so much about the royals?" I run a hand through my hair, feeling my chest tighten.

"My cousin Sarai was the queen's personal maid." Kieran places a glass under the running faucet and takes a big swallow before leaning against the wall to face us. He puts out his joint in the half-inch left in the cup.

I want to argue with them, but I know they're right. "You know I can't room with her and not hit on her," I tell them. *I want to do a lot more than that.*

"Then you'll have to leave." Deakan shrugs and yanks his comforter and pillow off the bed and makes his way towards the door again. "I'll take your place."

"What? No, I can't do that." I shake my head. "It's the nicest room on campus." *And I have to be her roommate,* not that I'm complaining.

"You have to." Kieran pushes off the wall. "Or do what you can to avoid thinking of her as anything fuckable."

I raise a brow at him. "Have you seen her?" She's easily the most beautiful fae I've ever seen. It's got to be the Luna magic in her blood. "Besides, I'm the only one who's going to room with her, and that's that." Dean Fallgren won't have it any other way. She'd have to voluntarily let me out of my fae promise, but if Rose's safety is at risk, she won't.

CHAPTER THREE

ROSE

The rise and fall of Mekhi's chest is the only sound in the room as I snuggle against him. We're both lost in our own thoughts, and tension radiates from him. He can only be here for another few hours before he must get back for his own orientation. He'd borrowed a portal stone from Bennett to get here since he's not a shifter and can't sift—or teleport—places. Where Bennett got it from, I don't know. They're so rare.

I finally ask, "What's wrong?" softening the worry in my voice as I trace circles on the shirt that hugs his broad shoulders. He presses his lips to my hair, but I can feel something is off. Tilting my head back, I look into his eyes and can see the fear hidden beneath them.

"Mekhi," I say, propping myself up on my elbow. "You know you can tell me anything."

"I know." He sighs, running a hand through his hair in frustration. "It's just ... I'm worried about you."

"They have protective wards on campus, babe," I remind him, frowning. "Nothing is going to happen. Most of campus has no idea who I am."

Mekhi's brow furrows and he shakes his head, unable to form words. He reaches out to clasp my hands in his, the warmth of his touch calming me in an instant. "I just don't want anything bad to happen to you. You mean so much to me," he whispers, his gaze searching mine for understanding.

My heart swells with emotion as I lean down and kiss him lightly on the lips. "That's the sweetest thing anyone has ever said to me." I pull away to look into his eyes, still burning with sincerity.

His shutter and he exhales a deep sigh, shaking his head. "I wish I could protect you from what lies ahead." He meets my gaze once more.

"You can't," I say softly, cupping his cheek, the stubble soothing. "Whoever is behind the threats to our family will reveal themselves eventually, and I'll handle it. I can't spend the rest of my life in hiding."

He nods slowly, a conflicted expression on his face as he looks into my eyes again. "I know," he says quietly, "but that doesn't mean I have to like it."

"No, it doesn't." A sad smile crosses my face and I squeeze his hand in reassurance. "But I appreciate your concern."

"I just want to keep you safe." His voice is rough with emotion. "It's really fucking with my head."

"Can you understand why I'm disappointed you didn't believe me about the text?"

He hangs his head in shame. "I let jealousy get the better of me, and you deserve better than that." His fingers twine with mine. "After I'd gotten that text, I was upset you were just writing me off. I treated you so poorly. I felt terrible and wanted to explain myself face-to-face. But I went kind of crazy seeing that guy in your bed, reconfirming everything in that text."

"It did look pretty bad, didn't it?" I wince. If I were in his position, I probably wouldn't have given him a chance to explain himself. He's a better person than I am. "Thank you for apologizing." I press another kiss to his lips.

"I love you, Rose."

My heart skips. We've said this to each other countless times before, but never as boyfriend and girlfriend. "I love you, too."

The alarm on his phone goes off, reminding him of the time. We both groan.

"You could always skip orientation?" I smile sweetly. "My full week of classes won't start until Monday."

"Tempting." Mekhi presses a kiss to my forehead. "But I need to get back. Bennett will kill me if I miss it. He has to return this portal stone to the guy he borrowed it from."

"I know." Sitting up, I sigh. "I'll walk you to the Witches Woods."

He hesitates. "Are we okay?"

I bury my head against his neck and breathe deep. "Yeah, we're okay. Just know I'd never, ever be so callous as to break up with you over a text. You're too important to me."

Mekhi's hands tighten on me for a moment before he forces himself to relax. "I know that, and I didn't react well when given a chance to prove it. I fucked up." His lips press against my temple. "I know you'll eventually find other guys you want to be with. Provided I'm still with you, too, it's something I can live with. Because, if you're happy, then I'm happy."

"You mean that?" I raise my head to look at him. "You borrowed a portal stone to confront me about being with someone else, and now you're still saying you'll share me?"

He smiles down at me. "I'd prefer to keep you all to myself, but provided you'll have me, too, I can't object to you taking more mates."

"Really?"

He nods. "I want you to be happy."

Mekhi and I aren't mates, which doesn't just mean two people who are having sex—I mean, there's usually lots of that between mates, but it's when two people have a mating bond. It's for life. And that's not something we'd ever force. But the fact that he's okay with the idea of me taking more mates fills me with hope for our future.

"Thank you."

We meander along the path through campus, taking our time as I soak up the last moments with him. Mekhi has a backpack slung over his shoulder and a hint of nervousness in his eyes; he's due at orientation for his classes soon. When we reach the edge of the Witches

Woods, he pulls me into a hug and holds me close for a moment. His voice is low and scratchy as he says, "I'll see you soon, okay?"

My throat tightens at his words, and I nod in agreement, offering him a small smile. "Give Bennett a hug for me," I whisper.

"I will." Mekhi presses a final kiss to my lips before he steps back, his image already blurring as he activates the stone in his palm.

I watch until he disappears before I turn and trudge back to my room. Quickly freshening up, I rush to the dining hall. Just as I enter, an earsplitting bell rings, signaling that breakfast is almost over.

"Rose!" a voice calls out.

Penelope stands across the room, her hand raised in a wave. Relief floods through me and I smile as I weave through the other students, my feet carrying me towards her.

"Hey." I breathe, relieved to see a friendly face. "I'm glad you're here."

Her eyes widen in surprise, and she tucks a lock of hair behind her pointed ear before gesturing towards the lunch line with a nod. "I've already eaten, but I can keep you company while you get something."

"Thanks." I follow her to the line and grab a tray. "What's good?"

"My omelet was alright." Penelope points to the long row of tall, thin, brightly-colored boxes lined against the counter wall. "But the cereal? Omigods. They've got Sugar Faes, Sprite Bites, and Blosso-mallows!"

"I'll take your word for it." I chuckle, picking up an omelet. "Anything else?" The scent of something delicious wafts my way, like a kiss of summer rain, but before I can turn my attention towards it, Penelope speaks.

"Some bacon and toast—oh!" Her eyes widen as she spots something over my shoulder. "Don't look now."

"What?" I try to turn, but she stops me.

"Just act casual." Penelope smiles, but it doesn't reach her eyes. "You've got a group of hotties looking your way."

I turn anyway, my eyes landing on Jax and his friends. Her grip on my arm is like steel. "I said don't look!"

Raising my voice so the three of them can hear me with their fae hearing, I meet Jax's intense gaze. "The big, beautiful one with curly hair has a tiny cock. The blond kid has a love affair with his pet goldfish—" I grin as their expressions turn murderous. "And the neanderthal one has metal poisoning that's affected his brain and he's super awkward in social situations on account of a raging hard-on that won't go away after he stuck it in a magical tree near the sand dunes. Poor guy." None of what I say is true, except the part about Jax being beautiful. But after their bullshit? It's deserved. "Remember that if any of them try to get in your pants, 'kay?"

"Rose!" Penelope's strangled whisper comes out as a reprimand.

Turning towards her, face plastered in a grin, I point a finger at the three jerks and then turn it towards her. "Protecting you from the monsters? That's my job today."

Her face flushes, eyes dancing with amusement as she shakes her head. "You're terrible."

Linking my arm with hers, I open my mouth to respond, but the words die in my throat as my attention catches on the far table. A gasp escapes me as I lock eyes with a beautiful man with golden eyes, glasses framing his perfect features. His dark hair is styled like he's spent a fortune on it, and he wears a tailored suit that emphasizes his broad shoulders. It feels like all the air has been sucked out of the room, and I can't look away. From here, I can see his pupils dilate, the same reaction taking over him as it's doing with me.

"Rose?" Penelope's voice sounds far away, but I can't take my eyes off the man. "Are you okay?"

"I'm fine." My voice grows faint as I stare in awe at the most beautiful creature I've ever seen. His features are captivating, as if he put some kind of spell on me. A faint shimmer over his skin briefly reveals tattoos lining his neck before they disappear again. I can't look away. Someone bumps into me from behind, and I stumble forward a few steps before I catch myself, finally managing to tear my gaze away from the man and look down at my tray. *Who* the hell was that? *What* the hell was that? My cheeks heat up, and I feel disoriented.

"You sure you're okay?" Penelope casts a troubled glance my way.

"Yeah." I nod, grabbing a few things from the tray before I head to the register. "I'm fine."

I stop in my tracks, my arm outstretched to grab a napkin, when I realize I'm glowing. Panic grips me, and I look around to see if anyone has noticed. The entire room stares my way with wide eyes, and I know they've seen.

My face burns with humiliation as I drop my tray on the counter and bolt for the door. The room is deafeningly silent, and I feel every pair of eyes boring into my back as I tear out into the bright sunshine, desperate to put as much distance between myself and the stares of my peers as possible.

"Rose?" Penelope's voice carries faintly in the distance, but I keep running, my breath coming in ragged gasps as I sprint away from the humiliation, not sure where I'm going but positive that I have to be anywhere but here.

"Rose, wait!" Penelope calls again as I dart around a corner, but I don't stop.

Not everyone has seen a Luna fae glow, but everyone knows why we glow; we're either healing, hurting someone, under the moon, or we're aroused. Considering it's daylight, and it's obvious I wasn't healing or hurting anyone, that just leaves one option. I've never glowed just by looking at someone before, but this guy ... there's something about him that sets my body on fire.

How long I run, I don't know, but eventually, I find myself in the Witches Woods. I slow to a stop, bending over to catch my breath as I lean against a palm, the smooth bark unlike most in this jungle. I'm no longer glowing, but my cheeks are still heated, and I can't stop thinking about the man with the golden eyes. Who is he? And why did I have such a reaction to him? And him to me?

I make my way to the sand dunes and flop down, burying my face in my hands. How will I ever show my face on campus again? The only consolation is that only a handful of people know who I really am. Maybe if I lie low for a few hours, they'll have forgotten all about it.

WHISPERS GREET me as I step into the dining hall at supper, and I keep my head down as I make my way to the food line. I tried to hold out as long as possible, but I'm a snack-based life form, and I've plowed through the stash I have in my room.

Filling my tray with as much food as it can hold, I shuffle to the cashier, my eyes constantly sweeping the room for any familiar faces. I pay quickly and make my way to an empty table, the clinking of my tray echoing off the walls of the cafeteria. I can feel eyes on me, and heat rushes to my cheeks as I try to appear unfazed. Shoveling food in my mouth, I barely taste it as I avoid making eye contact with anyone.

Suddenly, Snake Bite Guy appears. He leans back in his chair, studying me intently. I feel like an ilab caught in his sights, trying to keep still in hopes he won't notice me.

"You're the princess."

A shiver runs down my spine as I hear that rich gravel in his voice. I swallow hard and force myself to look up at him.

"Shocker, you spoke to Jax and Deakan." I reply coolly, even though my heart thunders in my chest. I wonder if he can smell my fear.

"What would happen if the rest of the academy found out?" He grabs an apple off my tray and cracks it in half with his fists before shoving a piece into his mouth.

I drop my fork and meet his eyes. "Haven't you ruined enough?"

His eyes narrow, and he leans forward. He considers me while he finishes chomping on my apple. "You have no idea what I'm capable of."

I snort. "Please. Why are you messing with me? Did my parents pass some kind of law that made your precious life inconvenient? Or are you just a bully because you can be?"

He says nothing, but the muscle in his jaw ticks. I've hit a nerve, and I know it. But before I can say anything else, he stands up and walks away.

I sit in silence for a few moments, letting what just happened sink in. I have no idea what his deal is, but I know one thing for sure: he's trouble. Our first encounter, he was hitting on me. Our second, he stole my phone to text Mekhi a picture of Deakan looking as though he's about to kiss me. And now he's threatening to out me to the entire school. I'll have to be careful around him from now on.

Is he the one behind the threats?

The rest of supper is relatively quiet, and I don't see mystery man anywhere. Good. Maybe he was just visiting campus. I can only hope. After supper, I head back to my room, but I'm not alone for long. A few minutes after I enter, Jax comes in, slamming the door and sulking.

"What's wrong?" I ask, setting my laptop down. "You know I was just messing with you earlier, right?

"Right." He flops down on his bed and stares at the ceiling.

"Oh, c'mon. Penelope knows I was just goofing around. I'm sorry. I was just pissed about the crap your friends put me through."

"Nah, I'm good."

Alright, then. Moments later, I get a video call from my dad, and I click 'Accept.'

"Hey, Dad!"

"Hey, Princess. How's campus life treating you?"

I'm not about to tell him the truth. "Really good, but I miss you all. Wish Mekhi and Bennett were here with me, too. Did you know they don't let us use our magic outside of class?"

"Finn mentioned that. Seems like they've got a good reason for it, though—"

"Dad, I've been using magic since I was practically in diapers."

"I know, but the others haven't, and you've got to remember that."

I huff a sigh. "Yeah, I know, it just sucks."

He chuckles. "We're all looking forward to seeing you at Parent's Day—"

"Dad, you can't!"

"What? Why not?"

I take a deep breath. This should be obvious, should it not? "They'll know I'm the princess?" It isn't safe; not while our family is under threats from an unknown enemy.

There's a long pause. "We're coming, but we'll disguise ourselves like we did for you in public. No one will know. You know we wouldn't put you or any of us at risk."

"No one will know I'm the princess when my mom shows up with all seven of my dads, even if disguised?"

He laughs. "Well, maybe we'll just show up in shifts."

I smile. "Thank you, Dad."

"Anything for you, Princess. I love you."

"I love you, too. Now let me talk to Mom."

She and I chat about my upcoming classes and the new friends I've made. She's excited to hear about herbology, but I leave out the part about mystery man. I'm not ready to share what he is, or isn't, yet. When my mom first came to Bedlam and was learning magic and combat, she got really into growing herbs because she kept accidentally injuring the soldiers. Now she's a great gardener and is even better at using magic—especially as High Queen of the Fae.

After hanging up, I get ready for bed, but sleep doesn't come easy. I don't hear a word from Jax the entire night, but his presence is still heavy in the room. Did I push things too far today? Maybe. He won't talk to me.

Sunday morning, I choose to skip breakfast and snack on the extras I'd grabbed from dinner last night. Other than using magic, there's no real way to heat food in my room, so I eat cold pasta salad and olives.

After cleaning up, I dress in workout gear and head to the gym for a lifting session. Tilting my face to the sky, I let in a deep breath. It's a beautiful day outside, with warm winds, fat, puffy clouds like cotton balls painted on an azure sky, and temperatures in the mid-seventies, which is a pleasant reprieve from the sweltering heat from yesterday, and I need to clear my head before my meeting with the dean this afternoon.

One of my dads, Auguste, is the one who got me into fitness. He's a vampire and doesn't require exercise, but he taught Bennett and me everything about combat as he helps train our vampire army when they come for retreats at our compounds. He served during Earth's second world war, and I guess his routine hasn't left him in all the years since.

The gym is empty, except for a guy I don't recognize sitting on the weight bench. Most students on campus are eating breakfast or sleeping in before classes start tomorrow. After lifting, I opt to run the trails in the Witches Woods instead of running on the treadmill. I tilt my face to the sky and breathe in deep. The heat is gentle on my skin today; tropical fruit hangs from the trees around me; in the distance I hear laughter from students walking by; sunlight glistens across the dew-damp palm leaves; sounds of birds sing in tune with Lady Gaga blaring in my ears through my earbuds—and it all makes up one beautiful day outside.

I take the path that leads deeper into the woods. The last time I'd been on this trail I was chasing after Kieran and Deakan. I'm not paying attention to where I'm going and before long, I'm lost. I stop to look around, trying to figure out which way leads back to campus. There isn't a soul in sight, as I'm surrounded by trees so dense, it's difficult to see the sun, let alone another person. Taking a deep breath, I try to calm my racing heart and steady my breathing. I've been lazier this week than I normally am, on account of leaving for the academy, so I haven't kept up my routine.

The first two moons have already risen in the sky, their pale white and orange hues stretching over the canopy. The other moons are still off in the distance and won't be seen for another hour. For a realm so dependent on them, they often take residence alongside the sun, depending on the time of year. I close my eyes and extend my senses, trying to feel for any magic users nearby.

I sense nothing.

Opening my eyes, I change directions and run towards what I think is East based on the position of the sun and the faint outline of our moons, hoping I'll run into someone who can help me get back. I'm rounding the corner when I run into a solid wall of muscle. My arms splay out as I try to catch myself, and my body lifts off the ground.

Oh no, not lifted off the ground. That's me falling on top of someone. In slow motion, I watch as we both hit the ground, me on top of him. His body is hard as a rock, and every contour of his muscles press into me, every nerve ending in my body on fire. I scramble to get off him, but his arms wrap around me, holding me in place. My hair slips out of its ponytail, framing our faces in a curtain of waves.

Gilded eyes meet mine, losing me in their depths as though I'm tethered in their orbit. Every moment narrows until it's just us, and I can't look away. His arms loosen their grip, and one hand comes up to tangle in my hair, while the other wraps around my waist. I'm unsure of what to do, and I don't want to leave, so I lay there, relaxing into his hold.

His lips part and I blink. "It's you," he whispers.

My eyes search his, trying to place how I know him. The way he makes me feel is nostalgic. His aura is a beautiful golden color, his hair jet black across his forehead, and I can feel the magic swirling around him, dancing with mine. Pointy ears tell me he's fae, that much is certain. But I don't know who he is. I couldn't begin to guess his fae order. He's not wearing his glasses or a suit like he had been in the dining hall. Instead, he wears cargo jeans and a tight white button-up shirt emphasizing every inch of muscle adorning his body, though several buttons have come undone, revealing a good portion of his torso.

Between us, the blue glow of my skin pulses, and his eyes widen in surprise. He leans closer, his face inches from mine, and his breath warms my skin. "Your aura," he whispers.

"What's it like?"

"A soft, cyan light radiates from you, illuminating the darkest of days. It pulses with a swirled pattern, like a whirlpool of colors, changing in intensity like the tide."

The air around us crackles with intensity, and I'm rooted to the spot. His eyes burn into mine, and I know he's going to kiss me. He leans in, and my heart beats wildly in my chest. Logic wars with instinct; I have no idea who this man is, but my body seems to trust him more than my mind does. I gulp in a deep breath, hold it for a moment, and then move closer.

As I lay in the bushes with him, his arms still encircling me, a million thoughts race through my head. Who is this man? What kind of fae is he? Why do I feel so drawn to him?

Is he an incubus fae? Is *that* why I'm losing my ever-loving mind over him?

His body tenses beneath mine when the laughter of students peals through the air, and we both freeze. We had been so close to that kiss—but it was not meant to be. He rolls us off the path and into a patch of bushes just in time.

We stay there, holding our breath until the students pass and their voices fade away. Then slowly, he loosens his grip on me and I roll off him onto my back. We both breathe sighs of relief. The warmth from his body still lingers on my skin as I stare up at the sky through the dappled shadows of palm tree leaves above us. My heart pounds in my chest as I replay what had just happened between us—what we almost let happen—and how wrong that would have been. I don't even know this man.

We lie there in silence for a few moments. "I'm Theo." He rolls onto his side to face me.

"I'm Rose." I turn so I'm looking at him. "It's nice to meet you, Theo."

He grins at me, and I can't help but smile back.

CHAPTER FOUR

THEO

My heart makes a racket in my chest as I grin back at Rose. "The pleasure is all mine," I vow. "I'd apologize for crashing into you, but I'd be lying. It's the best thing that's happened to me in a long time."

She laughs, and the sound is like music to my ears. *Who is this creature? And how can I make her mine?*

I help her stand, and she dusts off her shorts. "I should get back." She hesitates. "Where did your tattoos go?"

"I spell most of them on campus. Don't want people to get the wrong impression of me." Some of the professors gave me the stink eye for it. "Spend the day with me."

A blush creeps up her cheeks, turning her complexion a delicious shade of pink. "I don't know," she hedges. Her phone goes off, and she slips it out of her back pocket, checking it with wide eyes before tucking it away.

I see on her face the moment she decides she won't, and I try not to let it crush me. My reaction to her is so far out of my norm, and she might be feeling the same way—not quite sure how to tame whatever it is we feel. I try to give her an out. "I understand," I say, hoping she'll change her mind. "It's a busy week."

She nods. "Yeah, fall semester. But I've got a meeting with Dean Fallgren that I've got to get ready for."

"Of course," I say, trying to sound like it's no big deal. "Maybe another time."

"I'd like that." She turns on her heel, and heads in the direction the students came from.

A gasp escapes me, and I call out. "Rose!" She wheels around, a hopeful look on her face. "I didn't get your number."

She presses a hand to her chest and flushes. "Oh, you're right. Sorry." She inputs her digits into my phone before passing it back to me. Giving me a little wave, she disappears around the bend.

I stare at my phone for a moment, reading her name over and over again. She didn't give me a last name, but I've got her first name. *She is a rose, and her beauty is rare—her heart, a tender bud that only beauty can compare.* A grin splits my face as I tuck my phone away. *Rose.* It fits. We're jogging in the same direction, and once we make it to campus, I watch her walk into the staff dorms.

I'm going to make her mine.

∼

ROSE

"Rose!" Gideon's panicked voice barrels through the phone as soon as the call connects.

"What's wrong, Dad? I just got your text," I ask, heart in my throat. He'd asked me to call right away.

"How soon can you get here? Bumblebee is on the way!" There's an edge of both panic and excitement in his voice.

I knew my mom was close to being at full-term with my sister, but I didn't expect things to be moving so fast. "I can sift right now." My feet carry me as fast as possible in the direction of the staff dorms. "Can you give the Dean a call? She's a hard ass and won't sift me unless you ask."

KATHY HAAN

"Got it, kiddo. See you soon." The call ends just as I reach the staff quarters.

I shove my way past a professor who's leaving the building. "Sorry," I call over my shoulder as I make a beeline for the Dean's room. It's easy to find, not because of the gold posted signs, but from the trail of ice leading that way. I knock on the solid wood door, and the skin on my knuckles sticks on account of the small film of ice.

"Come in," a voice calls from inside, and I slip into the freezing room.

Her living room is tidy and filled with pictures of what I presume to be family.

The Dean sits at a well-kempt rolltop desk, looking over a file and glances up once I'm fully in the room and shuts the door. "Is everything okay? We're not supposed to meet for another two hours." Her brows furrow in concern. "In my office, not my dorm."

"My mom's—"

My explanation gets interrupted by her phone ringing, and she glances at the screen for a split second before answering. "High King Finn, what can I do for you?" Her already pale complexion drains of all color. "Of course, right away."

She sets the phone down and takes a deep breath before looking back at me. "Your mother is in labor, and your father has requested that you be sifted to their location."

"Thank you, Dean. I'm ready to go now." I don't waste any time.

She stands. "Of course." She holds out her hand to me, the cold felt from the distance between us. As soon as our hands connect, I'm dragged through a slip in space, and we land in the foyer of my family's mountain home on Rexuna. The first person I see is Oz, who rushes through the hall with a heating pad. He skids to a stop when he sees me, pulling me into his arms.

Oz is Sumerian, but was the first vampire ever created, so now he's enormous, though not as big as most of the fae in our family. My brother inherited his dark features. Though we're twins, Oz is Bennett's dad, and Gideon is mine. We treat all my mom's mates as our dads, though.

"Hey, kiddo." He squeezes me tight and then glances at my dean, who's standing there looking out of place. "Thank you for bringing her home."

"Of course." She glances around, taking in the foyer of our family's home, and then without another word, she's gone.

"Come on," Oz takes my hand and pulls me down the hall where we bump into my sister, Nova, whose expression is both traumatized and excited.

"How's Mom doing?" We enter the room where the rest of my dads pace back and forth in varying stages of worry, apprehension, and excitement. The father of this baby could be any one of them, but we'll never find out, because it doesn't matter.

"Mom is good." Gideon comes to a stop in front of me and pulls me into a hug. "But she's getting tired. She'll be pushing soon." He's the most handsome of the bunch, but I might be a little biased. I inherited his dimples.

Gideon steps back and Finn takes his place. "We're so glad you're here," he whispers before kissing my forehead and stepping back.

My other dads take turns hugging me as well, until finally I'm left standing in front of my mom. She lies in the bed, with a thin sheen of sweat on her beautiful face. Everyone tells me I look like her, and I can see the resemblance now more than ever. Her hair is a little curlier than mine, though, and she's thicker than I am, although I'm not thin either. I'm more muscular than thick, and my curves have enough padding to hold onto.

"Hey, Mama," I say softly as I sit down on the edge of the bed and take her hand.

"Hey, baby girl." She smiles at me, and exhaustion nestles in the bags under her eyes.

By the time baby Brianna arrives, it's four o'clock in the morning, and most of us are like zombies, save for Oz, Auguste, and Grandpa who are vampires and don't need sleep. The rest of us are fae (save for grandma, who's a witch) and need at least six hours to function well.

"How is she?" Bennett comes into the room and sits down on the other side of mom. He's got Mom's curls, and is as tall as Oz, though not as buff—yet. Another few months and he'll surpass them all.

I leap from my seat, embracing my twin brother. By the time he arrived, Mom was in full-on push mode, and he wasn't keen on being in the room for it.

"She's good." I lie back down. "Tired, but good."

"And Bee?" he whispers as he tiptoes closer and peeks at where our baby sister rests on Mom's chest. They're both passed out. A tiny pink hat sits atop Bee's head, and her cheeks already fill out like a little ball of dough.

"She's perfect." I breathe.

We share a moment in awe of the wonder that is our baby squish before Mom starts to stir. "Hey." The sleepy lilt in her voice doesn't detract from its melodic tone. "Come meet your sister."

We gather around the bed and take turns holding our new sister. Her eyes are like caramel drops and her skin so pale, it's almost translucent. Nova holds her like she's as fragile as a new leaf. She's not, as hours have passed and fae mature fast. It's a moment I'll never forget, and one that I'm grateful to have been a part of. I want a small army of children of my own, though not for a long time, and lots of mates to keep me on my toes.

Not long after, Mekhi arrives with gifts in tow. We haven't told my parents we're dating, but considering some of them can read minds, it won't take them long to find out. We've all been excused from school for a week to spend time with Bee.

"Hey, Khi." Nova blushes. She's the only one who calls him that.

He wraps his arms around her, spinning her. "How's my favorite Luna?"

She giggles, fluffing her dress when he sets her down. "Mom won't let me throw a birthday party for Bee." She pouts.

"Novaleigh," Penn warns from the doorway. "We're keeping Brianna's birth from the news until she's matured, for the same reason others don't know yet that you're a princess, either." He crouches so he's at her level. "Besides, it'll be a year before she gets an actual birthday."

"That doesn't even make sense, Dad."

I chuckle, sharing a look with Mekhi. Though fae births are at an all-time high thanks to my parents' soul-bonded union, it's still safer to wait the two years it takes for fae to reach maturity before we announce the addition of more heirs.

For now, I'm content to sit back and enjoy the peace and love that fills this room. This is my family, and I wouldn't trade them for anything in the world.

∼

"You've got two hours; I can't distract them any longer than that." Bennett tinkers with a skeet launcher at the edge of the waterfall that runs underneath our house. The floors are see-through, so we see the occasional spirit fish beneath our feet. "And keep your dick in your pants." He levels Mekhi with a stern look as he turns up the notch on his homemade toy.

"Jesus, Benny. We're virgins!" I whisper.

"For now," he mutters under his breath.

I elbow Mekhi in the shoulder, and he grins, looping his arm around me as we pick our way down to the lake. We fling off our shoes and dip our feet into the freezing water. This high on the mountain, it's already well into autumn.

"You know, I can't keep my dick in my pants if I'm not wearing any," Mekhi teases, pulling me in for a kiss.

"Mekhi!"

He chuckles as I shove him away. He peels his shirt off, baring his toned chest and abs. "Come on, Rose. It's not like anyone is here. Let's swim." He yanks his shorts off, revealing a pair of red boxers. Against his tanned skin, they stand out in stark contrast.

I can't believe him. I shake my head, laughing, but I don't object as I shuck my clothes but keep my bra and underwear on and join him in the ice-cold water. Thankfully, I wore my cute ones today.

Mekhi's heated gaze lands on my chest, and I blush, though I don't turn away. He closes the gap between us in three strides and pulls me into an embrace. My lips are on his, and a sudden warmth runs through my body, thawing the chill of the water. He hoists my legs, and I wrap them around his hips. His erection presses against my heat, and though two thin scraps of fabric still separate us, I feel it all.

I clutch at his shoulders and rock my hips against his. A low groan sounds in his throat. He rips his mouth from mine, breathing heavily as he rests his forehead against my collarbone.

"You're killing me, Rose," he whispers before pulling back to look into my eyes. I've never seen such heat in his.

"We don't have to have sex." I search his gaze.

"I know, but I want to. With you."

My heart flutters at the sincerity in his words. I press my lips to his, and as we kiss in the middle of the lake, surrounded by nothing but cool mountain air, starlight, and the glow of my skin. I know this is right. This is what I want.

Tightening my hold around his waist, I free one of his hands and he pulls back to see what I'm doing. But when I place it on my breast, he understands. I nod at him. He returns the nod, a silent agreement between us, and I know he will keep me safe. Slowly, we move out of the water, both of us shaking from the chill.

He lowers me to the blanket we've got set up on shore, and I unclasp my bra, exposing my breasts to his gaze. My nipples harden under his scrutiny, and I gasp when he takes one into his mouth. His tongue swirls around it, tugging it gently and sending a jolt of pleasure through me. I arch my back as he moves to the other breast, sending my hips in circles. His knee wedges between my thighs and I moan as I spread them wider, wanting more.

"You are so beautiful," he breathes before moving to my neck.

"I need you," I beg. "Where's the condom?"

He freezes before sitting back on his heels. "Fuck. I don't have one. I'm sorry, Rose."

I take a deep breath. We can wait and find one in town, or…

"Maybe, I mean," I pause, my cheeks flaming. "We don't have to use one."

He stares at me, surprise flashing across his face. Then he smiles. "Your dads would murder me if I got you pregnant."

I laugh. "Yeah, they would." Blowing a frustrated sigh, I sit up and use my magic to dry us both off before Mekhi settles next to me, our legs entwined.

His erection presses against my hip as his fingers trail over my bare skin, giving me goosebumps. I sigh and lean my head against his shoulder, enjoying the feeling of being so close to him.

We take our time exploring each other's bodies, kissing, and murmuring compliments as we study what each other likes. Finally, when neither of us can take it any longer, I take his hand and guide him down the flat plane of my belly. I nod, urging him to continue. His fingers trail over the small mound between my thighs before dipping further. My heart hammers in my chest as he drags his finger inside of me, and I moan. I grip his shoulders as he continues to move, slipping in another finger after I adjust to the intrusion.

"This okay?" he whispers.

"Don't you dare stop," I growl, earning a chuckle from him.

He leans down and captures my lips in a deep kiss before increasing the pressure of his fingers. My body moves with his rhythm, and I let out a loud cry when I reach the summit of pleasure. He smiles, triumphant, and presses soft kisses against my heated skin until I'm able to slow my breath.

"You have no idea how long I've wanted to do that." There's more gravel to his voice than normal, and it just does something to me.

I breathe a laugh. "Hope it was worth the wait."

He grins, eyes still smoldering. "Always."

We lay there in contented silence until the sun sets. Eventually, we dress and head back home, both of us glowing from our secret little rendezvous.

CHAPTER FIVE

JAX

"You need to listen to me! Rose hasn't been back to our room all week. She's not in her classes." I stop by Fallgren's office for the eighth time this week. I've also caught her sixteen times in passing thanks to us sharing some of the same routes across campus. Yesterday, I even skipped my afternoon classes so I could sift to Convectus Castle to see if she was okay, but the guards wouldn't let me in. "I'm worried something has happened to her. All her stuff is still in the room. Why aren't you doing something? You're the one who asked me to look after her!"

Dean Fallgren's lips press into a thin line, and the temperature in her office plummets, ice crystals twirling in the air between us. "You are not to breathe a word of this to anyone or you will be expelled and face punishment for treason. Do I make myself clear?" she hisses at me.

She's always been strict, even with her family. I swallow hard and nod. "Yes, Dean." What's going on? And why all the secrecy?

Gods, has something already happened to her?

"Good." She stands. "Rose has been excused from classes until Monday. I won't discuss why, but it has to do with the royal family, and that's all you need to know."

"So, she's okay? Nothing bad happened to her?"

"She's fine. Now get out of my office before I change my mind and pull you from tryouts for bothering me." She points to the exit. "If it weren't for your concern of another student, I would have by now."

Bowing my head, I leave her office, barely avoiding being hit in the face with the door as she slams it shut behind me.

I'm not sure what's going on, but at least I know it's not like she's been abducted or anything. I wish I'd gotten her cell number, so I could've checked to see if things were alright. A part of me is also upset she didn't give me a heads up either way. I know we're just roommates, but I've spent the entire week worried sick.

It's late Sunday night by the time I hear the electronic lock on the door to our room disengage. I sit up in bed, not bothering to turn on the light as Rose enters, but feeling immeasurable relief when she returns. The anxiety in my chest eases.

"Hey," she says softly when she notices me awake. Deep purple bags line her heavy-lidded eyes. We're plunged into darkness when the door shuts behind her, and I hear her set something down on her desk before she comes over to her bed and yanks the covers back.

"Hey." I turn over, too exhausted to come up with anything else. "Where were you?"

"Family stuff," she mumbles as she slides under the blankets.

"Is everything okay?"

"Yeah." She yawns. "Just tired."

That's all I get? No apology for worrying me all week? No explanation of what happened? I'm not sure what to say without making it sound like I'm a creeper, so I just lay back down and close my eyes.

"Goodnight, Jax," she says after a few minutes.

"Night, Rose."

I'm not sure what to think as I drift off to sleep. It's obvious Rose is tired, so I'll let her be for now. But come morning, she owes me an explanation.

ROSE

My alarm blares, a shrill reminder that Monday has come again. I groan and drag myself out of bed; I'm exhausted after spending most of the week curled up with my baby sister while mom got some much-needed rest. Even my dads had to fight for time with her; I wanted to keep her all to myself, just like I had when Nova was born.

Squinting into the morning light, I find Jax already up and dressed, sitting at his desk with a book open in front of him. His lamp casts a warm glow over his face, and if I weren't so heavy-lidded, I'd stand here to admire him a little longer; his square jaw, lined with stubble, and the small sweep of curls resting against his forehead. He really has no idea just how handsome he is.

"Mornin'," I mumble as I collect my textbooks and notebooks.

Jax grabs his backpack and swings it onto his bed. "What kind of family stuff kept you away all week? Everything okay?" He asks as he strides over to his dresser and rummages through it. His low-slung shorts hug the globes of his ass just right, and I avert my eyes before I'm caught staring.

I pause and shrug, not wanting to give anything away. "It's complicated." And I'm not ready to talk about it yet. Maybe never with him. I still haven't decided if I can trust him. Even though we had that heart-to-heart my first night, he'd ruined it the next day.

He runs a hand through his hair before leaning his shoulder against the wall, facing me. His jaw grinds in frustration and his nostrils flare as he takes a deep breath.

"You didn't call."

"I don't have your number." I pause my rummaging through my bag to study him.

"You could've gotten it from the school directory."

I shrug. "Didn't think of it."

He stalks over to my side of the room and yanks my cell off its charger on my nightstand before shoving it in my face.

"Unlock this."

I enter my passcode into my phone and hand it back to him. He types something in before putting it back on my nightstand.

"Happy?" I scowl.

"No, Rose, I'm not happy. Do you know how long it took before I started to worry?"

"I don't—"

"Three hours."

I whip my head back towards where he stands next to my bed with his arms crossed over his chest. "Why?"

"They were serving lasagna for supper, and I remember you saying how much you loved your dad's, so when you didn't show, I got worried."

"You remembered that?" I said it in passing during one of our conversations, but I didn't think he was really listening.

"Of course." Jax flinches, indignant. "And when you didn't come home, I went to the Dean's office, only for her to just dismiss me. She did it all week until Friday. She said it was a family matter. Now I'm sitting here, looking at you, and wondering if everything really is okay."

He steps closer to me, and I take a step back until my legs hit the edge of my bed. I sit down hard, clutching my bag to my chest as though it were a shield.

"Look, I'm not going to force you to tell me what's going on, but I want you to know that I'm here for you. Whatever it is."

He holds out his hand for me to take, but I just stare at it. I'm not ready to trust him yet, but his words touch something deep inside me. One of the last interactions we had before I left had me a little disjointed because he was acting standoffish, so I'm not sure what to think. I take his hand, letting him pull me into a hug. I let out a sigh and relax against his chest, the warmth of his body seeping into me. Jax runs his hand up and down my back in a comforting gesture, and I close my eyes, letting myself just breathe in his scent of pine and musk.

"Thank you, but I promise things are okay." I probably could've told him that before I let him hug me, but damn it, I wanted a hug.

And he did too if the way he's holding onto me is any indication. "If you ever need to talk, feel free to do the same you know."

He chuckles. "Yeah, I can do that."

"Good." I step back, but not before he gives me one last squeeze. "Mind if I hop in the shower first?"

"Nope, go ahead. I'm just checking out the assignment for my first class."

I head into the bathroom and use the invisibility cloak while I undress and get in the shower. I know he's been trying not to ogle me, but it's hard to ignore when someone is nude right in front of you.

The shower is modern, with stone accents, and Jax must've hung an aromatherapy plant from the shower head, because it wasn't here last time. It's like eucalyptus, but they call it seaspawn, and it grows near the windmill on the North Shore of Academia. Instead of green leaves, its leaves are blue and velvety. I take my time in the shower, enjoying the hot water cascading down my body and the heat seeping into my muscles. Once I'm out and dried off, I slip on a pair of denim shorts and a plum-colored, ribbed V-neck tank top before heading back out.

Jax lays sprawled on his bed, his long legs hanging off the edge. He wears a pair of red basketball shorts and a band t-shirt, highlighting his muscles as it clings to him like a second skin. He glances up at me as I enter, and I can't help but admire his chiseled jaw and piercing cobalt eyes with flecks of green and yellow. Even from here, I can make out the smattering of freckles on his cheeks, and I want to trace them with my fingers.

"You ready for class yet?" I gesture to the open books and papers strewn about his half of the room. I wouldn't call him messy by any stretch of the imagination, but he's got organized chaos going on. "What's your major, anyway?"

"As ready as I'll ever be, I guess." He sighs and sits up, running a hand through his short curly hair. "It's supposed to be finance, but I like collecting treasure, not managing anyone else's." His eyes dip to where I'm braiding the hair at my waist.

"Never been much for it myself." I stride to my side of the room to gather my things. "I'm going to grab some breakfast—Oh!" I throw my hands up to shield my eyes from where he's undressing, and I spin around, but not before I saw him there in all his splendor. He's all bulky, sleek lines, with tattoos accentuating much of what he's got hidden under his clothes. *Are they all that big?* Or just him? "See you later?"

"You can see me now, Rose." The warmth of his body pressing against mine adds to the intensity of his voice. Something about the way his finger traces my shoulder and then my arm sets off alarm bells and ignites something dangerous inside me.

He retreats, allowing a rush of cool air to hit me, robbing me of his heat. I make my escape before he has a chance to say anything else. The entire way to breakfast, I keep picturing the muscles carved into his tapered waist and the way his shorts hugged his—

"Hey, Rose." Penelope greets me as I get in line with a tray. "Everything okay? I haven't seen you in any classes yet."

"I'm okay," I smile, not really in the mood to make up any lies. She's been nothing but nice to me, but I can't tell anyone about baby Bee. "Just had some family stuff to take care of."

Her eyes widen a smidge before she gives me an almost imperceptible nod.

I fill my tray with fresh fruit, green juice, and oatmeal while Penelope sticks to her usual of every breakfast cereal known to fae, bacon, and toast. We head over to an empty table, trying to ignore the questions people ask their friends about me in what they think is a quiet tone, though I hear them just fine.

"Isn't that the Luna fae who freaked out at the beginning of classes?"

"I wonder what had her so worked up."

"Who do you think she has the hots for? You know they only do that when they're DTF."

"I heard she's from Earth."

"Is that why her accent is so weird? It's like Thor and Sofia Vergara had a baby."

My face heats as I take a seat, and I keep my head down, not wanting anyone to see the anger in my eyes. I know they're just curious, but it still hurts to be the center of gossip. It's partly why I don't want people to know who I am.

I'm too focused on my meal to notice her enter until she plops down right next to me on the smooth wooden bench. The girl with shock-white hair who'd seen through my invisibility cloak beams at me while she munches on a crunchy apple out the side of her mouth. I shift nervously, but before I can move away, she offers a hand in greeting.

"Hi, I'm Bella," she says, her mouth full of apple. With a shaky voice, I tell her my name and introduce her to Penelope. "First year?" she asks, as if she didn't already know.

Penelope and I both nod, and Bella hums in understanding. "I'm a fourth year, but I remember how hard it is to adjust. Especially since the school is so big."

"Yeah, it's a lot to take in," I agree, glancing around at the rapidly filling cafeteria full of students milling about. Though it's much smaller than any university I'd attend if I stayed on Earth.

My stomach clenches as I remember how easily Bella saw through my invisibility cloak during orientation in the auditorium. Why is she pretending like she didn't? Fear stirs inside my chest.

"So, what's your story?" Bella asks, and I can tell by the mischievous glint in her eye that she's thrown me for a loop. She seems more interested in speaking to me than Lopey—the nickname I've given Penelope—and it sends my hackles up even more.

"I'm from Earth," I hedge, and her eyebrows shoot up as though she's surprised. *What is her deal?* It's not a lie. I was born in Chile when my parents were just King and Queen of the Vampires. "My mom is from Minnesota, and my dad is from Italy." Biological parents. The rest of the table doesn't need to know I have six other 'dads' in addition to them.

"Wow! I'd love to hear all about it sometime. I've never been." She turns further towards me as a thought strikes her. "Have you met any movie stars?!"

Shaking my head, I chuckle nervously. "No, I'm pretty sure they don't hang out in the same circles as me." Although, that might've been a tiny lie. My parents are friends with many noble and famous people, and I'm sure I've met some during my childhood.

"That's a shame." She pouts. *Did I imagine what happened in the auditorium?* "If you ever do, make sure to tell me all about it. I bet you have some great stories."

"I'm sure she does. Rose is full of surprises. I'm from Luporia, mouse order." Penelope interjects, and I throw her a thankful smile for redirecting the conversation. My discomfort must've been obvious.

"Oh, how adorable." Bella giggles before she turns somber. "Shadow and storm order here."

I still and cock my head to take better stock of her. A close family friend is of that order, and it's super rare and not easy to control. Her white hair and midnight skin are similar, too.

Professors mix with students at the tables, and a few of them give me odd looks, but I'm not sure if it's because they know who I am—the girl who glowed in the middle of breakfast—or if they're just trying to figure out who I am since I haven't been in any classes aside from that half class two weeks ago.

"Excuse me, Miss?" a guy with blond, messy hair that's longer on top than the sides stops right next to me. I can tell right away that he's a vampire, on account of the no-breathing thing, and his preternatural movements. Some vampires attend the academy because they have witch blood but are not naturally adept at magic. "I heard your accent and thought you might be Rose."

"Hi." I don't confirm or deny who I am, but just give him a tiny shake of my head that I know he'll catch with his acute predator eyesight. I take in his football build, enormous hazel eyes, long nose, and square jaw. He has a sprinkle of freckles across the bridge of his nose and a jagged scar that runs down his cheek and disappears into the collar of his blue T-shirt, though it doesn't detract from his beauty. There isn't much that can permanently scar a supernatural creature—even tattoos must be spelled to stay— but this vamp bears a mark that must've been recent, or it's a curse. I'm guessing the latter. He must've come for the war, which means he already knows who I am, and who my parents are. Some of the fae used it against the vampires, and only time can heal it. "What's your name?" I gesture for him to have a seat. He won't tell anyone my real identity, or he'll face the wrath of our entire coven. Something no vampire wants.

"Eli." He slides in next to Lopey, whose cheeks turn bright red, and the next thing I know, she's disappeared.

He makes to comment on it, but I give him a tiny shake of my head to not draw attention to her cloaking herself. She's skittish around new people.

"Where are you from?" He's got that Southern American thing going for him, where he's all boyish charm, take him home to Momma, and he'll leave you with a broken heart? Paired with his accent, I'm betting on Texas.

"Dallas," he drawls, his grin showcasing a perfect set of straight, white teeth. *Called it.* "Part of Maeve's line."

Huh, my aunt's line. "How old are you?" Vampires stop aging when they're turned, but Eli doesn't have a wrinkle on him, so he must've been young.

"Twenty-two, but I was turned the night of my twenty-first birthday." He offers me a grape from the bunch on his plate and I decline. Vampires don't need food, but they love to eat. Everything on his tray he keeps separated from each other, and he eats one food group at a time. Peculiar creature.

The bell rings to give us a five-minute warning. "Maybe I'll see you around." I stand.

"Hope so." He grins. "Say bye to your friend for me."

Bella says her goodbyes and goes to join her friends at another table because she doesn't have a class until period two.

Penelope and I head to our first class of the day, which we have together. I hadn't noticed her in Professor Blush's class on account of Deakan and Kieran drawing so much attention to themselves.

"Do you think anyone else will figure out who I am?" I ask her as we walk, feeling a little anxious about it.

"Doubtful." She ties her hair into a bun using a pencil she had tucked behind her ear. "You're just another student here. Besides, your family does a good job of keeping you out of the public eye."

"Yeah." I give her a tight smile. Let's just hope Kieran doesn't out me like he's threatened to.

～

THE HUMIDITY in the greenhouse causes the hair at my nape to stick to my skin as I try to focus on the task at hand. We're supposed to be finding and classifying different types of roots, but it's hard to focus with so many distractions. Like the fact that my arch-nemesis—Kieran—just happens to be in this class with me.

The weight of his attention makes me uneasy, and I can tell he's just waiting for an opportunity to strike. I should've known he'd be out to make me feel uncomfortable. Hanging my royalty over my head like a noose, trying to out me to everyone. It's not like I can just leave the class, though. I need the credit for it.

I'm so wrapped up in my thoughts that I don't even hear Penelope until she's right next to me, speaking in a low voice so only I can hear. "He's been like that all class." She nods her head in the direction of Kieran. "I think he's just trying to get a rise out of you."

I want to roll my eyes, but I manage to keep them trained on the gnarled root in front of me. I'm pretty sure this is the same one my mom grows in a pot in the kitchen of our family home. "Does he always have to be such a jerk?" I mutter under my breath.

"You know what they say about guys like him," Penelope responds sagely. "They're just projecting their own insecurities onto others."

"Yeah, maybe," I grumble, but I doubt it. This feels personal. Like I've done something to hurt him enough to retaliate.

Professor Blush holds a plant up for us to see and starts naming off the different parts, while I take notes. Until my phone buzzes, anyway.

Pulling my phone out under the table, I tap the display to see who it is, and Theo's name sprawls across the screen in a text.

> I'd like to make you dinner on Friday. Can I pick you up at 7?

My chest swoops unexpectedly at the question, and I have to force

KATHY HAAN

myself to breathe. It's just a date, I tell myself firmly. *A date with someone who isn't my boyfriend.* But Mekhi told me I could pursue other men, as long as he's got a seat at my table. Even so, I want to run it by him first.

> Hey babe. Alright if I go on a date on Friday?

His response back is quick.

> Go ahead, but I'd prefer it if you didn't ask. I don't want to hear about any randoms, only if things get serious.

I want to tell him I'd never entertain a random guy, that they'd have to be serious contenders for a permanent place by my side, but I don't. Instead, I just send him a kissy face emoji and an "I love you!" back. The next time I see him in person, I'll have that conversation.

> Love you, too. Be safe.

I type out a response to Theo before I can overthink it too much. My face heats, and I can't help the tiny grin that pulls at the corners of my lips.

> How about I meet you in front of the North entrance to Witches Woods?

I type back and hit send. If he picks me up, I feel like there's more pressure to end the night there, and I don't know him well enough. He doesn't give me stalker vibes, but you never know. I have a lot to protect.

> Perfect. Wear jeans and boots if you've got them. See you then.

Interesting. I shove my phone back in my pocket before anyone can see the ridiculous grin plastered on my face. I'm sure Kieran or

Deakan would just love to use this against me. They already tried to mess with Mekhi. I won't let them do it to Theo, too.

∼

IT DOESN'T TAKE me long to find the locker room so I can change into workout clothes for my next class. It's combat training with Professor Thorn. That's one thing I need very little of thanks to my dads always treating Bennett, Mekhi, and me the same. When we weren't training for war using both magic and weapons, we were sparring in the ring. Bennett usually won based on sheer size alone, but I was a close second. The last war in the realm was between the vampires on Earth and the fae in Bedlam. Penn, Casimir, and Grimm, now three of my dads, had stolen my mom's memories and kept her from us, and we brought war to their doorstep to get her back.

Locker sixteen sits in the far corner of the room, and I wade through the packed space to get there. My hand grips the metal combo lock, ready to turn the dial and enter in my code.

But then I notice something strange. There's a piece of lined, yellow paper tucked into the doorframe. A chill races down my spine as I glance at my classmates and shove the paper into my pocket without reading it. I take my time getting dressed, letting the area clear out. Once I'm alone, I open the paper with trembling hands.

It's a clear warning with a simple message written with what smells like fresh blood:

Every Rose has its thorns,
but does every Thorn have its Rose?

My heart thunders as I take in the implications. Are they talking about Coach Thorn? Or is he the one sending me threats? I change then stow my bag and grab a pair of red gloves, wrapping them around my hands.

The sun beats down on the arena, the heat stifling with no wind.

Sweat already plasters my hair to my face, and not just from the temperature. With cautious steps, I approach Coach Thorn, who gives me a once over before turning back to the clipboard where he's making notes. He's got short black hair, a clean-shaven face, and an athletic build. He's not ugly, but he's got an off-brand Tom Holland look about him. "Name," he says without looking up at me. "You're the woman who was on family leave?"

"Yes, sir." Instead of saying my name out loud, I point to it on his sheet. *A yellow, lined sheet.* My stomach lurches.

Thorn glances at it and then looks back at me before his attention flickers to the gloves I'm wearing. "Welcome back, Rose. You'll be working with the level three women today."

I furrow my brows. "Why?"

He caps his pen and tucks it behind his ear before leveling me with a stare. "The Dean said you've had training. Is that not the case?" *Is he assessing my threat level?*

I'll show him I'm no damsel. "Why are the men getting different treatment?" I demand. "We're all here to learn. We should all be on the same playing field."

Thorn gives me an unimpressed look. "Women are just as capable as men," he says plainly. "But they're not as strong, and they don't have the same stamina. It's a colossal waste of time to put you in with them."

I open my mouth to argue, but he cuts me off. "If you want to prove to me that you're just as good as the men, then I'll put you in with them. But if you can't hack it, then you'll be stuck working with the women." *What's his angle here?*

I square my shoulders and tilt my chin up. "Fine. I'll prove it to you on one condition."

He humors me, and I continue. "Let the other women prove it to you, too."

Studying me for a beat, he nods his head. "Fine." He tucks the clipboard under his arm and pulls the whistle out from under his shirt. "We'll put it to a vote."

"Careful, Rose, your tyrannical roots are showing," a deep voice purrs in my ear, and I stiffen.

∽

I KNOW THAT VOICE. It's the one that's been haunting my dreams and my waking moments for the past week. It's the voice of my nemesis. Pivoting around, I come face to face with the green-eyed fae. He gives me a devilish grin, and my stomach does a little flip-flop in response. No, it can't be Coach Thorn. It's got to be *Kieran*. He must've stuck the note in my locker before anyone got in there.

"What are you doing here?" I hiss. "This is a combat class."

"I know," he says, his eyes flickering over my body in a way that makes heat pool low in my belly. "I'm—"

"Kieran, over here please," Coach calls out, and Kieran runs his tongue over his lip rings as he trains his eyes on me while he walks backwards towards the center of the room.

"You, too, Rose."

Kieran turns around, and I reluctantly follow him to the center of the pitch. Coach Thorn hands us both a staff before walking over to the sidelines where the other students gather.

"Alright, class," he shouts. "Today we'll be doing a little sparring. I'll be calling out pairs, and you'll fight until one of you is disarmed for at least fifteen seconds or submits. Rose and Kieran, you'll be up first."

I shoot a death glare at Kieran, but he just smirks at me in response. How he expects to keep all his piercings intact during combat class is beyond me. But I guess that's part of his appeal—not that I'm noticing he has any whatsoever—he's always up for a challenge. If he thinks a few little threats can scare me, I'll show him.

We circle each other, taking measure of our dominant sides based on which foot we lead with, and when Coach Thorn blows the whistle to start, Kieran is the first to strike. He aims for my head, but I duck out of the way and swing my staff at his legs. He leaps over it with ease and comes at me from the other side.

I parry his blow, and we continue to circle each other, attacking and defending in turn. A wrong move on my part sends my staff flying behind him, and before I can even react, he's got me pinned against the wall with his staff pressed so tight against my throat, I can't even swallow.

"Yield," he growls, his eyes boring into mine, breath hot on my neck.

I glare at him and clench my teeth. There's no way I'm giving up, no matter how good he looks when he's being all dominant like this. No, definitely not good looking.

"Never," I spit. "I'll yield when you do," I grind out, and a rumble of laughter vibrates through his chest but cuts off quick when I press my hips against his.

He never sees it coming. I bring my knee up hard into his groin, and he blocks it at the last second—he saw *that* part. Kieran doesn't see what's next. He's so proud of himself for blocking that feigned attack that he doesn't even see my fist connect with his nose until it's too late. He staggers back, clutching his nose in pain, and I take the opportunity to disarm him.

I sweep his legs out from under him and press the broad end of my staff to his throat. My knees pin his shoulders to the grass, and no matter how much he bucks, he can't escape my hold. It's hardly fair. I'm a Luna fae, and my magic regenerates when I'm healing and harming. So, as his exhaustion mounts, mine fades just as my glow dims.

"Yield," I snarl, savoring the victory. The whoops and hollers from the other students drown out his words, but it's there on his lips, clear as day.

He yields.

CHAPTER SIX

ROSE

There are two things I'm certain of in life. One is that I'll never back down from a fight, especially knowing my Luna order makes me incredibly difficult to defeat. And the other is that Kieran will never stop trying to get under my skin. He's relentless in his pursuit of me, and that only makes me more resolved to stop him. But I can't deny that there's a part of me that likes it. Maybe even enjoys it.

Does that make me a sadist, or a masochist? Either way, I'm in for a world of hurt with Kieran. Because he's not just my tormenter—he's my attractive, tempting bully. I haven't figured out why he's sending me threats, but as long as he doesn't out me to everyone, I can handle everything else.

Coach Thorn tends to Kieran's wounds while a brunette with short, spiked hair faces off against an orange-skinned fae with a series of ridges on his forehead. Their movements are slow, and perspiration flies off the guy, just missing a group of students cheering them on. I take a seat on the sidelines next to Raven, a witch from Occasus. She's a short red head with more freckles than skin, and a fast-talking, high-pitched voice that grates.

"So, what do you think?" I nod towards the two students who are still going at it.

"She'll yield first," Raven blurts. "She's already favoring her right side, and he's barely touched her."

Sure enough, a few minutes later, the female does yield, and the male is declared the victor. As they both walk off the field, Coach calls out for the next two students.

For the rest of class, Raven and I make predictions and give commentary on the fights. It's more fun than I thought it would be, and when Coach approaches me after class about joining the Spar Games team, I don't hesitate to say yes.

Spar Games is an Academia-wide tournament where teams of six compete in a series of one-on-one matches. The winner is the team with the most points at the end. It's not all sparring, though. Teams take part in three kinds of bouts: non-lethal magic, unarmed combat, and strategy. A champion from each team must also compete in all three types of matches, so it's not just about being the best in any one category.

"We already had tryouts over the weekend and I'm posting the roster in the commons tomorrow morning. I think you'll be a valuable asset to the team." Coach Thorn has me follow him to his office after class. "You've got impressive combat skills, and I believe you have a natural talent for magic if what the rumors say is true."

My steps falter. "Rumors?"

"Oh, yes," He adjusts the stapler on his desk until it's square with the edge. *What's up with everyone's perfectionist tendencies?* "I overheard some kids talking about a Luna fae who conjured a ball of water and used it to splash Deakan in the face. Considering the animosity Kieran seems to have for you, I figured you were the culprit. Those two are good friends."

I flush. "It was just a ball of water. And I got in trouble for it, which I'm kind of hoping the Dean forgot about."

Professor Thorn chuckles. "I'm sure she did. But I'll let you in on a secret; the Dean is quite fond of you. She came to me personally to let me know you were out last week and to tell me you'd make a great fit for the team. She never does that. Besides, a first year who can conjure a ball of water, send it flying towards its intended target whilst avoiding other students?" He shakes his head in disbelief. "That's some control."

"I'm not so sure about the Dean." I bite my lip, thinking about how she came after me and nearly dragged me back to her office for using magic. "But I am interested in joining the Spar Games team."

"Excellent." Coach Thorn pauses digging through a trunk of uniforms while he checks a spreadsheet on the wall. His office is immaculate, with every book in its place and not a speck of dust to be seen. It smells faintly of lemon and cloves, and on the corner of his desk sits a small potted plant. "We have our first team meeting Wednesday morning before breakfast. We'll meet on the pitch every morning and afternoon." He tosses me a green and silver uniform. "This should fit."

"Thanks." I clutch it to my chest. "Can you tell me who else made it?" I'd been shocked to learn Lopey tried out. She said she did well.

"You'll have to check the roster in the morning. I'm not at liberty to say, and it's best to keep it to yourself until then." Coach shoos me out of his office.

I head back to the locker room to shower and change before lunch. As I'm walking out, Kieran leans against the wall, waiting for me.

"Have you been waiting here this entire time?" I walk past him. My eyes follow the large glass window that overlooks the pitch. The frosted glass blurs the shock of green turf and stands of bleachers.

"What if I have?" He falls into step beside me. "What did Coach want?"

"Nothing." I sling my back over my shoulder. "Why are you following me?"

"Did he offer you a spot on the team?"

"No."

"Liar."

I stop and turn to face him. "What do you want, Kieran?" I start walking again. "Leave me alone."

"Nah," he challenges, keeping pace with me. "I wanted to ask something of you."

"What?"

"Stay away from Jax and Deakan."

I snort. "What makes you think I want anything to do with them? Besides, it's a little hard to do that when Jax is my roommate." I yank open the cafeteria door and storm inside, Kieran close on my heels. The smell of greasy French fries and pizza wafts up from the lunch line. It's full of students, loud with clanging dishes, the scraping of chairs, and the chatter from a hundred different conversations.

"I don't care if you're roommates. The two of them don't deserve to get tangled up in your little royal games."

I yank him aside, eyes darting to those around us. "Keep your damned voice down. What the hell are you talking about?" I hiss. "And if you threaten me again, I'll gut you."

"You know exactly what I'm talking about." Kieran steps closer to me, and I must crane my neck to meet his eyes. The heat of his body envelops mine. "You're playing a dangerous game, Princess. And I don't want my friends to get hurt."

"Are you insane? What game?" I demand. "I'm not playing any games."

"Anyone involved with your family just ends up hurt," Kieran spits. "I don't want that for Jax or Deakan." His eyes take on a serpentine quality, and I take an instinctive step back.

"What are you talking about?" I shake my head, trying to clear it. "My family doesn't hurt people."

"No?" Kieran puffs his chest. "Your family started an entire war just to fight over your mother. That must be some magic pussy if—"

Rage consumes my vision, and I tackle him to the ground before he can finish that sentence. All I see is red, and all I can think about is shutting him up. I pelt him, my hands flying at his face while the roar in my ears drowns out the chants of students gathering around us. My skin glows a bright blue, and Kieran's eyes widen in fear as something inside me snaps.

Strong hands come around my torso and lift me straight off the ground. "That's enough, Your Highness," Jax growls in a low voice, too low for anyone else to hear over the crowd. His grip is firm but not painful.

A hush falls over the cafeteria as Jax marches me out, arm banded around my waist, my feet in the air and Kieran's blood smeared across my knuckles.

Kieran's words echo in my head as I try to make sense of his animosity towards my family. Mistakes were made—there's no denying that—but wouldn't anyone start a war, no matter the cost, if their mate were taken? I would.

Then again, I'm not necessarily a good person. My heart is pounding wildly in my chest, and I'm shaking with adrenaline as images of what just happened replay over and over in my mind. I take in the blood smeared on my hands, and they tremble as my mind replays seeing my brother dead on that mountain pass. It was my fault. The whole reason we were up there in the first place is because I wanted to go. My fau—

"Rose!" Jax's voice breaks into my thoughts, and I blink, taking in his cobalt blues. His brow furrows, concern etched into his features. "Are you okay? What happened?"

As I'm coming back to the present, air expands in my lungs, and I can breathe again. "What? Yes, I'm fine. Just lost in thought." I try to shrug out of his grip, but his only tightens.

"What were you thinking about just now?" His eyes bore into mine, and I have to fight the urge to squirm under his intense gaze.

"N-nothing," I glance around at the people who'd followed us outside. "Just, uh, the fight."

"What did he do?" Jax's voice is tight, and his hold doesn't loosen.

"He just said some stuff that I didn't like," I hedge. "About my family. No one talks about my family."

"You're damned lucky none of the professors were in the cafeteria yet," Jax tucks me under his arm. "You could have gotten expelled for starting a fight. Deakan is in there now trying to keep the entire student body from sharing the videos they took on their phone on social media."

"What?" My heart sinks. I wipe my hands on my jeans and try to ignore the stares of the other students. "I didn't even think about that."

"Yeah, well, you should start thinking about it," Jax snaps. "You're not on Earth anymore. You're at a school for supernaturals, and one wrong move could get you, or someone else, killed."

I swallow hard, his words sinking in. He's right. I need to be more careful. But it's hard to be careful when I'm constantly on edge, waiting for the other shoe to drop. Especially when that shoe is usually in the form of a six-foot-something, tattooed, green-eyed bully.

But is that true? Is Kieran the bully ... or am I? That's the second time I've bested him today.

"We should go," Jax says after several moments of uncomfortable silence. He turns away without waiting for a response, and I scramble to catch up with him as we make our way back to our dorm room. His face is unreadable, gaze fixed forward as if nothing out of the ordinary had just occurred.

Back in our room, Jax closes the door behind us and takes my hand, bringing me to his unmade bed. I sit while he reaches into one of his drawers and pulls out a soft t-shirt. He kneels in front of me, taking care to clean away the remaining blood on my hands.

My throat is dry as I watch him work silently in front of me. After a few minutes he's done, and he meets my eyes with a soft expression that catches me off guard.

"What happened back there?" His voice is gentle yet tinged with worry that makes me drop my gaze to the ground again. "You don't have to tell me if you don't want to …"

I shake my head softly before gathering up enough courage to meet his gaze again. "Kieran said something about my family." I swallow thickly before continuing on in a small whisper. "He said they started a war over 'some magic pussy'."

Jax's expression darkens at these words, and he curses under his breath. His arms close tightly around me, and I sink into his embrace. He doesn't say anything, but the tension in his body speaks volumes. I can feel the anger radiating off him, but I'm grateful for it.

Finally, Jax pulls away, looking down at me with an intensity that takes my breath away. "I'm sorry," he says softly. "No one should talk about your family like that. I'll talk to him."

"It's fine. I'll handle him myself." If Kieran is going to keep spouting his mouth about me, that's fine. But I won't let him talk about my family. I wipe at my eyes before taking a deep breath and standing up. "I'm going to take a nap."

"You sure?" He takes my hand as though he doesn't want to let go.

"Yeah. Mind if I turn out these lights?" I gesture to the fluorescent bulbs suspended from the ceiling.

He nods and reluctantly lets go of my hand before flicking off the light switch. I just need some time alone to think. To try and sort out the mess that is my life.

I spend my lunch and the next two free periods in my dorm room, curled up in a ball on my bed, trying to make sense of what's going on. Kieran's words keep echoing in my head, and no matter how much I try to push them away, they just keep coming back.

Anyone involved with your family just ends up hurt.

Is he right?

Taking out my phone, I browse through pictures of our family's adventures at Cerulean Isles before I text Mekhi. It was at the Isles I'd figured out his feelings for me were more than an infatuation.

> Hey babe, how are classes going?

I hit send and then spend the next few minutes staring at my phone, willing it to light up with a response. But it doesn't. I huff out a breath and toss my phone on the bed, flopping back down when I remember he has some kind of water magic class right now, so he won't have his phone on him.

∼

IT'S late afternoon when I head to Dark Arts 101 held in the Witches Woods near the sand dunes. Nestled in a dense grove of trees, the squat building looks like it's made of sticks and stones. The canopy is so thick, there isn't a lot of natural light. The front door is an archway with no door, and the only thing that indicates it's a classroom is the small, hand-painted sign that reads "Dark Arts."

It's a little ominous, but I'm not deterred. After everything I've been through—Bennett's death, my mom's kidnapping, the threats, and the war—a little dark magic is nothing. Just as I pass through the entryway, a brush of something caresses me across my lower back.

"What the—" I start to say, but before I can finish, someone cups the back of my neck.

I yelp and stumble forward into the darkness, tripping over something and landing hard on my hands and knees. Pain radiates up my arms, but I push myself to my feet and try to see who touched me. My skin gives off a faint Luna glow as my body works to repair the tiny abrasions, but it's not enough to see much in the darkness.

"Who's there?" I call out, but there's no answer. "Kieran?" I whisper-shout.

A group of students hop off the path from the trees and start to file into the building, chatting, and laughing. I get a few strange looks, but no one says anything to me. For hundreds of years, it was a novelty to see a Luna fae in person, but thanks to my parents, it's not so rare anymore.

I dust myself off and follow the group inside, trying to act like I'm not rattled. But my heart roars in my chest, and I can't shake the feeling that someone is watching me. Glancing around, I spot no one, other than a dark bird taking flight over the trees.

As I walk into the Dark Arts classroom, I'm enveloped in the thick smell of magic and herbs. It's an earthy, heady combination that makes my skin tingle. Along the walls are all sorts of potion-making supplies: cauldrons of different sizes, shelves full of colorful bottles, and tables lined with greenery.

In the center of the room is a large fireplace with an iron kettle suspended above it. I've hardly ever done any potion-based magic, except for a few weeks where I helped witches with potions during the Realm War. The war lasted less than a year, and while there were many casualties on both sides, it could've been a lot worse if it weren't for my mom putting a stop to it. She makes a great queen.

Most of the students are already seated around small tables, talking quietly amongst themselves. There are a few empty seats, so I choose one in the back corner. I slip into the chair and pull out a pencil, running my thumb over the smooth wood. Next to me is a short witch with bright pink hair. She's furiously doodling in a notebook and doesn't look up when I sit down.

"Hi," I say, wanting to be friendly.

She looks up at me with a raised eyebrow, as if she's trying to figure out why I'm talking to her. "Hi," she says finally, but she doesn't smile.

I pull out my textbook and try to focus on the itinerary, but it's hard to concentrate with the feeling that someone is still watching me. I keep glancing over my shoulder, half expecting to see someone lurking in the shadows, but there's no one there.

I'm so lost in thought that I don't even hear the professor come in until she speaks. She's a tall woman with olive skin and she's wearing a long, black dress with a purple scarf draped around her shoulders. Her dark hair is pulled back in a tight bun. Her eyes are shrewd, and she has a sharp nose that seems to sniff the air as she walks.

"Most of you will fail this class," she says without preamble, her voice booming in the small room. "Dark magic is not to be taken lightly. It's dangerous and unpredictable. It has, by far, the most casualties out of any class taught on Academia. If you can't handle that, then you need to leave now."

Oh, I think I'm going to love it here.

A few students get up and leave, but most stay. Part of me wonders if the ones who got up are witches or fae without wings. Some are easy to tell, others, not so much. Adults can be brought back to life with feathers from fae wings, and the more powerful your magic, the fewer feathers you need to revive someone.

"I fully expect that half of you will either fail this class or perish trying. Now, let's get started."

The professor starts the lesson by giving a history of dark magic.

"Not all dark magic is the work of evil." She pauses. "Who can tell me when one might use dark magic for good?"

I already know, but don't raise my hand. I've seen the work of it several times, and I don't need to draw any more attention to myself.

The professor calls on a blonde woman with short spiky hair. "Our feathers use dark magic to resurrect."

"Correct." She projects a timeline on the wall. "It was first used in the war between the gods and the fae. The fae won, but at a great cost. Many innocent people died because of the dark magic that was used to win the war. After that, the fae decided to ban some of the worst dark magic." She grins. "But there are always those who break the rules."

The professor goes on to talk about the different types of dark magic. There's blood magic, which is using your own blood or the blood of others to cast spells. There's death magic, which is using the life force of others to cast spells. And then there's soul magic, which uses the souls of others to cast spells. Now that I think about it, there are only two people who can harness the three different types of dark magic at the same time.

My parents.

It's then I notice a quote on a black poster on the wall, written in what appears to be red acrylic paint.

"But he that dares not grasp the Thorn should never crave the Rose." – Anne Bronte.

A chill runs up my spine. Thorn and Rose are capitalized, suggesting proper names. What if it isn't Kieran, and it's Coach Thorn? Is he obsessed with me? Glancing around, I check to see if anyone else has seen the quote, but they're all engrossed in class.

Fear settles in my stomach. We're given our syllabus and a list of supplies we'll need for the semester. Apparently, they never give this ahead of time so that only the students who are truly dedicated to learning dark magic will stay. I have a feeling that half the class will drop out by the end of the week.

The professor dismisses us so we can gather ingredients after class and I pack up my things, eager to get out of there. As I'm leaving, the unfriendly pink-haired witch falls into step next to me.

"Hi, sorry about being a jerk earlier. I'd just gotten an upsetting text from home."

"Oh, it's okay," I return her smile. "I know how that is."

We chat for a bit, and I learn her name is Sienna. She's from a family of witches on Earth, but she's the only one who has come to Bedlam to pursue higher education, and her parents live on Sundahlia, the sunniest part of Bedlam. Some witches never come to Bedlam at all, while some come much later in life like her parents and never attend a college for magic.

Together, we work through the list of ingredients we could find in the Witches Woods. The rest, we'd need to head to the campus store for. I'm about to suggest that when I spot a familiar figure in the distance. Deakan—the mischief-maker himself—flashes me a megawatt smile and steps in my direction. Despite his good looks, I mentally mark him as off-limits as I remember the mess he caused with Mekhi and me. I still haven't learned why he pulled that stunt.

"Hey, beautiful," he says when he's close enough. "What are you up to?"

I level him with an impassive stare. "We're headed to the student store. Excuse us."

"I was just on my way to see you," he throws an arm around my shoulders, and I shove it off me.

"What do you want, Deakan?" I snap.

Sienna ducks her head with a grin on her face as she trots off, leaving me with this asshole. *Brat.*

"I wanted to apologize for what Kieran and I did." He jogs backwards to keep up with me as I try to walk away from him. "It was a prank gone wrong, and we didn't mean to hurt you."

"You didn't mean to hurt me?" I stop and glare at him. "You humiliated me and nearly caused Mekhi and I to break up. For what? A laugh?"

Deakan has the decency to look sheepish. "It wasn't just for a laugh. I was jealous."

"Jealous, Deakan?" I gesture wildly. "I didn't even know you. And you know what? I still don't know you! Don't really care to. Excuse me."

I try to push past him, but he catches my hand. "You had this smile on your face." He brings our conjoined hands to his chest, and I don't breathe. *Can't* breathe. "It nearly robbed the air from my lungs. I wanted to see if I could make you smile like that. It took me a moment to realize you were smiling at your phone, and another second to realize it was probably a guy. So, when Kieran asked for help, I told him yes. I'm sorry."

Maybe it *is* Kieran messing with me?

I jerk my hand away from him, feeling both anger and something else I can't quite place. "You're sorry?" I scoff. "You think a sorry is going to fix this?"

"No," he admits. "But it's a start. Let me make it up to you. Can I buy you dinner?"

For a moment, I debate saying yes. It would be the mature thing to do, and it would give me a chance to get to know him better, and maybe even dig a little more into Kieran. But I can't forget the way he's made me feel, and I'm not sure I want to let him off the hook that easily.

"No," I say finally. "I don't think so, Deakan."

Deakan watches me walk away with a forlorn look on his face, and I can't help but feel a twinge of guilt. But I push it away. He's made his bed, now he can lie in it.

CHAPTER SEVEN

ROSE

"What are you all dolled up for?" Jax pauses in the doorway to our room, watching me apply a coat of no-smudge, red lipstick.

"I have a date." I don't bother looking at him. There's no denying our mutual attraction, so it's best not to rub it in his face any more than I have to.

"With whom?" Jealousy is clear in his voice, though he tries to hide it. He lets the door slam, stalking over to his bed and dropping his bag onto the floor next to his bed.

"No one you know." Although he might. Just because I don't see Theo on campus, doesn't mean Jax doesn't. Besides, Jax is a second-year student, and most of our classes are different. I meet his eyes in the mirror. The last thing I want to do is entertain caveman tendencies from a man who has zero claim over me. "I'll be back late."

"Where are you going?" He flops down onto his bed, and I can tell he's trying to act casual, but he's failing miserably.

"Not sure. It's a surprise." I turn to face him and give him a sweet smile. There's a tic in his jaw where he clenches and unclenches it. "Don't wait up for me, alright?"

I don't give him a chance to respond before I'm out the door and down the hall. Wiping my palms on my jeans, I take a deep breath to try and calm my nerves. *This is just a date*, I remind myself. It's not a big deal. I've been on plenty of them before. Sure, they were with Mekhi, and it was before we admitted our feelings together, and they weren't technically dates...

Oh snap. This *is* my first real date. Like, with a guy I actually like and who likes me back. Holy crap, no wonder I'm so nervous. A slight breeze picks up, and I smooth my hair down as best I can as I make my way across campus and to the path where I'm to meet Theo.

My heart rate picks up as I stroll past the library, the smell of freshly cut grass wafting up from the center of campus. I reach into my purse and pull out a small, round mirror, checking for stray eyebrow hairs and making sure my lipstick is still intact. I slip a peppermint into my mouth, hoping it's not too presumptuous. After a few moments of quiet contemplation, I take a deep breath, smile, and continue on my way.

I decide how much I want to tell Theo before I arrive. Too many people know who I am already, and they learned by accident. I have a choice with Theo. If things don't pan out for us, there's no sense in telling him about who I am and risking him telling others. This means I'll have to steer our conversations around these questions until we've had more time together.

He's there by the time I arrive, the deep set of his dimples on full display as he beams at me. "Hey, beautiful." He's wearing all black; jeans, a fitted T-shirt under a leather jacket, and boots. Like Sons of Anarchy meets GQ.

Butterflies take flight in my stomach, and heat rises to my cheeks. "Hey."

He takes my hand and laces our fingers together, and the simple gesture does the opposite of what I expect it to. It calms me. It's soft and warm against mine. "Shall we?"

I nod, and he leads me down the path into the woods, away from campus and towards the sand dunes. We walk in silence for a few minutes, the only sound the crunching of leaves and twigs beneath our feet. The sun breaks through the clouds in parts, and the ray of light lands in between us. The black and white contrasts of the clouds give the sunlight even more powerful of a presence.

"So, where are you taking me?" I turn to face him, trying to make small talk.

"You'll see." His grip tightens on my hand, and he quickens the pace.

We wander through the Witches Woods, hand in hand, until the palm trees thin and we reach the edge of a clearing. He drops my hand and steps forward, gesturing at the large tree in front of us. He starts chanting an incantation in a strange language and sparks of magic illuminate the sky. Suddenly, a loud grating sound fills the air, and the tree pulls away to reveal a large black motorcycle hiding behind it.

"You have a motorcycle?!" This must be why he asked me to wear jeans and boots, though it's sweltering here. Vehicles are outlawed in Bedlam because of strict anti-pollution laws. We don't even have planes. People sift or use their wings to fly if they're lucky enough to have them.

"Yep." He grins at me as he pulls a helmet out from under the seat and hands it to me. I put it on, and he helps me with the straps, his touch sending a jolt through me. "You ready?"

I nod, and he swings his leg over the bike, patting the seat behind him. I hesitantly climb on, wrapping my arms around his waist. Having been on a motorcycle only once before in Australia, I know just enough to hold on tight and not freak out.

Theo's muscled arm reaches out and flips the switch, and the engine growls to life. I feel the vibrations of the powerful engine reverberate through my body as we pull away from the tree, the wind whipping through my hair. The scent of the palms, crisp and clean, fill my senses as he expertly navigates the twists and turns of the winding forest.

His tight abs move beneath my grasp as he steers the bike, and I find myself leaning closer to him in this moment of exhilaration. He's taller than me, so I can't quite see over his shoulder. Instead, I rest my head against his back and close my eyes, enjoying the rush, and the feeling of being free. He cuts a path through the woods until we come to a stop in front of another small, secluded clearing.

He kills the engine and helps me off the bike before taking off his helmet. "Welcome to my secret spot."

I look around, taking in the beauty of the place. It's like a scene from a fairytale, with wildflowers blooming and the gentle sound of a stream nearby. High over us, the trees form a sort of roof where the branches meet and entwine. Flowers hang from them, brushing our heads below, with fragrant petals and long, green leaves that cast a dappled shade over the grass. "It's gorgeous." There's an echo of the vibrating engine still coursing through me, and my body hums with excitement.

Theo takes my hand and leads me to a large tree trunk, where he motions for me to sit down while he slips the pack from his shoulder. "I come here to get away from the campus and clear my head."

"It's perfect." My stomach chooses now to rumble, and I hide my face behind my hand, embarrassed. "Sorry, I didn't realize how late it was getting. I don't care for the soup they served for lunch today, so I only had a snack."

He chuckles as he pulls out a blanket from his pack and lays it down on the ground in front of me. "I've been eating off campus, because while some of the food is good, I prefer my own cooking."

He pulls out a glass container and a couple of forks, and my stomach growls again. "Awe, you're going to feed me, too? And is that why I never see you on campus?"

Theo chuckles. "Nah, my classes don't start until January. I was only on campus for orientation." He opens the container and hands me a fork before taking one for himself.

I take a bite of the steaming pasta dish and I am overwhelmed with a medley of spices and flavors as they burst in my mouth. I moan in delight, and I can't help but to praise the chef, "It's so good. You're a great cook." It might just be that there's chicken, bacon, and carbs, my favorite combo.

"My mom taught me. She's the one who got me interested in food and cooking." He smiles fondly, and I can see the love he has for his family in his eyes.

"What's she like?" I'm curious to know more about him, and his family seems like a good place to start, though I'm hesitant to talk about my own.

"She's amazing. No matter what I want to do, she is always supportive. She's an artist, so she understands my need to be creative." He pauses, and I can see the sadness in his eyes. "My dad died when I was younger, so she's been both mother and father to me."

"Oh, Theo, I'm sorry." I reach out and touch his hand, offering what little comfort I can. His dad must not have had wings. Our feathers can revive us, though ours don't grow back, so once we use them, they're gone for good.

He shrugs, and the sadness is replaced by a determined look. "It was a long time ago. I don't like to dwell on it." We sit in silence for a while. I want to press him for more information, but I can see that he doesn't want to talk about it, so I let it go. Before I can ask him another question, he asks about my parents.

I don't want to judge me for being the princess, so I keep it surface-level. "My mom is really smart, and my dads are ... protective."

Theo's fork pauses halfway to his mouth, and he considers me for a moment. "Dads?"

"My mom has a lot of mates." A grin tugs at my lips while I wait for his reaction. I take great pleasure in watching people squirm over this. It's not a traditional take on relationships, but it's one that works for my parents.

"Huh. That's different." Theo takes a bite of his food and chews thoughtfully. "It must be nice to have so many people who love you."

I shrug. "It has its moments. Though I have siblings who help take the attention off me sometimes."

He captures me with his gaze, and curiosity fills his eyes. "I have a hard time believing you're not the center of everyone's attention."

I bite my lip and look away, turning my attention to the fae flies dancing just above the damp ground, their butts aglow. Not sure how to respond to him, I change the subject instead. "How'd you get a motorcycle in Bedlam?" I'm not about to admit it's my mom's mates who enacted the law banning vehicles with internal combustion engines to help combat pollution. Fae fly, sift, walk, or take boats to where they need to go. I don't think I've ever seen an engine-powered vehicle in this realm—ever.

Theo hesitates, and the hesitation reveals the conflict in his head. The moment he lets his guard down, he answers. "I, um, I built it."

"You built *that*?" I gesture to the sleek metal beast parked nearby. It's all matte black, save for a few well-placed stripes along the front of it, and its gold handlebars.

He nods, and a hint of pride shows in his expression. "It wasn't easy, but I figured it out off an old manual I found at a market on Sundahlia." Figures. Most witches from Earth settle there, on account of the beautiful weather year-round.

I'm impressed, and my opinion of him skyrockets. "That's wild, though I didn't peg you as a rebel." He has a studious look to him, with his perfect posture and perfectly groomed goatee that's less a beard and more of a shadow, but now he has a mischievous glint in his eyes. Though, the tattoos peeking above his collar, the leather jacket, and jeans have really thrown me off.

There's so much to unravel about him, and I want to know it all.

He chuckles and takes another bite of his food. "I'm not a rebel," he says around a mouthful of pasta. "I'm just ... curious."

"Curious about what?"

"Everything." He hands me an apple slice dipped in caramel and sprinkled with chocolate chips. Forget the pasta, I might need to marry this man. At least lock him up in my kitchen, anyway. "I want to know everything about this world, and I'm not content to sit back and let others tell me what's true and what's not."

I can respect that. "I think that's admirable."

"Thank you." He hesitates for a moment, clearly deep in thought. "What makes Rose tick?" He taps his fingers against his thigh, a nervous tic that I've come to recognize.

A sigh escapes me. "That's a loaded question." Instead of answering,

I shove the whole apple slice into my mouth, caramel dripping from my fingers.

Theo's thumb comes up and wipes at my bottom lip, gathering the caramel and pushing it back into my mouth. I close my mouth around his thumb, tasting his skin, and watch how his eyes darken. His attention stays transfixed on my mouth until I swallow, then he presses forward and takes my lip into his mouth, sucking on it. Everything in me combusts with the desire to taste him, to feel his mouth, and all I can think is: *more*.

Before I can let greed get the better part of me, he pulls back, and along with it, his warmth. I'm left with a burning need to devour him. He hands me another slice. "I want to know you, Rose." The hand he held tight to his thigh reaches out and covers mine, his grip gentle yet firm. The heat of his touch radiates through me, toying with my nerves.

As I inhale deeply, the barriers I've built shatter and crumble. I'm teetering on the edge of a cliff, and I know that if I take the leap, there's no going back.

"Adventure," I hedge, still wary about divulging everything in one fell swoop. "Always chasing the next thrill and the unknown. Freedom is important to me, too. To do and be whatever you want?"

Grinning, he looks at me with newfound understanding. "I know that feeling." The gesture is so genuine that I can't help but return it.

"I think you and I have more in common than either of us realize," he says, and there's something different in his voice. Something that wasn't there before.

"Maybe we do."

Taking the container of apple slices, I feed him, rather than handing him his own. All the while, our magic entertains itself. With each brush of skin against skin, the air between us becomes more charged, with our magic pulling us towards each other.

I've got to get a hold on my emotions or I'm going to tackle this man, and I'm not sure how much longer I can play the game of feeding him without attempting to do something far more out of my comfort zone. He seems to notice my shift and uncaps his bottle of water before handing it to me. But my self-control slips when he reclines against the tree trunk and spreads his legs, making room for me to sit between his thick, jean-clad thighs.

I take the invitation, positioning myself between his legs so I rest my back against his warm chest. The scent of clean, fresh laundry and sun-kissed skin lingers around him as I inhale. His arms come around me, the strong fingers of one hand digging into my hip, the other holding the water bottle to my lips. I stare at his tanned forearm, where he's rolled the sleeves, and inspect the tattoo as I drink. It's a moon ... or more like it's a man cradling a woman in his arms and walking on the surface of the moon.

Running my fingers over the ink, I ask him about it.

"My order is loyal, and we save ourselves for our mate. I got this as a reminder that I'd give her a moon if I could."

"Your soul bonded mate?"

His fingers intertwine with mine. "Yeah."

"Do you know if you have one yet?" Memories of the day my grandmother brought Bennett back to life all come back to me, as does the moment she whispered something in our ears about our mates.

"I do."

My chest cleaves with an aching sadness. Sitting up, I scoot away from him, back to the other side of the blanket, and to a place of safety. Tucking my heart back into its shell, I think of the word "nostalgia," that longing for what is gone.

"Did I say something wrong?"

I shake my head, willing the tears not to fall. Why am I reacting this way to someone I don't even know? The heart is a sentimental organ that sometimes misleads us into thinking we've met the person with whom we will spend the rest of our lives. Mine is a fool.

Theo kneels in front of me, tilting my chin so I must gaze into his kind gold eyes framed in dark lashes. Fat tears spill down my cheeks and make a dark patch on my top.

"Rose," he starts, but I shake my head, unable to speak.

What the hell is wrong with me? Is it the approaching Bedlam Moon messing with my emotions?

"What if it's you?" His thumb caresses my cheek.

My heart thrashes in my chest, desperate to claw itself out and volunteer as tribute at his feet. The glow of my skin flashes in quick succession, bathing him in an alluring cerulean hue. I can't even be embarrassed. His magic responds in kind, casting his form in a breathtaking golden light.

"What are you doing to me?" I whisper, searching his eyes.

His grin shows off his dimples, and I fight the desire to press my lips to each one. He leans in, eyes closed, just as a twig snaps in the canopy overhead. A crow takes flight and swoops over our heads, but not close enough to give us a scare.

"Guess that crow doesn't want you kissing me, huh?" I tease.

He chuckles, returning to lounging against the trunk of a willow. "Why Bedlam Academy?"

"Oh," I think about this a moment. There was no question as to which academy I wanted to attend. I only wish Bennett and Mekhi could've gotten in, too. "It's the best, isn't it?"

"True. I'd considered Moonfire Academy, but ultimately ended up here because I had top pick of rooms."

"I love mine."

We remain silent for a few minutes as we finish the rest of our picnic, and I can't help but wonder about the strange connection we have. My imagination runs wild as my attention catches on the bow of his top lip; an image of his soft mouth pressed against mine flashing through my mind. Against my neck, tangled sheets, and the sole desire to feel him, to—

He's grinning.

Why is he grinning?

Blinking to clear my thoughts, that's when I notice the blue gleam of my skin, like a radar, advertising exactly what's on my mind. My pulse skips with the uncomfortable heat of embarrassment crawling up my chest. I haul myself to my feet, humiliation washing over me as I flee towards the path that led us here. It's one thing for my skin to flash when he and I are actively making out, but for it to do it when we're sitting there eating? I can't control myself around this man, and I'll be damned if I'm going to let it continue.

The sound of Theo's voice calling to me barely registers over the static drowning out my thoughts. I can't bear to turn back. My booted feet carry me through the woods when a gush of wind, accompanied by the sight of a giant half-lion, half-bird-like creature, stops me in my tracks. Reeling back, I nearly stumble as a startled shriek cuts through the noise. Its talons are the size of my hand, and its beak is even larger. A scream is about to erupt from my throat when the beast transforms into Theo, hands outstretched like he's the one trying to calm an unpredictable animal.

"It's okay." His eyes twinkle with laughter. "You don't have to fear me." He reaches where I'm frozen in place, and his warmth radiates against my skin.

"What are you?" I whisper, still not able to believe my eyes. Gone are the giant wings, long tail, and fur. In front of me stands a man who still is, more than anything else, one of the most beautiful men I've ever seen.

～

Theo steps closer, so close I can see flecks of blue in his golden eyes. I don't think they were there before. "I'm a griffin," he says, the words a gentle caress against my skin. "I could never hurt you." He reaches for me with a tentative hand, and when I don't shy away, he cups my cheek. "You don't have to hide your order from me, Rose." The press of tears blurs my vision. "There's no reason to be embarrassed." His thumb brushes against my jaw. "You wear certain thoughts on your skin, and I'd be lying if I said I'm not incredibly flattered. Unbelievably lucky, too. If you knew half the things that run through my head when I look at you, you'd blush. I can promise you that."

A sizzle of magic zaps the air between us, a fae promise if I've ever heard one. It's risky to make such blatant promises about something so vague, something that neither of us can control. A broken fae promise means death for whomever breaks it.

For a moment, there's nothing but the two of us, standing in this jungle and allowing ourselves to be something more than what we have been. A moment of freedom, a moment of possibility.

Warmth seeps into my cheek where Theo's hand rests. Whether it's him who leans in, it's me, or we meet in the middle, our lips press together before I know what's even happening. He tastes like caramel apples and sunshine, and I melt into him, heat pooling low in my belly where our lower halves meet. His thickly muscled arms band around me, the sensation comforting as we explore each other's mouths. When I reluctantly pull away to catch my breath, I rest my face against his.

"I'm glad you stopped running," he whispers against my cheek. "If it were much further, my beast would've pounced. And I'm not sure either of us wants that yet."

I laugh, the sound echoing in my chest and radiating outward. *Oh, but I do.* "No," I say instead, the lie leaving my lips before I can think better of it.

Theo's grin widens as he takes a step back. "Good." He runs his thumb along my lower lip. "Because I'm willing to wait for you." He hesitates. "Though if I'm being honest, my beast is barely restrained right now. He's pacing the hallways of my mind, waiting for the moment he can take over."

"Does that happen a lot?" My voice is soft and curious. I'd heard about shifter fae whose beasts are more sentient being than wild animal, but my order goes feral. It's a deeply engrained part of our psyche that shuts off our humanity and focuses on a few key things to aid in survival. Naturally, it happens when we're defending our loved ones or fighting for survival.

Is that what happened when I attacked Kieran?

"No." He sighs, a gentle gust of air that carries the scent of summer. "Though he's been difficult to contain since the semester started."

"Why is that?" I finger the collar of his button-up shirt and meet his intense stare.

"I'm not sure," he glances behind me before returning his attention. I'm uncertain he's being totally forthcoming. The way he hesitated gives me the impression he's keeping something from me. That's fine because I have my secrets, too. It's bad enough my roommates and his friends know I'm the princess, even worse if they ever learn I have a newborn sister and the wrong people find out.

"I have one more place I'd like to take you, if that's alright?" He takes my hand, lacing our fingers. I nod, trusting him to keep me safe as he leads me further into the jungle. The trees here are thicker, older. Magical energy greets me as we walk near their tangled roots, their strength and stability far more powerful than the saplings that try to push through the underbrush and vines. It's quiet here, a peacefulness only found in the depths of nature, the thick canopy creating a barrier between us and the sea. The silence is the kind that can only be found deep in nature.

We walk in peace as I take it all in, though my awareness of his presence never fades. His grip is tight and reassuring; our fingers are entwined. I'm reminded of the strength found in vulnerability, of the beauty of letting go and allowing something bigger than myself to take the lead.

Theo stops abruptly, and I follow his gaze. Ahead of us, sheltered by a cluster of trees and protected by a thicket of vines, is a hidden temple. Its columns are covered in ivy, and the steps leading up to them appear worn by age.

My breath catches in my throat as Theo leads me closer, a feeling of reverence and awe taking over. We exchange a look, and the same feeling passes between us.

"Welcome to Sanctuary." He smiles, the sight of it enough to steal my breath. "My personal haven."

He moves aside to give me space to observe everything. I'm not sure what I was expecting, but this wasn't it. It's like a refuge, the kind of place you'd go to get away from it all and just be for a while.

"It's beautiful," I whisper, speaking aloud my thoughts. We stand in silence for a few moments, studying the stained-glass windows, touching the icons, and drinking in their jewel-like colors. Attached to the older structure is one that's new, and it, too, is beautiful, with its white stone columns, huge wooden doors, and tiled roof. In front of a row of windows are flower boxes that fill the space with vibrant blossoms. I'm almost hesitant to speak and break the spell this place has woven around us.

Theo takes my hand, and we walk up the steps together. Magic emanates from this place, greeting me, and a deep knowing settles in my bones the moment my foot touches the rough-hewn landing: I know that no matter what happens, I can always find refuge here. Like a weight lifted off my shoulders, I feel lighter than I have in ages. No longer does an invisible load strain my shoulders. Had I been carrying a burden this entire time? And why does it feel as though it's gone?

We take a few more steps, passing under a stone archway and into a courtyard filled with flowers. A fountain stands in the center, the sound of trickling water soothing to my ears. A spray of wildflowers lines the edges, giving it an ethereal feel.

"Come." Theo beckons, his voice just as soft as before. I follow him, my eyes lingering on the calming surroundings. He leads me to a marble bench and motions for me to sit. The cool stone is a welcome relief beneath my skin, and I settle into the moment with ease.

Theo rests beside me, our bodies touching as he takes my hands in his. I look up, mesmerized by the intensity of his gaze. He holds me there for a long moment before speaking.

"This is a place for you to come when things get too overwhelming." He gestures to the area. "A safe spot away from the noise and chaos of life. Whenever you need it, come here, even when I'm not with you." There is a moment of silence as he lets his words register. My shoulders loosen as I feel their truth resonating within me. "The entire area I've imbued with magic," he adds, squeezing my hands. I'm filled with a sudden warmth, and goosebumps run down my arms. "It has a way of shouldering your burdens, if only for a little while."

"How'd you find this place?" I whisper, barely able to contain the emotions bubbling up inside of me.

"I don't know, it just called to me. This summer, I came back and built that." He inclines his head towards the small house in the far corner.

"You what?!" I approach the structure. "It's beautiful." Spinning back towards him, I shake my head. "I wish I had half this talent." I can make some really cool things with magic, but even with a vivid imagination, I couldn't dream of something this elaborate.

Theo approaches me, taking my face in his hands, and his thumbs wipe the tears that have spilled down my cheeks before pressing his lips to mine.

We stay there for what feels like an eternity, our kiss communicating more than any words could. He pulls away, but his fingers remain intertwined with mine as we continue to sit in silence together, watching the sky darken with hues of orange and pink. The moons rise in the sky, my Luna order more at peace than ever and glowing a bright blue. Theo's fingers trace my skin, marveling at the gleam of it.

"Where did you grow up?" I ask him.

"Rexuna. My great grandparents settled in Serapi City, and my family just never really left it. Where on Earth did you live?" Serapi City is less of a city and more like a remote village on an archipelago in the Southwestern part of the continent. To encourage more settlers, the people built a land bridge connecting the islands to the mainland. I'd only been there once, and it still has its old world, tiny village charm.

Tucking me into his side, he listens as I tell him tales of my life before Bedlam, leaving out anything too incriminating. The air cools, granting us a pleasant evening. We stay like that until the sky fades to a midnight black, and reality starts to creep in.

As we make our way back across the courtyard, I pause just before leaving and turn back to him.

"There's something I need to tell you," I say, my voice barely audible. I've dreaded this conversation all night, and let our good time get in the way of it.

As his eyes scan me, I take a deep breath and start talking. "I probably should've said something before our date," my palms begin to sweat, "but I have a boyfriend."

He blinks a few times before speaking, confusion evident in his features. "You what?"

Taking a deep breath, I explain the situation, my stomach lurching as his expression goes from confusion to disbelief to upset. The sting of tears presses against the back of my eyes, and I swallow hard before continuing.

"I'm sorry," I whisper. "You really deserved to know up-front."

He grips his hair and spins to face me. "You think?" He paces. "Did it ever occur to you I might not be so willing to share?"

Shame washes over me and I lower my head. "It did, but I couldn't help myself," I confess. I'm selfish. Always have been. I do things with little regard as to how others will feel about it, and sometimes, people get hurt.

He stops pacing and sighs. After a moment, he walks over and takes my hand.

"Come on," he inclines his head, his voice strained. "Let's get you back to campus."

After returning his motorcycle, we walk in silence until we reach the courtyard and I draw up short. "I'm going to stop at the store to grab a few things before bed. Goodnight, Theo." I have to force the words out, because my heart wants to reel him back in and never let go.

He glances back at me, surprised. "Goodnight, Rose." He gives me a tight smile before turning and walking away without another word. A chill runs down my spine as I watch him go, and I can't help but feel like something between us just shifted for the worse. If the chasm in my chest is anything to go by, I'm crushed.

After picking up some chocolate and a few bags of popcorn, I walk back to my dorm alone, my steps heavy and thoughts troubled. I should have done the right thing, but instead, I chose selfishness and lies by omission. I dread the thought of facing Theo again, but I know I need to apologize and try to make things right. For now, though, I'm going to bed, hoping tomorrow will bring a new start.

An enormous weight settles over me, seeping into my skin and leaving a metallic taste in my mouth. My heart pounds in my chest as I inch my way forward through the deathly still alley between buildings, and a chill runs down my spine as I sense an unknown figure shrouded in shadows lurking close by. The hairs on the back of my neck stand on end and I freeze, helplessly drawn to the door by the alley entrance, without knowing why. Every muscle in my body screams for me to turn back and flee, yet something sinister keeps me rooted to the spot.

Why can't I move? I attempt to conjure a ball of light, but I'm unable to bring even the faintest spark into being. With each passing second, my panic grows until I'm sure I will suffocate from fear. Just as I'm about to give up and succumb to whatever awaits me, a large hand clamps onto my shoulder, a bag is thrown over my head, and the next thing I know, I'm being dragged away into the night.

My captor's grip is unrelenting and my heart races, questioning their motives as I'm forced into a chamber. The door slams shut, and I'm left in darkness, surrounded by nothing but my escalating fear and my inability to use my magic. Minutes stretch into hours, and just when I think I can withstand the silence no longer, the door groans open and a figure shrouded in white steps into my purgatory.

I recognize the glamour immediately, based on the way their face shimmers and changes shape in the soft light that pours in from the hallway outside, and I know they are fae. But who?

My questions remain unanswered, as the figure closes the door behind them, and my magic responds to their presence. It surges my veins and I shoot up, no longer restrained by an invisible force. In a single moment, the oppressive silence is shattered, and I'm given back control of my body. They hurl something at me, but I dodge it, flinching as it sails right by my face and bounces off the wall. They lunge for me, and I rake my nails across their face, leaving scarlet trails across their skin. The figure staggers back and I take my chance to run, out of the chamber and away from the fae who sought to imprison me.

Shrieks peel from my throat as I throw open the door to freedom and stumble out into the night. I race away, heart pounding and blood dripping down my skin as I desperately try to escape the terror of my captor.

I round the corner, barreling straight into a wall of muscle. I yelp when hands come to steady my shoulders and I look up to find Jax.

"Are you alright?" I thought I heard you scream. He holds me steady, and his gaze alights on the blood running from my nails to my neck and soaking the fabric of my shirt. His expression turns to rage. "Who hurt you?" he demands, his entire body trembling with fury. He yanks me to his chest, his arms encircling me. I let the tears fall and melt into his shirt as he tightens his grasp. He's here, and I'm safe. "Tell me who he was, Rose, and I'll spend the rest of my life hunting him down."

Jax scoops me up and carries me to our room, where he cradles me in his lap and holds me close until I calm down. He strokes my hair and murmurs gentle words, soothing me with a tenderness I haven't experienced in a long time. The fear begins to ebb away and warmth blossoms inside me that feels oddly like comfort.

"What happened?" he asks, his voice still shaking with anger. I tell him about my encounter, and he listens intently, his jaw clenched as I describe the attack. When I'm done, he breathes me in deep and holds me closer.

"Was it your date?"

"What? No. This person was smaller. Still fae, though."

Jax nods and tightens his grip on me. "I'm so sorry I wasn't there to help you," he whispers, pressing his lips gently to my forehead. He cleans me up before bringing me to his bed and pulling me down with him.

As his arms encircle my waist, I feel as if I've been let in on a secret. I feel the warmth of his embrace and the gentle rise and fall of his chest as I rest my head against it. The tension in my muscles eases, and my eyes grow heavy as I drift off to sleep.

CHAPTER EIGHT

JAX

Waking with Rose in my arms would be heaven if it weren't for what she'd gone through last night. Rose's hair is a tangled mess, strands strewn about her face, and her lips part as she breathes slowly, lightly. Her head rests against my shoulder, her eyes furtively shut as she dreams.

She's at peace now, with bits of sunlight fingering through the crack of the blinds, her brow smooth and her limbs languid where she's plastered to me. I'm afraid to move, to break this moment of tranquility for fear that the pain she endured will come flooding back.

But I must. I ease myself from beneath her and stand from the bed, feeling her warm absence behind me.

I make a few phone calls before I wake her.

"Rose." I caress her cheek. It's so smooth and delicate compared to the armor she wears around her heart and soul. "We're going to see a seer, to help figure out who hurt you."

Her eyes flutter open, a hint of fear still lingering in their depths. I offer her a gentle smile and cup her cheek.

"Where?"

"There's an old witch on Luporia my family knows. Bayer the Seer. She can meet us in twenty minutes."

"You can sift?" She props herself on her elbow and peers at me, eyes wide.

I nod and take her hand in mine, pressing a tender kiss to her knuckles. "We'll figure out who hurt you."

And with that, we set off towards the meeting. We sift to a timber forest, the fingers of winter already tangling the trees and clinging to the earth.

The frozen seas of the north are on our left, rumbling with giant breaks. We weave around the looming mountains and their snowy caps, a misty winter morning fog beginning to rise.

Rose shivers, and I pull her under my arm, cranking up the heat of my dragon order to warm her. Her little nose burrows further into my chest, and I'm reminded of how precious this creature is to me.

Finally, after a few minutes of trudging through three feet of snow, we come upon the seer's cottage. It looks like it has stood in this same spot for hundreds of years—the stones weathered and chipped, the windows caked in frost.

I knock on the door, and the old witch calls us inside.

We enter the seer's small room, which is tucked away in the back of her cottage. She sits perched at a desk; a leather-bound book clenched in her knotted hands. Deep wrinkles crease her face, and her eyes are sharp with knowledge.

The air is heavy with the dust of hundreds of years of potions, magical powders, and incense. It coats the floor like a thick blanket and hangs in the air like a forgotten ghost.

Rose shrinks into my side as we approach the seer. Her eyes are wide with fear and anticipation—fear that comes from not knowing what lies ahead and anticipation that she might finally find out who hurt her.

"Sit," Bayer commands.

Rose glances at me and I nod towards the worn, corduroy couch covered in a thick film of dirt. She steps over oddly shaped bottles and vials scattered around the room and settles onto the couch, her hands quivering in her lap. I settle in next to her, twining our fingers together to help steady them.

"Payment?" the crone barks. Her grey hair hangs in thin braids, and looks as though it had been once blue, but was now faded by the sun and hardship of the world.

Rose makes to grab for the copper-colored purse slung around her neck, but I stop her with a hand on her forearm. She looks at me and I shake my head. "She doesn't take money."

"What does she take?"

"Take?" The seer scoffs. "I trade in secrets, girl." The giant hoops of her earrings jangle as the witch leans forward, her milky white eyes dancing with anticipation. "I take the things that you keep hidden, the things you lock away, and in exchange, I tell you what you need to know."

I swallow thickly, knowing that this payment won't be easy. We need to give away something very personal in order to get the answers we seek.

Rose takes a deep breath and speaks. "I killed my brother."

Bayer slams a knotted hand onto the table, startling us both. "I know all your secrets, High Princess of the Fae. You wear your heart on your sleeve, and a murderer you are not, but a liar you may be. Let this falsehood go and be at peace." The witches' eyes meet mine. "But you, boy, you're full of secrets, aren't you?"

My breath catches in my throat and fear rises inside of me. I nod once, slowly, and Rose's hand tightens around mine.

"I don't ... I don't need to be here to listen to this." Rose rises from her seat but freezes when the witch snaps her fingers.

"You, sit."

Rose sinks back down onto the couch and takes a deep breath. "Sorry," she whispers and glances at me, taking my hand again.

"It's alright." I smile down at her, some semblance of comfort that the witch put her in her place about Bennett. She's carried that guilt for so long, and it was only an accident.

My pulse quickens, and I suck in a breath, praying Rose won't hate me when we're through here. I have to be brave enough to tell the witch something that I have kept hidden from everyone else, even Rose. Things I haven't even told Kieran or Deakan.

The seer rests her hands against the table and looks me in the eye. "Well? Don't keep me waiting, boy. Let's hear it."

Training my attention on the flames licking the fireplace walls, I begin, even as shame invades my blood.

"Last summer, I made a deal with a god." My voice is quiet, but each word I speak feels like I'm ripping out my own heart. "A dark god," I continue. "And I promised my soul to gain something that I wanted."

As I confess my sin, I swear I can feel the weight of the deal pressing down on me, threatening to suffocate me. My traitorous confession is the loudest sound I've ever heard in my life. The words echo in my head, a prison cell closing in around me.

The crones' voice feels close, as though her breath were on my skin. It hangs in the air around me and whispers, "And was it worth it? In the end?"

The fire pops and sparks among the blackened logs, and I tear my gaze away from the flames, burying my shame deeper within my heart.

"Some days I wonder if the god delivered. And others, I just pray I never die."

~

ROSE

My heart cleaves for Jax in this moment. Whatever it was that his heart desired so desperately he'd give up his soul must've been huge. The weight he must carry around with him each day is more than I can begin to fathom. I draw him closer and hold him as his words tumble out of his mouth like shattered glass.

Tears prick my eyes, and guilt courses through me for not knowing the entirety of Jax's burden. I should've sought to comfort him about any problems he'd been facing sooner, rather than it always being about me.

"Interesting," Bayer croaks. She turns to me. "Give me your hands, girl."

I squeeze Jax's before pulling them from his grasp and offering them to the seer. I steel myself, grateful I'll soon know who's after my family, but afraid it may be someone I trust.

The seer's icy fingers clasp around mine, and an eerie sensation travels up my arm. She closes her eyes and begins humming a strange melody. It's a bit like a lullaby, but it feels more like an incantation than a song. After what feels like an eternity, her lips stop moving and her eyes fly open as she tears her hands away with a gasp.

They're no longer milky, but inky black. Her face is pale, and her lips are trembling.

"It is as I feared," she finally whispers, her voice barely audible. "There is dark magic afoot, and it aims to harm your house. Someone powerful, someone strong," she murmurs, narrowing her gaze at me. "Someone surrounding you, in the shadows of your home. You must hurry."

My heart races faster and faster as the realization that this is real hits me. "Who is it?"

The witch shakes her head and jumps to her feet with far more stamina than her age suggests. "I cannot see it, child. But be warned. The closer you get to your truth, the greater the danger."

I open my mouth to respond, but the seer turns away before I can. She pulls a key out of her pocket and unlocks the barred door.

"Leave." Her voice is cold and firm. "Go now, as quickly as you can. Every second you waste could mean disaster."

"Mom? Bring Bennett home, now. Where are you?!" Hysteria laces my voice.

"The castle. Honey, what's wrong? Where are you?"

"Which castle—"

She doesn't get a chance to respond before my battery dies. Fuck.

I'd forgotten to charge it last night since I was sleeping in Jax's bed. I'm trembling so badly I can barely hold onto it.

"Can you sift us to Convectus Castle?" I turn towards Jax.

Worry etches his brow. "Only just outside the gates. I've never been inside it."

"Hurry!"

He nods in reply, and soon we're tearing through space, the ancient stone walls of the castle appearing in a flash. I jump out of his arms before he even sets me down, and rush towards the retinue of guards patrolling the front gate, Jax right on my heel. "Stop!" A guard shouts and I skid to a halt.

The castle is surrounded by a high stone wall, standing at least ten feet tall and topped with spiked iron. A thick wooden door is the only break in the wall. I can just glimpse the tops of trees inside.

The stone walls are dusted with soft green moss, a few plants hanging off the edge of the deep-set windows, and a deep brown hue shellacking the outer surface.

"I'm High Princess Rose Ankida Drake," I pant, my chest heaving. "And I need to see my mother!"

"And I'm the tin man," he chuckles, widening his stance and glancing at the guards beside him. "Move along."

Fucking glamor me my entire life, so when I need my guards to recognize me, they don't!

"Let me in!" I shriek, my voice cracking from desperation. I feel my power swell within me, begging to be unleashed. I can't control it now. I won't be barred from my home.

I strain forward, pushing against the guard's chest. Jax gasps and wraps his arms around me, holding me back before I can do anything I might regret.

But he's too late. I feel it before I see the blast of magic that hits me square in the chest, plowing me into Jax and sending us both flying. My skin flares on contact as a sob wrenches itself from my throat at the pain radiating through me.

But I don't have time to wallow in my misery. The guard's attention has sharpened, and he kneels down, examining us both closely. And then his expression shifts, realization flashing in his eyes.

"Your Highness." He gasps, his face pale. He scrambles to his feet and bows deeply. "Please, forgive me. I had no idea—we weren't expecting you."

He reaches out to heal me, but Jax grabs his wrist. "You lay another hand on her, and I'll roast you where you stand."

"It's okay, Jax, he was just doing his job." I rub at my chest, my body doing its own work to heal me.

He stiffens and steps back, offering a curt nod before gesturing to the door. "Right this way, Highness."

The guards surrounding the doors step aside, allowing us entry into the castle grounds. I take a deep breath as I make my way through, taking in the thick scent of lavender and something else I can't quite place.

"Stop." Jax's hand flies out. "Do you smell that?"

He strides away from me and approaches the main door with cautious steps, hand outstretched, telling me to stay back. His body shimmers and ripples like water before suddenly transforming into something much bigger—a giant, blue dragon.

He stands tall, wings spread wide and powerful legs ready to defend us both at any sign of danger. A thick fog seeps through the cracks around the edges of the door, giving off an eerie chill that I'm not sure I'm prepared for.

What the hell is going on?

Jax sniffs the air carefully before his head snaps up to meet my eyes. He charges at me with the full capacity of his beast, and I cry out as he rears his head, opens his giant maw, and snaps it shut around me. I'm too stunned to do anything until his enormous tongue presses me against his fangs.

An explosion rocks the air seconds later and I cling to his teeth. A scream peels from my throat as the force of the blast barrels into us, and I hang on for dear life as we tumble. When we skid to a stop, I'm thrown from Jax's mouth and onto the ground.

He lay lifeless on the charred grass next to me, his body cloaked in blood and soot. I can hardly see his face, as it's hidden beneath the scales that had flown off his skin, but I know it's him. "Jax," I choke, my voice a whisper. Terror grips my heart as I scramble to his side, searching for his faint pulse. I heave myself up the scales of his massive body, my fingers clinging to each plate as I go. My foot slips and I catch myself before falling.

"No, no, no," I choke as I reach the top and throw my arms around his huge neck, a sob rising from my throat. Tears pour from my eyes as I gently lift away a loose scale. "Jax," I whimper, sobbing uncontrollably as I feel for his pulse point. The smoke fills my lungs and tears blur my vision. The sweetest feeling in the world stirs beneath my fingertips as his heartbeat beats softly against my hand. But it's too weak.

Desperately, I begin to heal him, praying he won't leave me.

"Help," I scream hoarsely, hoping someone can hear me. "Mom! Dad!"

Guards come running, mounting the giant beast as they try to remove the debris from Jax's body. Skilled healers immediately begin their work, but I know it wouldn't be enough — and as I watch Jax fight for his life, my heart fills with dread that he won't make it out alive.

Moments later strong arms pull me away from Jax and I open my eyes to see Penn, my mom's dragon mate. He holds me close as he speaks soft words of comfort in my ear: "It's okay, Rose. You did everything you could—he'll be alright."

Penn turns back to Jax and continues the healing process while my own heart breaks with fear and sorrow, tears streaming down my cheeks.

A thunderous roar shatters my heartbreak and my eyes snap open. Jax stares down at me with an intense look, his cobalt eyes smoldering like a fire. I can feel the deep connection between us, the unspoken love almost tangible in the air.

My hand grabs onto his snout, my grip tightening with each passing second as if I never want to let go of him. I cling to him as if my life depends on it, wishing I could hold him forever.

He stands on wobbly legs, and the guards jump off him. Jax shifts into his human form, and I'm left holding onto his neck.

"Don't you ever do that again," I shriek. My voice doesn't sound like my own; it's almost unrecognizable as I give into my emotions. "If I die, my family can bring me back to life. If you die, you're gone. Forever!"

His lips curve into a soft smile and his arms wrap around me as he whispers in my ear: "If I'm gone, you'll be able to live on without me. But if I had to live even a second without you, I wouldn't survive it."

I'm left in the wake of his confession, barely able to breathe as our moment is interrupted by palace staff and guards rushing to tend to us. They escort us away, and I take one last glance at Jax.

Admiration pools in the depths of his gaze, flashing that same smile that I'd almost forgotten how to return.

I learn from Penn that my parents weren't even at Convectus Castle, but at the one on Rexuna. But when the call dropped, my dads sifted to each of the castles to intercept me. This was the only one hit.

Jax sifts back to campus while I meet my family on Rexuna, but we have plans later once I get back to our room. First, I need to see my whole family with my own eyes and know that they're safe.

CHAPTER NINE

ROSE

*P*assing a few students in the rec room, lounging in their pajamas and sharing a bottle of fae wine, I make my way up the stairs and scan my irises before slipping into my room. A yelp escapes me when I bump into Jax on the other side of the door, and he steadies me with his hands on my shoulders to keep me from toppling over.

He freezes when I meet his gaze, and he grows concerned when he sees my face. A lock of curls rests on his forehead, and I want to run my fingers through it, but don't.

"What happened?" He swipes his thumbs under my eyes, gently wiping away the tears I hadn't realized were still falling.

Shaking my head, I give him a weak smile. "My parents almost pulled me from school."

"Permanently?" Jax takes my hand and leads me over to my bed, where we both sit down together. He puts his arm around me in a comforting embrace. "Because of the threats?" His eyes narrow, and his grip on me tightens.

"Yeah. They're worried, but I told them I'm safer here, where most people don't know who I am. It's a closed campus so only those authorized to be here can be." I lean into his touch.

"Maybe they're right," he whispers. "I don't want to see you hurt."

"I can't keep living in fear, Jax. And besides, my dads have a few leads on who it might be. It won't be long before they're captured," I assure him, and smile when he relaxes a bit. "Sometimes, I think it's Kieran."

He stiffens. "What?"

"It wouldn't be the first time he's threatened me."

"He did what? When?"

I shake my head. "Not physically. He just threatened to out me to the school. Said I need to stay away from you and Deakan." I rest my head on his shoulder.

"Kieran is a lot of things, but he isn't stupid. Are you sure it wasn't your date? Who was it with?"

My cheeks flush, and I avert my gaze. "Just a guy I met before the semester started." He's more than just a guy. The connection I feel with him is so intense, my only thought was to hold on to him as tight as I could, even if it hurt him in the end.

Jax is silent for a moment before standing up. "You should be focusing on your studies," he mutters under his breath, and then stops at my dresser. "Not dating," he mumbles.

I flop back onto my bed and groan. "Believe me, I know."

Jax turns to face me and tosses a pair of pajamas at me. "No more dates until you graduate," he says, his voice firm.

"Did you just go into my drawer?" I arch a brow, and he shrugs. "And who are you to say who I can and can't date?"

The cool floor kisses my feet as I pad my way to the bathroom to wash my face and brush my teeth. When he doesn't respond, I meet his gaze in the gilded mirror above the sink.

"I thought you'd need something to sleep in. But feel free to wear something of mine instead," he winks.

Rolling my eyes, I finish in the bathroom and change into my own pajamas. When I approach the bed, Jax has the covers thrown back on one side of my bed, and the other is where he lays, under my white duvet.

"What are you doing?" I plop down onto the mattress.

"We're going to sleep." He tucks me under the covers and pulls me close until our bodies are touching. The heat from his bare torso seeps into my skin, and I feel a soothing calm wash over me.

"You can't stay here all night." I don't have the heart to push him away. Not that I want to, anyway. Whatever this is between us? It's nice. Especially after this massive fuckup of a day.

"Sure, I can." His breath tickles my ear. "I'm going to turn your night around."

"You said I can't date until I graduate," I goad him.

He chuckles and tightens his arm around my waist. "I'm the exception to that rule."

A smile creeps onto my face, and I turn my head to press a kiss against his shoulder. "You and Mekhi are the only exception," I whisper before snuggling into his body.

"Did you just kiss me?" Jax sounds shocked, but his laughter makes his chest rumble against me.

I shrug, my eyes heavy from exhaustion. "Maybe," I mumble, already half-asleep.

"Does this mean I can return the favor?" His lips brush against my temple.

"Maybe," I whisper again, the bright glow of my skin illuminating the space between us. The shadows accentuate the deep planes of his smooth chest.

With a cupped hand, he lifts my chin so that he can look me in the eyes. His lips press hungrily against mine with the force of a thousand thunderclaps. I can feel my defenses crumbling as I surrender entirely to him. His hands reach my body with a fiery passion, blazing a trail of molten desire as I shiver with pleasure in his embrace.

Jax pulls away, his cheeks flushed, breathing heavy. He's quiet, his eyes searching mine for something. For what?

"I've never, um…" I trail off, not sure how to finish that sentence. Doing so implies I think we're about to take things further with each other. I don't want to set myself up for embarrassment if it's not his intent.

He beams, his eyes crinkling at the corners as he leans in to press a soft kiss on my forehead. "Me, neither," he murmurs.

My skin flares, and my heart does a little flip at his response. I want him, and for the first time in a long while, I don't feel guilty about it. My mouth is on his before I can even consider all the implications of it.

Swinging my leg to straddle him, my center presses against his length, enjoying the heat between us. His hands grip my hips, his thumbs tracing circles on my skin. He moves me like a marionette, his grasp dragging my body against his, angling me just so that I can feel the press of his need against me.

The hunger between us is palpable, and for a moment, I forget about the threats, the bomb, and the way I almost lost him. I allow myself to give into my selfish needs, and Jax pulls me close, deepening our kiss. His tongue trails along my lower lip, and I sigh against his mouth, my hands gripping his hair as I bury my face in his neck.

"Can I have you, Rose?" His voice is rough against my ear, and I moan in response, my body trembling with anticipation.

"Yes," I breathe out, near feral with need. With fumbling hands, I lean over him to dig in my nightstand for protection. My fingers close over a cool foil packet, and I toss it onto the pillow near Jax's head. Mom sent me to school with a drawer full, just in case. My dads don't know.

Jax helps me peel my shirt off, his eyes drinking in the sight before him. "So beautiful." He cups the back of my neck to pull me towards him. Instead of kissing me, he uses the momentum to flip us, so he hovers over me. "Tell me, Rose, have you ever been kissed?"

Furrowing my brows, I'm about to answer when he brings his knee against my heat. Have I ever been kissed *there*?

"No." My cheeks heat up in embarrassment.

He gazes down at me, his hands caressing my face before skating lower to my waist. "Good. I want to be your first everything." He grins.

"As long as that goes both ways," I whisper, my breath catching in my throat as his lips trail down to the crook of my neck.

His smile fills me with warmth as he nods in approval. "It does."

Sitting up, I reach behind me to undo my bra, my skin tingling in anticipation of his touch. I arch into him as he cups my breasts in his hands, and a sigh escapes my lips as he traces circles around them with his tongue. His mouth moves lower still, following the trail his hands take to remove my shorts and underwear.

My face flushes as I'm bared to him, and he sucks in a strangled breath. He curses, running a finger along my slit. I fight the urge to close my legs, to draw myself away from his stare, his touch.

"Tell me where it feels good, Rose." The hunger in his gaze nearly undoes me.

Gliding a trembling hand along the curve of my hipbone, I bring it to the apex of my thighs, pressing a finger against the small nub of pleasure. Moving it in a small circle, I close my eyes, feeling into the bliss of it. Jax's hand cups mine, applying slight pressure as our fingers intertwine. He drags them to my center, hissing when he dips into my core. "So fucking wet for me, aren't you?"

My hand falls away, and my back arches when the warm press of his tongue laps at my clit. My chest rises and falls in fits, and my eyes fly open when he coaxes a thick finger inside me, beckoning it towards him. Gripping his hair, I watch as he works me over.

His thumb replaces his tongue for a few moments as he whispers wicked things against my mound. *So fucking sweet. You don't know how many nights I've dreamt of this. I love watching you fall apart beneath me.*

The moment his words meet my ears and his tongue nudges against my skin, a wildfire's ignited that burns through me. It's all-consuming. It's an inferno that blazes, him stoking the flames until I'm consumed in a body-shattering release.

Sweat dampens my skin, and I barely register Jax kneeling between my legs until he speaks. "How'd I do?"

A laugh escapes me, bordering on hysteria. "Please don't let that be the last time you do that to me," I plead as I bring myself up onto my elbows. "I'm not above begging."

"Fuck, you're going to undo me." A wicked gleam dances in his eyes. "I'll do it every night if you let me."

"Promise?" I grin. Kidding, of course. Fae have to be careful about making promises they can't easily keep, as breaking them leads to death.

"Would you settle for as often as I can?" His lips press against mine, and that's when I notice he's still got his pajama pants on.

"Yes, so long as we get you out of these." I tug on them, and he helps me slide them over his firm ass.

My attention catches on the heavy erection between his legs, where it bobs gently against his cut abs. I've never actually seen a cock in real life, save for a peek or fifteen when he's changed in front of me. It's been our unwritten rule; we can sate each other's curious glances, but we never talk about it, nor do we linger too long. Up close, it's bigger than I thought it'd be. I reach out for it without thinking and am taken aback by how smooth the skin is.

Jax sucks in a breath, his stomach muscles contracting at the contact.

My fingers close around it, testing the weight of it while I meet his eyes. "Tell me what feels good, Jax." My voice comes out huskier than I intended.

He pants heavily, his breath coming in short bursts as he wraps his hand around mine, guiding me to caress him in long strokes. He stops me, and it looks as though doing so pains him. "I don't want to come until I'm inside you, Rose."

"Okay." I withdraw my touch, and instead pull him to me. He settles between my thighs, and his mouth is on mine. Tasting myself on him, instead of feeling embarrassed, I groan and suck on his tongue.

He pulls back, pressing a finger to my lips. "Where's the condom?"

Reaching over my head, I feel for the foil, and find it under my pillow. "Can I … Can I put it on you?"

He rips the packet open and pulls a rubber disc from it. "Yeah." He hands it to me. "Please."

I roll it onto his length, and I can't help but cup his balls when I finish. They're heavier than I imagined, and while soft, not as smooth as his cock. Falling onto my back, I tug him with me. His weight presses against my chest before he lifts his pelvis and I guide him to my center. The thick head nudges my entrance, and he pauses to meet my eyes.

"You sure about this?"

I whisper, "One-hundred percent."

That's all the encouragement he needs to press into me until he meets my resistance. The breath seizes in my lungs, and he groans, "I don't know if it'll fit, Rose. Fuck. You're so tight."

I gasp for air in short spurts as I try to get used to him. Everyone knows your first time is painful, but Luna fae have it a little easier because our magic fills when aroused, inflicting pain, or when we're healing. Jax seems to remember this, and pauses, allowing my body time to do its thing before pressing further into me.

The second he pushes past my hymen, a sharp pain makes my entire body flinch. "Are you alright?" He stills, about to draw back, but I keep my legs firmly wrapped around him.

I can't speak, so I nod, gripping him as tight as I can to prevent him from moving. It's not long before my body heals itself and my legs loosen their vice-like hold.

"I'm good." I sigh, able to feel the pleasure of this moment now.

The fit is still tight, but all it brings is bliss. We moan in pleasure as we move together, our bodies melding into one as we savor the sensation of being skin to skin. Jax moves within me, slow and steady; each thrust filling me with a primal need that neither of us can deny. I gasp into his mouth as he speeds up the tempo, my body trembling and responding in kind. My fingernails dig into his skin as he continues, driving me closer and closer to the edge.

Jax pulls out. "I'm going to come, but I want our first time to last, so give me a minute." His mouth closes around my left nipple, sucking and nibbling as he slides his hand in between us, finding the hot button of my clit. "This okay?" He pinches it between his finger and thumb and tugs down just hard enough to drive me right over the edge, and I don't even have a chance to respond.

My back arches off the mattress, and I'm unable to muffle a scream against his chest as my orgasm rips through me. His fingers dip into my center before he brings them to my mouth as he sheathes himself inside me again. I taste the remnants of myself on his fingers and meet his gaze with my lips parted. "I want to make you feel good, Rose." His voice is rough, thick with lust, and something else.

Jax sits me up, supporting my back as he positions his legs under me, so I'm in his lap, sliding on his cock. My legs wrap around his waist, grinding our bodies together. He speaks, and his words are sin, luring me in with the baddest of intentions.

I'm the first to reach the finish line, but we come together, our breaths mingling and becoming one as we collapse into each other's embrace.

Silently, we both understand that this is a new beginning for us. Whatever it is, it's something special. From this day forward, wherever life takes us, we'll always have been each other's firsts.

～

ROSE

Sunlight filters through the curtains, and Jax stirs against me when my phone buzzes on the nightstand. I've got a text from Mekhi telling me he's glad we're alright and letting me know he can get away for a few hours to watch my first game in a few weeks. He'll tag along with Bennett and my parents (disguised). We make plans before I scroll to the next name on my text notifications: Penelope.

> My parents took me to Occasus this weekend and I picked us up a box of Fae Grahams!

I chuckle at the text. Each week, she and I have been taste testing each box of cereal the realm has to offer. Before meeting her, I hadn't eaten cereal much, but now it's a thing between us.

> Isn't that made by Merlin? I hated his Pegasus Poos.

I type out and hit send. I've never been a fan of chocolate cereal.

Yes, but we need to try it. For science.

I grumble.

Fine, I'll try it if you try the Hexes and Ohs.

Easiest deal I've made in months.

Scrolling to the next text I've received, my hands still on a name that makes my heart clench: Theo. I've thought about him and our disastrous date every day since I fucked it up.

Can we talk?

My thumbs hesitate over the keypad, unsure how to respond or if I should. Before I can decide, a knock sounds at our door, waking Jax.

"Go away!" he grumbles and tucks me into his side. His mussed hair falls over his forehead before his brow smooths out.

"Open up!" someone shouts from the other side, and I can't tell if it's Deakan or Kieran.

I don't have to wonder long because the knob wobbles a few times before a bolt of magic jimmies it open and in struts both. *Second years and their fucking freedom to use magic.*

Jax yanks the duvet up to cover my exposed chest and I shout at them to get out. Kieran's nostrils flare, and his cold, green eyes glare at me. It's such a contrast compared to Deakan, whose gaze doesn't break from mine once I meet it. His pupils blow wide as he cups himself on top of his jeans.

"What the fuck are you doing?" Jax and Kieran shout at the same time.

"We—" Kieran gestures between the three of them, "—were supposed to meet two hours ago!"

"Shit." Jax stumbles out of the bed, getting tangled in the sheets and effectively baring me to our intruders once again.

Kieran's attention falls to my lower half and his eyes widen before he whips his head to where Jax is busy pulling a pair of jeans on. "You took the high princess' *virginity*?!"

Heat crawls up my neck and tears gather in my eyes before I can remember to cloak myself to hide from their scrutiny. They can no longer see me, but I see them, attention fixated on the evidence on the bed.

Jax's shouts for them to leave pierces the room, and he drags them out of the door. I'm left hugging my knees as tears spill down my face and onto my legs. In a matter of seconds, he's back, yanking me onto him and shushing me though he can't see me.

"I'm so sorry, Rose. No one should've violated your privacy like this," he whispers against my head.

I'm too humiliated to speak, and he seems to sense this. "Please don't hide from me, beautiful. Have you any idea how much it means to me we were each other's firsts?" His hand fumbles for my face before he locates my chin, bringing my tear-stained lips to his. His kiss is insistent, coaxing. He pulls back when he realizes I've dropped my cloak, his gaze searching mine as he brushes the tears out from under my eyes.

"Don't cry," he whispers. "Not over them. They're just being dicks. I don't regret a single moment of this. Of us, okay?"

Something inside me thaws, and I nod. His features relax, relief written on his face before he kisses me with so much tenderness, I fear I might break in half.

He never meets up with his friends, and neither of us leave the room today. We're both caught up in exploring each other, finding new ways to give and receive.

CHAPTER TEN

JAX

Rose and I spend the next few weeks being almost inseparable except for classes and practice; talking, exploring, and learning more about each other. She's captivating, and I can barely take my eyes off her when she talks. I know that what we have is special—it's different from anything I've ever experienced before.

When Monday morning arrives, it brings with it an unwelcome reality: Rose and I must deal with the Kieran situation before he outs her as princess or keep whatever it is between us a secret. With the threats against her growing more credible, we can't risk the rest of campus finding out.

Rose and I promise each other that we will figure out the best way to share our feelings with everyone else when the time is right. In the meantime, our rendezvous will only occur in our room, and I'll work on Kieran and the dean to ensure no one can use a spell to unlock our door again. If I must pull the princess card on Rose's behalf—citing her safety—I'll do it.

After classes, Kieran and I are in the locker room with the rest of the Spar Games team. Deakan didn't try out, though Coach Thorn,

Kieran, and I wanted him to. He has natural talent for it but prefers to stay on the sidelines.

"What's going on between you and Rose?" Kieran slides his head through the hole of his workout t-shirt. "I thought we agreed she was off-limits?"

"You agreed, Kieran, and you just took the rest of us along for the ride." I pause and glance around, but the other guys are too busy with their own conversations to pay attention. "All I'm going to say right now is that Rose and I have been getting to know each other better for the entire semester. Assumptions beyond that are your own."

"So, you taking her virginity was just my imagination?"

"I'm not having this conversation with you." I slam the locker shut and start for the door. The only reason I'm not pushing the issue is because I've got a plan to warm him up to the idea of her, but it'll take some time and a little help from Deakan.

The sun bakes everything in sight as we make our way over to the practice pitch. Rose is already there, running drills as the rest of the team watches. I can see the admiration in their eyes, but what I feel for her is far greater. She may be a princess, but she has earned my respect and loyalty—even if no one else knows it yet.

No one looks our way, and I catch Kieran checking her out, his attention on her form as she glides across the field with a staff in hand. Sweeping it in graceful arcs, she controls the weapon like an extension of her own body. Her dark hair swings from her ponytail and contrasts sharply against her fitted white tank top, her snug black workout shorts, and her bare, tan legs. She's barefoot against the lush green of the field. Without even seeming to realize what he's doing, Kieran's eyes glaze over, his jaw slackens, and he just stares at her like a fool in love. Though a staff is her weapon of choice, today she appears as a ballerina, one who dances through the field with a swaying of hips and legs, her movements poetry in motion.

My mood sours when I catch a group of guys near the locker rooms scoping her out. They're not on the Spar Games team, so they're not here to practice; instead, they're leering, drooling, and discussing her assets as if she's an object. Kieran takes notice, and before I can storm over there, he does it for me, leaving me shell-shocked in his wake.

He flashes his venom-tipped fangs at the lot of them, and they take off. I was too busy watching what they were doing to notice the coach divvying up pairs already. He paired Rose with a blond kid named Eli, though I know nothing about him other than that he has a weird accent. The way the two of them interact, they must know each other.

We're the last to take our places on the field, so Coach pairs me with Kieran, and we're to work on strategy. This is the most difficult of the three things to practice. With combat and magic, you're making a physical effort and pushing yourself to your limits, whereas strategy requires an intellectual effort and an awareness of the state of the pitch.

For our strategy practice, Coach has Kieran and I dismantle a magic bomb. When it goes off, it will release a multitude of small, brilliant, multi-colored bubbles. If popped, these bubbles will float up and gather into a cloud, trapping players beneath them and hindering their ability to play. It's a rare game, but one of the few that requires all players on the field, and it's the first game played during a bout when activated.

The rest of the team continues their training while Kieran and I kneel beside a ticking device with six minutes on the countdown timer. There's an easy off button, but it's trapped under a puzzle with one hundred pieces containing different chemical components you must match before you can place the piece. Kieran won this game last year with two seconds to spare, but that all goes to shit when I catch him sabotaging the puzzle. It was a sleight of hand, and I would've missed it if it weren't for one of my chemical senses inherent to my dragon order. It's not until the trap springs that I realize why he's done it:

That Eli guy has Rose pinned beneath him; her skin alight in hues of blue.

The bubbles release, and everyone on the field rises into the sky, arms and legs flailing as we hover twenty feet off the ground. We remain here for the next six minutes, but it's a small price to pay. Is

Rose attracted to that yeehaw? She's not glowing anymore, but everyone is more than a little distracted while we explain why everyone is suddenly up in the air.

When we descend, Coach gives new pairings to everyone. This time, I get Rose, and as soon as we touch down, I head towards her. Eli keeps glancing her way, and she seems to like it.

"Are you doing that on purpose?"

"What?"

"Flirting with him."

"I'm not flirting with him. He's from Earth and is a vampire." So that explains some of the connection between the two of them. Her parents are the King and Queen of Vampires.

"You aren't attracted to him?"

"I didn't say that."

Using this as an opportunity to spar, I tackle her to the ground before she sees it coming, and I wedge myself between her thighs, wrists pinned over her head. Breathing in that heady scent that I love so much, she whispers in my ear, "I was wondering when you were going to do something like this."

"My cock isn't enough for you?" I emphasize my point by pressing my erection against her heat and smashing my bare chest against her breasts.

She smirks. "I didn't say that either."

"Keep smarting off, and I'll show you what you can do with that pretty little mouth of yours."

Coach blows the whistle, signaling our attention. "Leave it to the bedroom, you two. Don't make me have to hose you off."

The team laughs, and I release her wrists just as she swings her leg out, so I'm thrown onto my back with a thud. All the air escapes my lungs, and a triumphant Rose pins my shoulders to the grass.

"I think I quite like you between my thighs, Jaxy Baby." She winks before popping off me and she struts off, giggling as she approaches the group who applaud her win.

Though the sparring can be intense at times, there's a mutual understanding between us that this is all in good fun. We're both trying to better ourselves and help the team win.

After we spar with others, me with a third-year witch we call Basher, and Rose with a fourth-year incubus fae named Corson, Coach calls everyone over for combat magic. Rose is only one of two first years who made the team. The other is another shy girl who appears on friendly terms with Rose, judging by how she calls her Lopey instead of Penelope. Lopey is a mouse order of some sorts, which will come in handy during games when we need someone small, fast, and nimble.

Our first field magic lesson is how to use our spells in conjunction with one another, and while it takes me a good hour to catch on, Rose seems to be a natural. She's practiced magic for a while now. We drill until sunset, with Coach praising us both for our prowess as the skies darken and we make our way back up the hill. It's an unusually hot late fall day, with a warm sea breeze doing little to cool us off.

Rose and I part ways at the gate without saying goodbye but exchange knowing looks full of the promise of more to come in the room. We both know that we have something special between us, and it's up to us now to make sure that everyone else knows it, too, in due time. I can only hope that Kieran will be on board soon enough because Rose deserves to be seen for who she really is. Him denying the way he feels about her is bullshit. He wouldn't have done half the things he did today if he wasn't crazy about her. Right?

An inkling of doubt stirs inside me. What if he *is* the one who made threats? Is it because he wants her?

Just before the turn, the Dean meets Rose on the path in front of me. I overhear their conversation and can't help but smile as she tells her about how well she did in practice and how proud the school is to have such a talented student on our team. It's moments like these that make it all worthwhile seeing the high princess shine in her own right, without relying on her title or family name. This is what true—

"Though, you must know you're well overdue for our meeting, and I've tallied at least forty-six instances of you using magic outside the pitch," the Dean says, ending the pleasantries.

The smile falls from my face as I watch their interaction, and doubts creep in. Have I made a mistake by keeping Fallgren updated?

~

ROSE

Sweat clings to my brow as the Dean lectures me on using magic recklessly. I can't help but smile, though, as I look down at her—though stern, she's a kind fae with an air of authority around her.

Using a hand towel to wipe my face, I listen, planning to do whatever it takes to earn her trust. She's the one in charge of my future, after all, and I don't want to mess this up.

With a nod of understanding that I'll meet her in her office in ten minutes, I thank her for her time before turning on my heel and heading back towards the pitch. I've forgotten my water bottle and I want to grab it before the sun sets.

As I walk, my thoughts drift back to my family—my parents and siblings, so far away from me now. It's a strange feeling to be here without them, but I know that with the help of this academy and its faculty, I can learn to be the powerful fae my parents want me to be. Anything to keep them safe.

Just as I'm about to enter the pitch, I hear a voice behind me—it's Kieran. He and I went at it hard today during sparring, him barely holding back his magic each time Coach wasn't looking. He wasn't supposed to be using it for our session, but I could feel it as though it were my own magic, prodding and trying to coax mine out to play. I turn to find him standing before me, an angry scowl on his face.

"You think you're so special, don't you? You and your high-and-mighty family," he sneers. Anger radiates off him in waves, but I refuse to be intimidated by it.

What did I do to him that makes him hate me so? Or is it all royals in general?

Though my thoughts waver, I stand firm, cocking my head in challenge as I cross my arms. "Would you rather I forget who I am, Kieran? That's not going to happen."

He looks taken aback for a moment before his face settles into a smirk. "Don't worry, Princess," he says with a wink as he turns to leave. "I know what you are, and it's not going to be forgotten any time soon. Not when the rest of campus will soon know they've got rotten blood in their midst. The stench of it never goes undetected for long." He walks away while I'm left with a faltering smile on my face. Why is he always so hot and cold with me? Sometimes, it's as though he can't wait to fuck me, and others, he's devising ways to ruin me. He's got to be the one threatening me. Though, I'm not sure about the bomb. The way he treats me seems personal, and the bomb could've been for anyone at the castle. There was no note.

Knocking on the door to the Dean's office, I startle when Coach Thorn lets me in. The way his face is twisted into a frown gives the impression that he isn't thrilled with whatever my punishment is. No matter what it is, it must be bad.

With a deep breath, I look up into his tormented gaze and nod my head. "Let's do this," I say quietly, steeling myself for whatever comes next as I turn to face the Dean.

She stands and looks down at me, her eyes seeming to see right through me. "Rose, you have no idea how powerful a being you truly are," she begins.

Without pausing for thought, I respond, "And that's why I need this school." I want to learn how to use my abilities for good. Already, I feel the burden of my careless use of magic, a cost I will bear in my subconscious for all of eternity. No one who takes a life should forget it. This is also the reason why Oz no longer possesses any magical abilities of his own.

"Forty-six times you used your magic against the rules of the school," Dean Fallgren interjects. "Forty-six times you put yourself and others in danger."

"If I may, Dean..." I wince. "Some of those times, I was healing myself or others. As a Luna fae, my magic regenerates as part of my autonomic system. When the moon is out, when I'm healing—"

"That's correct. However, you aren't here at school to heal yourself or others," she cuts in.

I pause and look up into her eyes before I remember the words Kieran whispered to me moments ago—*you think you're so special.* My brow furrows as determination seeps through me. "No," I stand straighter and square my shoulders. "I'm here to be the best fae I can be and use my magic responsibly."

Dean Fallgren nods her head in approval before motioning for me to sit down. She turns her attention to Coach Thorn and the two of them discuss the details of my future. All I can do is sit and watch, hoping that this meeting is going to end with a better outcome than it began. They've put a silencing bubble around themselves, and it looks as though Coach is on my side based on how heated he's getting.

Soon enough, the bubble dissipates and the two of them turn to me. I can tell from their expressions that things haven't gone my way. "Rose," Dean Fallgren begins in a somber tone. "You will no longer have the ability to use magic at Bedlam Academy outside of the pitch or in class as necessary."

Stilling, I wait for the rest of what she has to say. I'm already not permitted to use magic except in those circumstances, so I'm not sure where she's going with this. It's when she reaches behind her neck with both hands to unclasp a necklace hidden under her blouse that I pay closer attention. Attached to it is a key she uses to unlock the bottom drawer of her desk. The sound of the lock gives way to a small clinking noise as she removes a large black velvet cinch bag. She sets the bag on her desk and slides a circlet out of it.

My pulse thunders in my ear as I recognize it for what it is—it's the same type of suppressant necklace the King of Werewolves used on my mother when she was his captive.

My breathing gives way to panic as Dean Fallgren turns my way and gestures for me to come forward. "Rose," she says, her voice firm but gentle. "This is the only way we can ensure your safety until you prove yourself."

No, I want to scream. My subconscious cries for it. She wants to scratch, rip, maim, and kill to get away. *Maybe there's more beast in me than I thought.* My throat tightens as I nod my head in agreement before I rise and move towards her desk. Each step I take threatens to buckle my knees, and tears fall freely down my cheeks as I reach her.

Everything happens in slow motion, as though I'm beside myself and not here. I fight the urge to scream, to claw my way out of the room and away from the darkness coiling around the edges of my vision; away from the sinister magic pouring off the jewelry.

Dean Fallgren takes the necklace and places it around my neck, locking it in place with a click. This causes the ends of the necklace to lodge into my skin as an extra layer of precaution. A sob escapes me as I sink to my knees, the weight of her actions pressing down on me like a heavy burden. The oily sensation of the suppressant seeps through my skin and circles my throat, choking me until I can hardly breathe before it fills every cell, cutting me off from source. The moon beams filtering through the picture window no longer warms me, and I'm left in the cold, barren void of my own desperation.

With a heavy heart, I gaze up at the two of them. They both wear expressions of sympathy, and though I know they have my best interest in mind, all I can think about is how broken I feel.

As if sensing my thoughts, Coach Thorn crouches beside me and takes my hand in his own. "I'm sorry, Rose," he says, his voice soft. "But this is for your own good. You'll make the most of it, I know you will. Each of your professors has access to the key to unlock this when needed." Though he tries to appear as though he was for this method of suppression, the way his eyes shine with unshed tears tells me he's almost as pained as I am about it.

Stunned, I can do nothing but stare at the moons hanging high in the sky, who've been my friends and confidants since I was a child. I suppose even they can't protect me from the trials of life, and that's when I know this is only the beginning. With a deep breath, I face forward and accept the challenge that lies ahead of me.

Even if I'm dying inside.

Before I turn to leave the room, I catch a giant crow watching me from a palm tree outside the window. Its eyes are wise and knowing, and it cocks its head to one side before flapping away into the night.

The sight strikes me as unusual, as this isn't the first one I've seen. Earth-side crows don't like dense jungle. I don't know enough about the fae ones to know if this is normal for Bedlam or not.

Instead of returning to my room, my feet carry me through the Witches Woods after I've pulled on a sweater to cover the necklace. Though it's sweltering, I don't want anyone to see, or they might think I'm out of control.

When I'm walking, time seems to stand still, and it's only when my foot strikes rough stone that I look up and realize I've arrived at Sanctuary. My burden lightens as I make my way to the bench where Theo and I sat, where signs of life and nature glow around me. It's a pocket of peace in my bleak outlook.

Crashing to my knees, I let the tears pour out until I'm too exhausted to cry anymore. I'm scared of what is to come and unsure if I'll be able to make it through this. But I know one thing for certain—I will not be silenced. Even in my darkest hour, I'll continue to fight for the freedom I crave and that my parents worked so hard to give me.

Following in my mother's footsteps, I refuse to give up. Standing, I take a deep breath of the fresh night air and raise my arms to the heavens in supplication. I long to feel the kiss of Luna's beams on my skin, the hours feel like an eternity without her, and I whisper a plea for guidance.

The wind carries my voice away like music, and I close my eyes, believing in my grandmother's magic. For hours, I beg on my knees for the help she promised me not too long ago. And for hours, I'm met with silence.

Can she not hear me with this on? I reach behind my head to unclasp the necklace just like we did my mother's, but instead, I'm met with a sharp wave of pain that begins at my fingers and radiates through my entire body, as though I were getting tazed. A sob wrenches itself from my throat and I collapse against the bench, my face in my hands.

The feeling of displaced air greets me then, and I look up to see the giant crow from earlier. It alights on the bench beside me, its eyes gentle and knowing. Instead of beady black marbles, its eyes are pools of silver. Though I cannot understand its language, I can feel its strength and ancient wisdom, and for the longest time we sit in silence.

Just when I gain the courage to reach a hand out to see if its feathers are as soft as they appear, a heavy whooshing sound breaks the silence, and the crow takes flight. The noise didn't come from the crow, though.

I feel him before I see him. Swathed in a cloak of midnight, his face hidden beneath the hood of a leather jacket, he stands at the edge of Sanctuary.

CHAPTER ELEVEN

THEO

She's here.
When I saw Rose on her knees at our bench, I hadn't planned on rushing to her side and pulling her into my arms. But I do just that when the light from the moons catches the fresh tear streaks marring her cheeks. A single sob escapes her lips before she fights down her sorrow, and it nearly sends me to my knees.

"Are you hurt?" I whisper against her hair, grateful that she doesn't pull away.

When she looks up at me, I can see the silver flecks that now dance in her deep blue eyes, and it's then that I understand. She's not just a woman who's managed to snare my heart, no matter how much I want to deny it. She's one of *them*, a fae with enough power to be noticed by the gods. *This is why* I can't contain my beast. He knew long before she'd been chosen.

The mere idea creates a cacophony inside my chest, even though it aches for her pain. For millennia, griffins have served the ones the gods have marked in secret, never daring to let them know of our presence. Is this why I feel this pull towards her? Why I felt called to come here tonight? She didn't have those sparks in her eyes during our date. Does she even know who's marked her?

"Theo?" Rose murmurs, breaking me out of my thoughts. I peer down to find her studying me, her gaze questioning and vulnerable.

"Yes, love?" I reach a hand up to cup the side of her face.

She leans into my touch and closes her eyes. "I thought you were still mad at me."

Her words drag me back to reality, and I can't help but chuckle.

"I am mad at you," I admit. "Sure, I'm upset you kept it from me that you're dating someone else and still went out with me, but I'm more upset you never returned my text."

"Your tex—ohh," she winces. "Sorry, I had a couple of guys break into my room just as I saw it and—"

"Someone broke into your room?!" my beast shrieks inside of me, barely restrained as it fights to keep her safe.

Rose bites her lip, her eyes widening as they meet mine. "Yeah," she says softly, pushing a strand of hair from her face. "But it's taken care of now."

I exhale, calming my beast and giving her a concerned frown. "Why were you crying?" My nostrils flare, catching the faintest hint of blood. Panic seizes me, and I grip her arms, turning them to inspect the skin beneath.

"Theo!" Rose scolds and tries to pull away when I reach her shoulders. "I'm fine, I just scraped a knee."

She's acting cagey right now. What isn't she telling me? I can feel her distance and it's killing me, so I force myself to take a step back.

"Rose," I begin slowly, searching for the right words. "I'm here for you, no matter what."

Her lips quirk into a sad smile as she looks away. "You weren't, actually. Not that I blame you," her voice barely carries in the night air.

As though I've been slapped, I flinch, and my beast whines inside my head, wounded. I want to reassure her, tell her we'll figure it out together, but before I can say another word, she continues.

"My whole life, I knew I wanted to be just like my mom." Her voice takes on a reverent tone as if she's speaking of a goddess. "She has many mates, and it's all I've ever known. Her normal is my normal.

The way my dads all work together to make sure we're all happy and cared for, it's the most beautiful thing I've ever seen. But here," she gestures to the grounds, the trees, and the sky. "Here, we don't have that. We're so alone."

Taking a deep breath, I steady my hands, which have been shaking ever since she started speaking. I reach out and take hers in mine, squeezing before letting go.

"You don't have to be alone." I caress her cheek. "I'm here, and if you let me, I'll do everything in my power to make sure you never feel alone again. Forgive me."

Rose looks up at me, her eyes wide and unreadable. I can see the gears turning in her head, weighing her options. She's hesitant and unsure, but I can also see the tiniest glimmer of hope in the depths of her gaze, and it's all I need to know that she's considering it.

"Theo." She turns her head so I can't witness the tear tracking down her cheek. "No one male is enough for me, and you won't share. I'm sorry for not being upfront with you, but I'm not sorry about my needs."

My beast stirs again and for a moment, I'm tempted to just take her in my arms and tell her everything will be okay. But I know better.

Taking a deep breath, I force a calmness I don't feel into my voice. "It may sound difficult, but I'm confident that if we all put our heads together and figure this out, we can find a way to make it work. You don't have to be alone. It's new to me, too, and I'm sure with your mom's guidance and a little bit of trust, we can get through it."

She gives me a slow nod, her lips curving into a bittersweet smile. "I'm selfish, Theo." She faces me, her voice barely above a whisper. "I'm not sure I can offer you what you deserve, and I refuse to share."

"Rose." I take her in my arms, holding her as a tear streaks down her face, and I whisper into her hair. "I'm not asking you to. You have your own unique form of affection to give, and I'm here for it. If you don't want to be like your mom, then you don't have to. And if you do? That's okay, too. You just have to be you."

She sniffles and pulls away, her cheeks still wet. I wipe them before pressing a kiss to her forehead.

"We can figure this out." I cup her chin, my voice resolute. "The other day, I was caught off guard and didn't realize what I'd be losing when I walked away. For weeks, it's eaten me up inside, and I haven't slept or eaten properly since. I want to be here for you, and this situation is far from ideal, but it's worth the effort. You're worth the effort."

Rose's lips quirk up into a genuine smile, and she throws her arms around me. "Thank you," she mumbles against my shoulder. "Are you sure though? I can be a big pain in the ass."

"I'm more certain of this than anything else in my life." Emotion radiates off her in waves, and I pull her onto my lap when I sit down. "So, your boyfriend ... what's his name?"

"Mekhi." Her eyes are distant as she looks out into the night sky. "We started as friends and over the summer, grew into something more."

Dismissing the jealousy I feel, I take a deep breath and smile.

"Tell me more." I tuck a stray wave of her hair behind her ear, wanting to know everything about him so that I can be the kind of mate he isn't. What kind of life does she want? What does she need from me that he doesn't provide?

As she fills me in, I take careful note as my feelings of admiration for her expand in my chest. No matter how things started between us, I'm happy for her that she found someone who loves and cares for her.

"Do you want to meet him?" Rose interrupts my thoughts. I nod, answering without hesitation. "Then let's make it happen." She smiles, and I feel my cheeks heat up in response before she continues. "Are you coming to the Spar Games match this weekend? He'll be there."

"Can't make it this weekend because I'll be headed to Shatterlee Market so I can pick up some supplies."

"Oh, alright. Next time, then."

I give her a gentle squeeze. "Next time."

Rose and I talk for hours, until a midnight storm chases across the sky and we realize just how late it is. We'd both been determined to make our relationship work, no matter what kind of roadblocks life threw in our way. When she glances at her phone, she freaks out at the myriad of missed texts. I don't pry, as things between us are new and precarious. Best not to stress her out before we even begin to make progress.

"Do you mind if I make a quick phone call? I'll meet you inside." She nods towards the giant stone door draped in vines.

I nod, waving her off, and I turn to the stairs leading to the small home I built. Being with Rose feels right—like coming home after a long journey. The only question that remains is if she feels the same.

∽

ROSE

Watching as Theo slips into the darkness, I take a deep breath and dial Jax's number. He picks up after half a ring, his voice on edge with worry.

"Are you alright?!" he demands, his tone hard.

"Yeah, sorry," I reassure him, trying to infuse my voice with as much pleasantness as possible. "I lost track of time. I'm out of sorts from the drama with the Dean and ran into my date from the other night. Just wanted to let you know I'll be out a little bit longer."

He sighs, softening a bit. "Do you need me to come get you?"

"No, I'm alright. Just wanted to let you know," I explain, feeling sheepish. While I'm not keeping things from him, this is Theo's place, and it doesn't feel right to out it to Jax. "And to let you know things are alright between him and I now."

Jax is so quiet, I have to check to make sure our call didn't get disconnected. "Okay," he finally says, his voice heavy. "We can talk more when you're back home," he adds before hanging up.

I sigh, feeling guilty for keeping the full scope of my evening from him. I'll tell him everything when we're face-to-face.

I make my way up to the door to the small room inside the stone building. Its bone-white walls give the appearance it's larger than it really is, with its vaulted ceiling, but the dimensions of the place are still fairly small. A bed is set up in the corner, a few overstuffed leather chairs and a worn table take up the rest of the space. For being in the middle of the jungle, hidden from the world, it's sure cozy. The room is much cooler than the sweltering heat outside, thanks to a series of interconnected caves that create a natural air-conditioning system.

I find Theo seated on the bed, and join him, feeling calmer than I had since the day began.

"Everything alright?" His golden eyes focus on me.

Nodding, I give him a gentle smile as I stretch out next to him. "One of the other guys I'm seeing had been worried when I didn't check in after meeting with the Dean, so I told him I'd be a little while longer. I can't stay long because I've got an eight a.m. class."

"Alright." He tucks a piece of my hair behind my ear." This guy you're seeing ... it's not Mekhi?"

I shake my head, feeling a blush creep up my neck. "No, his name is Jax."

He chooses his words carefully. "And it's serious?"

"Yeah." Shrugging, I play with the strand of hair he'd just put away. It's drenched from the rain, along with my clothes, and I can't even use my magic to dry myself off. "We've slept together, if that's what you're asking."

He nods, looking away. "I see." He looks back at me, a half-smile playing on his lips. "Do you three ... share?"

"As in...?"

"At the same time?"

My entire face heats with the implication and I nearly choke on my own spit. "Um, no. I mean, not yet anyway." I consider his question for a moment. "Mekhi and I have never been intimate in that way. Jax is the only one I've ever slept with."

"Wait, you didn't sleep with your boyfriend, but have with your non-boyfriend-but-serious-lover?" He chews his lip. "No judgment, just trying to sort everything out in my head."

After a moment of silence, I fidget and mutter a silent groan at how terrible this sounds. "Mekhi gave me the green light to do what I want, but that doesn't mean I'm going around sleeping with anyone. I love him. And Jax knows about Mekhi, has met him, and understands the dynamic we're working with. I'm not saying I'm mating any of you. What I am saying is that I'm trying you on for size?" Wincing at how horrible that sounded, I close my eyes.

We're quiet for a while before he turns to me. "Do either of them know about me?"

This question, at least, I feel fine answering without screwing it up. "Both know I went on a date with you, and it didn't go well because I didn't mention Mekhi up-front. I'm talking with them both when I get back to my room about you joining the potential fold."

"Sounds like you've got it all figured out." His fingers interlace with mine on top of my thigh.

I blush and shake my head. "I've got no idea what I'm doing, or if I'm even doing it right." Checking the time on my phone, I tell him I should head back.

I stand and he follows, his arms pulling me into a tight hug. "When can I see you again? And can I walk you back to campus?"

"Soon, to the first, and sure, to the second." I hug him back before slipping out of his arms.

When we arrive at the courtyard, I spot Kieran on the path towards our dorm. With him not knowing what's going on between Jax, Mekhi, and I, I want to avoid a run-in, so I turn to face Theo.

"Thanks for walking me back. One of Jax's friends is here, and he doesn't really know about the whole dating-multiple-guys thing yet. Is it alright if we part ways here? I promise this will all be sorted soon."

He takes one of my hands in his, giving it a discreet squeeze. "Of course. Take care and let me know when the dust settles."

With a nod, I leave him to head for the dorms while he goes towards the bell tower. I can't help but wonder if I'm strong enough to handle what I'm putting myself through and decide then and there that no matter the outcome, I'll be damn proud of myself for even attempting it in the first place. I've just got to survive not having my magic to lean on.

CHAPTER TWELVE

JAX

Rose comes back to the dorm, wiping tears out of her eyes. She sees me, and runs into my arms, sobbing into my chest. I scoop her into my arms and carry her over to my bed before setting her down.

"What's wrong, love?" I stroke her hair, clinging her to me.

She sniffles before peering up at me with the saddest eyes I've ever seen. "This." She takes off her sweater, and laying on her neckline is a thick, steel-colored necklace.

My fingers lightly trace the edges of it. "What is it?"

"It's a magic suppression necklace from the realm of Romarie," she whispers, her voice despondent.

My eyes widen in alarm. "The Dean made you wear this?" Hysteria bubbles in my chest.

"Yeah. Each professor has a key to remove the necklace when needed during class, and I don't have to wear it during games, but otherwise ... it stays on. Probably the rest of the school year." Her expression is heartbreakingly vulnerable, and my anger swells inside me.

"We'll get it off you, love. I promise." I trace her jaw with my thumb. "We'll find a way."

She nods before burying her face in my shirt again, and I just hold her until she's relaxed enough to sleep.

That night, I lay awake in the dark, my mind racing with ideas of how to get that necklace off her. I'm not going to stop until it's done, and for the first time in a long while, I feel like I have a purpose. I'm going to protect Rose, no matter what it takes.

∼

BEFORE ROSE WAKES, I slip out of bed to visit the dean about the necklace. It's cruel, and I'm no longer convinced of Dean Fallgren's intentions.

Blinded by rage, I sift to the Dean's office and pound my fists on her door.

"It's open," she calls from the other side, her voice muffled as though she were eating.

I storm in, eyes burning with anger. "Is it you?"

"Don't take that tone with me, or I'll have your mom and dad on their way here so fast—"

"Good. Call them. Since when do you take a fae's magic if they don't bend to your will? What the hell would Prairie and Gerard think?" I slam my hands on her pristine desk, leaning forward until I'm inches from her face.

Fury blazes in her cool eyes and the temperature in the room plummets so fast, my breath plumes in front of me like vapor. "If you think for one second I haven't thought about my children every moment of every day in every interaction I've had, you are sorely mistaken. Everything I do is for them, and they'd want me to ensure those with out-of-control power can't disrupt our world."

She slams her hands down on top of mine, her power swelling through my body, locking my muscles in place. An icy coldness spreads through my veins and freezes my bulk. "You will not question my motives or my methods," she says.

I glare at her, pushing back against her power with my own, but I can't seem to break free. "And what of Rose? She's not out of control. You're punishing her for her potential power," I challenge.

"I'm protecting her!" She surges to her feet, ice cracking on her lips. "Trackers can't track her with this on, Jax Cavë. I believe this is how someone was able to know her whereabouts this whole time."

"Trackers?" I whisper, defeated as I lean back, and slump to my knees. "You're certain?"

She inclines her head, and the room's temperature begins to stabilize.

So, the Dean has just been trying to protect Rose all this time. And if it isn't her, who else has the ability to track magic?

The blood in my veins runs cold.

"Has anything else happened, Jax? You haven't given me an update in weeks," she scolds.

The attack after her date? And the attack on the castle? She'd want to know, but I just can't open my mouth to speak the words. I put my head in my hands and shake my head. "No, nothing else has happened. She just goes to her classes," I lie instead. Nausea climbs in my throat, the consequences of breaking a fae promise immediate. My skin is on fire and my lungs burn with every breath I take. I must stop lying. I have to tell the truth.

"There have been some incidents, but nothing we couldn't handle."

The pain eases slightly.

The Dean's brow furrows, her eyes narrowing. I can sense her probing magic and I brace myself against the pain of her questioning me further.

"What kind of incidents?"

I take a deep breath as my skin prickles with heat. "At—

"Grandma?" A voice calls from behind me. One I know as well as my own.

CHAPTER THIRTEEN

ROSE

My breathing is almost labored as I step into the Fae History 101 classroom. It takes place at the top of the windmill-turned-lighthouse, in a drafty room full of musty books and ancient artifacts. I take a seat in the back row, my eyes tracing along the high ceiling with its carvings of ancient symbols. With every spin of the revolving beacon, the symbols on the ceiling seem to move. Tall windows let in the cold wind and the soft smell of the ocean.

Professor McColt clears his throat and the class hushes. He wears a light-brown suit, his dark hair slicked back. "Today, we shall discuss the history of Bedlam and how our culture has evolved over the centuries."

I've yet to figure out Professor McColt's fae order. His pale skin, paired with straight, dark hair and a shaved face, makes him appear as though he'd be more at home in a boardroom than in a fae academy classroom. His tailored suit is at odds with the casual clothing most of the other professors wear.

The professor tells the story about my grandmother, the Luna goddess, and how she wasn't the first of her kind. Long ago, her ancestors made a deal with Chaos, the creator of all fae. "We didn't always have magic. But through a fae promise, Chaos granted Lunas with power, and then Luna fae shared it with the rest of the fae. Naturally, Luna fae are most powerful, and first settled on Rexuna, where they formed the first magic-based culture that still stands today."

Magic manifests itself differently in each of us, helping to make up the different classes of fae orders.

"Does anyone know the rarest fae order?" Professor McColt asks the class.

My stomach threatens to climb up my throat as I raise my hand with hesitation. "The Tolden?" I whisper. Prior to a year ago, only one person knew about this small group of fae.

The professor's piercing gaze fixes on me, and I can feel the weight of it as he nods slowly. "Correct." He presses a small panel on the wall, and a series of sounds like sliding metal cause a portion of the ceiling to lift. He steps through the secret door, motioning for us to follow him. The arid scent of dust and decay assaults my nostrils.

You can't even tell this is here from the outside of the lighthouse.

He leads us down a dimly lit hallway until we come across a room that's filled wall-to-wall with *stuff*. There are swords, utensils, armor, bottles, vials, papers, books, perfumes, dried flowers, flowing gowns, jewelry, and other contraptions I don't know about. The professor pauses in front of a simple wooden box with a large, silver lock.

He opens the box and pulls out a delicate bracelet. The chain is made of small, silver links, and the pendant is a brilliant white stone with intricate carvings.

"This bracelet." He holds it up for all to see. "Was a gift from Chaos himself. Only those who are god-touched can wear it."

"I'm obviously god-touched," a blonde-haired student says, stepping closer to the professor and snatching the bracelet from his hand. She yanks her hand back, wailing in pain as the metal burns her.

I feel my eyes go wide and my heart hammers in my chest as I stare at the blonde woman's hand, the metal having marred her skin into oozing blisters that drip a black substance onto the floor. It sizzles on contact. "What does this have to do with the Tolden?" My words are barely audible as I lean over to Penelope, the professor's stern voice cutting through the shock as he reprimands the woman for her actions.

I'm very protective of the Tolden, as they lived in secrecy for hundreds of years below the Wastelands in an underground ecosystem called Castanea until my parents got rid of the werewolf curse. Previously, werewolves could only cure their affliction by eating the hearts of the Tolden.

Penelope shakes her head and shrugs. "Beats me."

Another student escorts the blonde woman to the office so she can see the nurse. I turn back to the professor and raise my hand.

"Yes, Rose?" He places the bracelet back into its wooden box and removes the gloves he wore to protect himself.

"What does this have to do with the Tolden?" I knew they'd probably teach about the Tolden in fae history 101, but I don't want them exploited. In fact, it's a huge reason I'm even in college. I want to learn how best to integrate them with the rest of Bedlam without eradicating their cultures and customs.

Professor McColt smiles, as if he's been waiting for this question. "As I just said, only those of the god-touched may wear this bracelet. The Tolden are the only other order who can wear this if they aren't god-touched."

"What does the bracelet do?" A short witch named Eran asks.

"It grants the wearer power over all royal fae," Professor McColt explains, and panic paralyzes me. "It's been long thought of as a legend, but it *is* real. Whoever wears the bracelet will have ultimate control over royal fae."

"Wh-why do you have it?" I squeak. Nausea climbs up my throat, and my head spins.

"My family has held onto it for centuries, and it's now my responsibility to keep it safe," the professor answers.

"Then why are you showing it to a bunch of first years?" I hiss. The rest of the class gives me strange looks, but I don't care. This is reckless, and I'm certain my parents don't know he's got this. If this got into the wrong hands while I'm wearing this suppression necklace? I don't even want to think about the consequences.

"I'm showing you this because knowledge is power. I want to make sure you know the importance of the Tolden, and that you protect them." He locks the box and tucks the key into his pocket. "Now, let's head back to the classroom, and I'll tell you about the war that started the bargain between a god and the fae."

Still gripped by fear, I follow the rest of the class back to our classroom. The Professor may or may not know I'm the princess, but it isn't until now that I truly understand the danger my entire family is in.

The lighthouse creaks and sways in the wind, and I sink in my seat as Lopey keeps casting me worried glances. She's the only person in this room who for sure knows who I am, and the implications of that necklace the professor so carelessly showed to a class of untrained fae and witches.

When the class ends, I rush to the North Woods for Elemental Magic 101 so the professor can remove my necklace before the rest of the class arrives. I'm eager to get this off me and I make a note to call my mom about the necklace Professor McColt has.

CHAPTER FOURTEEN

ROSE

Professor Rowan is a short, bearded man with a pointy nose and keen eyes that misses nothing. He's the most powerful witch at Bedlam Academy, but he also has a reputation for being strict and uncompromising, though some say he befriends those who try hard to learn.

He's the only one in the room when I arrive. He glances up from the book he's writing and gestures at the seat next to him.

"Come, Rose, let's get this off you."

My muscles ache in anticipation, tired of carrying around my body without the help of magic to take the strain off. He slips a key out of his pocket while I lift my hair and face away from him. He unlocks the necklace, and a rush of magic fills my veins as he removes it from around my neck. My skin pulses bright blue, as though it were starved and it's sucking in air to breathe.

"There." He hands me the suppression necklace and I place it in my bag.

Taking a seat at the back of the classroom, I relax into my chair. I can already feel how much easier it is to concentrate without the suppression necklace on. My senses sharpen, and I no longer carry this irritating edge. I'm determined to make the most of this period while I have it off.

The scent of cologne wafts in my direction as someone drops into the seat next to me. I recognize the scent as belonging to Deakan, and he gives me a grin when I glance his way. "Hey, gorgeous."

"Hi." I put on a casual air. I should make more of an effort to be nice to him since he and Jax are so close.

He wears board shorts and one of those loose tank tops that shows off far too much of his rib cage and where his muscles dip and move. I can't help but stare for a little too long and he clears his throat, the grin tugging wider.

"Want to hang at the beach after class? You can share my board." He leans back, causing the shirt he's wearing to ride up the front and showcase his abs before gesturing towards the door, where a giant surfboard sits.

My traitorous eyes return to him, traveling lower as he chuckles.

As soon as my skin flashes blue does it disappear when I avert my gaze. "What gave you the impression I'd be interested in spending any time with you? And besides, why are you even in a 101 class? Aren't you a second year?" I ask, trying to regain my composure.

He leans in closer, his eyes twinkling. "C'mon. Jax and I are basically the same person. Only he's all dark and broody and I'm light and fun. Two sides of the same coin. Even our orders! His is all scary, badass, and mine is all badass, majestic."

Leveling him with an unimpressed stare, I cross my arms and lift an eyebrow. "Yeah right. I swear, guys like you are the same no matter what realm they're from."

"Oh, and what's that? Hot, kissable, and irresistible?"

I allow myself a small smile. "Exactly." I grab my bag, grinning as I stand up. Deakan's eyes are wide in shock at my blatant compliment. I lean close to him and whisper, "Maybe if you grovel, I'll consider it."

With that, I cross the room and plop into a wooden chair someone carved a proverb into.

> *A thorn defends the rose,*
> *harming only those who*
> *would steal the blossom.*

Either someone is really obsessed with roses and thorns, or it's a little less innocuous than that. I let out a deep breath, shake my head, and glance over my shoulder. Deakan is still staring at me in wonder, as if he can't believe what just happened. Am I serious about the groveling? Absolutely. Will I forgive him for his little prank? Maybe. Will I entertain his advances?

The jury is still out on that one.

Professor Rowan gets the classes' attention when he allows a giant fireball to erupt from his palm and be put out with a ball of water coming from his other.

The class looks at him with awe, completely transfixed. "Today we'll focus on the four basic elements of magic: earth, air, wind, and fire. Everyone choose one partner and practice. Sort yourselves. As adults, I'm sure you can manage this."

I stand by as everyone tries to pair up. No one bothers me, but then a voice calls to me from behind.

"Well, what do you say? Want to give it a go?" Deakan stands behind me, offering his hand with a confident, yet hopeful look on his face.

I sigh and take it. "Sure, why not?" His palm is warm, and he doesn't let go as we head for an empty corner of the room.

Sliding my hand out from his, I get to work. "So, what element do you want to learn first?" I ask him as he takes a seat next to me. "And why are you in 101?"

His smile falters. "My magic didn't come in until this summer."

"Oh, I'm sorry," I say, feeling guilty for my earlier assumptions. I'm not sure I even know what his fae order is.

"It's okay." He shrugs. "As for the elements, I think I'd like to learn fire first."

I nod, smiling. "That's a great place to start." I love that Deakan is competitive like me.

On the sheet the professor passed out is a series of exercises to help us master the element. Most pairs choose wind, which I suspect has to do with the fact that it's the easiest for beginners. Fire is the hardest because of the potential for harm if done wrong.

We take our time and make sure to cover each of the exercises thoroughly before moving on. The first lessons involve the basics of channeling and drawing from the elements, as well as controlling and manipulating them. We practice sending fireballs into the air that dissipate after a few seconds and making a small fire that flickers to the beat of music.

"See how well we work together?" Deakan grins with pride.

"Yeah," I admit, feeling a little guilty. After months of dodging him and avoiding the way he looks at me, it's nice to be able to work with him.

"Will you let me take you to dinner tonight?" His amber eyes land on mine, hopeful.

"Can't. I have a date."

Deakan is quiet for a moment, contemplative. "Bring Jax with."

"It's not with Jax."

The fire in his palm extinguishes. "Then who are you going out with?"

"Theo."

His voice is hushed. "Who the hell is Theo? And when did you and Jax break up?"

"We didn't. Theo is another guy I'm seeing."

"Does Jax know?"

"Of course, he knows!" I hiss.

"Sorry, it's just news to me. Will you join me after lunch then? I'll teach you how to surf."

"You know I lived in Australia, right?"

"So?"

"On the beach."

"Oh."

I grin. "I'm teasing. We did live on the beach, but I've never surfed. You can teach me."

He grins. "Deal!"

We make plans for after lunch, and I place a call to my mom before my next class to tell her about Professor McColt's royal fae control bracelet. She and my dads will pay him a visit while I'm in combat training.

∽

I SPIN TOWARDS MY MOTHER, my voice rising.

"What do you mean it's GONE? Professor McColt said it was here waiting for us!"

My mind races with possibilities and dread swirls inside me.

She wraps me in a hug, but I feel her fear even as she smiles with reassurance.

"But—I just saw it." Anxiety coils inside my chest.

"Your dads will track it down, not to worry. I'm sure it's nothing." Mom plasters a smile on her face, but it doesn't reach her eyes.

"But who could have taken it?"

"It might be whomever is sending us those threats." She checks her phone. "I've got to go, honey. I'll keep you posted. In the meantime, keep an eye out."

The small paring knife I'd been using to cut my apple slips and buries itself deep into my palm. I clench my teeth against the excruciating pain and press my shirt against the wound, trying to stifle the tears threatening to spill.

"Are you okay?" She takes my hand in hers and gasps as she sees the cut.

"Just a small cut—"

"Why aren't you healing?" Her eyes meet mine, searching for answers.

I reach up to the suppression necklace hanging under my shirt collar. "Dean Fallgren is making me wear this so I can't use my magic."

"She's what?!" Mom shrieks, her entire being lighting up as healing power hums through her fingertips.

Before I've finished blinking, Mom has sifted us to the entrance of the Dean's office. She slams the door open, her eyes burning with rage.

"What makes you think you can keep my daughter from using her magic?! Don't you know how dangerous this is for her?"

Dean Fallgren gawks at us in disbelief. When she finally collects herself, she says, "I gave your daughter the necklace to stop her from using her magic outside the classroom, as all first-year students must, but also for her protection. I'm afraid someone is trying to track her through her own magic."

Mom gasps and grips my hand so tightly it feels like my bones are going to break. "Who?"

"I don't know," answers the Dean. "But it could be related to the royal fae control bracelet that Professor McColt lost recently. It may have been taken by the same people."

Jax must have told her what happened.

Mom's face pales and she turns to me. "Rose, I think it's time for you to come home."

"No!" I protest. "Mom, please don't make me leave! I'm finally making real friends here."

My mother takes a deep breath, considering what's best for me. She knows she can't protect me from here and that if I stay, she'd be too far away to help.

"Alright," she finally concedes, "but you have to be careful. I wouldn't be able to bear it if something else happened to you."

"I will, Mom. Don't worry about me."

Exiting Dean Fallgren's office with Mom, I feel the fog of fear and uncertainty hovering around me. She sifts home to meet my dads while I head to lunch. I sit in the cafeteria and pick at my food, listening to Lopey talk about Eli. She's got a small crush on him, and I've tried to convince her to just talk to him, but every time she gets close to him, she disappears.

It's a nice distraction from my fear. I'm worried about the threats and the stolen bracelet, but I'm also determined to find out who's responsible.

Even though I'm scared, I'm not ready to give up. I've finally found a place to belong, and I refuse to let it all slip away.

∽

JAX AND DEAKAN make their way to our table, and each settle on one side of me. Lopey's face flushes and she gives me a wink before making an excuse to leave. I roll my eyes, smiling.

"Hey." Jax squeezes my leg under the table, his hand warmer than usual.

"Hi." I grin. "You coming with us?"

He shakes his head. "Nah, I'm going to go take a nap. I'm not feeling so well."

I furrow my brows; Fae rarely get sick. "Are you okay? I can stay back and take care of you?" The concern in my voice is palpable.

He shakes his head, but his movements are sluggish and lack his usual enthusiasm.

"Nah, you two have fun." He flashes a weak smile.

"Okay, I'll bring you back some soup for supper?" I place the back of my hand on his forehead and feel the intense heat radiating from his skin.

"Okay," he says, the word coming out more like a sigh than actual speech. "See you later." He steps away, looking paler than when he arrived at the cafeteria.

I turn towards Deakan, my brow still furrowed. "He doesn't look so good."

Deakan shovels a whole slice of pizza into his mouth, and I just look at him, wondering where it all goes. On his tray, he has another entire slice of everything meat pizza, a salad bigger than a basketball, and a whole burger with all the fixings. "He's never been sick a day in his life," he mumbles after swallowing. "It was bound to catch up with him."

Theo won't be happy I'm canceling dinner tonight, but I can make it up to him tomorrow. With one last look in Jax's direction, I drop my empty tray onto the little conveyor belt leading into the kitchen. By the time I make it back to the table, all the food on Deakan's tray is gone.

"Did you..." I glance around. "Did you just eat all of that between the time I walked to the kitchen and back?"

He glances at me, his cheeks slightly flushed. "Maybe."

I can't help but laugh. "You're going to make yourself sick."

He just shrugs, stuffing the last piece of burger he had in his hand into his mouth and chewing it quickly. "Lion shifters like to eat," he says around his food.

"Come on." I shake my head, taking him by the hand and leading him to where he's got his board propped up by the double doors. It's a giant surfboard, with enough surface area for at least three people.

Passing the dorms and the lighthouse, we trudge through the sand and tall grass, the ends tickling my thighs. When we get close to the beach, the sound of the waves crashing is almost deafening. The white sand is dotted with people in various states of sunburn and swimming, some in the water, some in the sand, some just rinsing off. I peel out of my jeans, hoodie, and t-shirt, taking the dry suit he tosses at me. It's too cold to go without, and my clothes are too bulky to fit under it. His lion order runs warm, so he can generate enough of his own heat.

Deakan rushes towards the shoreline, his board balanced on one shoulder. He places it in the water and pats the top. "Hop on up here," he calls.

I hesitate for a moment, but then I do as he says, hopping onto the board between his legs. He wraps his arms around me, and we paddle out to the waves. Once we reach a good spot, Deakan lets go of me, standing up on the board and riding the wave with me holding onto the sides for dear life as the board beneath us cuts through the waves with ease.

It's a surprisingly freeing feeling, and I find myself growing more and more comfortable with the sensation with each passing wave.

"How does a lion shifter become so adept at surfing?" I lean against his chest while our feet dangle in the water.

His breath fans my cheek. "I struggled for a long time, trying to control my beast. When I first got to Bedlam Academy, I didn't have magic, and I couldn't shift. But just under my skin prowled a different sort of power—something fierce and wild. I found when I was out in the waves, that wildness was tamed. It calmed me and made me feel more in control. The surfing became a way for me to practice controlling the beast inside of me."

"So, you just picked up a board one day?"

"Kind of. I felt like I was crawling out of my skin, and I couldn't figure out how to gain control. So, I did the masochistic thing, and threw a cat into the ocean to face its fears."

"That's some cat," I tease.

He laughs and leans back, his arms wrapping around me. "Yeah, I guess I am."

We stare at the horizon for a long time. The rhythmic sounds of the waves are calming, and soon Deakan's breathing deepens. I lean back, closing my eyes, feeling the rise and fall of his chest against my back.

We catch more waves, and by the end of our session, I'm practically standing up on the board, even if I don't quite manage to stay up for too long. We ride back in, our shared laughter echoing across the beach. Deakan takes my hand and I realize that, somewhere along the way, we went from two strangers to friends. In time, maybe something more.

"You're a natural, you know that?"

I smile, turning my face to look at him. "Thanks."

We collapse on the sand, exhausted from our day. I turn onto my side, propping myself up with my elbow, and find him staring down at me, his pale amber eyes intense.

His lips twitch slightly, and my heart starts to race. I'm not unfamiliar with the feeling, and I know what it means. It's a moment that could turn into something else if we both wanted it to.

I sit up and check the time on my phone. It's early in the evening, and the sun is setting in the sky. I clear my throat, breaking the spell. "We should probably head back soon," I say softly.

Deakan nods, gathering himself up from the sand. We walk back, side by side, and I can't help but feel a bit of regret at the moment slipping away between us.

We stop in the cafeteria—open round the clock—to grab some soup for Jax. When we reach my room, I unlock the door with my irises, and Deakan follows me in. The drapes are drawn, and we find Jax curled up in bed, his face slick with sweat.

I prepare his soup, and Deakan helps me get it to him, his eyes full of concern. We sit in the dark, watching Jax eat.

When he's done, Deakan stands up and steps towards me. I look up at him, my heart beating fast. He gently takes my hand in his, and for a second, I'm transported back to the beach. We share a moment, our breath mingling before he places a kiss on my cheek and heads for the door.

"See you later," he says.

"Goodnight," I call.

"You two were gone a while," Jax remarks between spoonfuls as he watches Deakan leave. A smile plays across his lips.

"He taught me how to surf," I explain, my cheeks burning.

"I'm glad you two are getting along." He sets his spoon down and reclines against the headboard.

"Oh?" I raise a brow.

"Oh." He grins. "He'll be good for you."

"Wait." I glance at the door. "Did you put him up to this?"

He shakes his head. "No, but I encouraged it when he brought it up."

"Uh huh." I level him with a look. "You want to share him?" I grin.

"Nah, but I'll share *you* with my best friend."

I laugh and shake my head. Though the idea is growing on me.

"I'm going to shower. Care to join me?" I glance over my shoulder, stripping out of my clothes and leaving a trail on the floor to the bathroom.

"Not sure how much fun I'll be," he calls.

"That's fine with me," I take my hair out of my messy bun, letting it cascade down my back. "Shark week is here, anyway."

"Shark week?"

A laugh barrels out of me. "Sorry. It's an Earth thing. I'm on my period."

He crawls out of bed and makes his way towards me, his movements slow. Dark bags hang under his eyes as he cups my cheek. "So?"

"That doesn't bother you?"

His arms wrap around my waist, a lopsided grin on his face. "Nah, Princess. I'll fuck you, eat you, and love every second of it. Period or not."

My eyes widen. "Noted."

He nuzzles my neck before leading me to the shower, both of us laughing. Together, we wash away the sand, salt, and sun from the day. As we rinse the soap from our bodies, I can't help but feel a little more peace in his company, despite the rough start to the day.

Jax starts coughing and turns his head towards the tile wall. His eyes close and his breath grows shallow, his body trembling against mine.

I press my palms flat against his back. "Jax? What's wrong?" I grab a towel and gesture for him to step out of the shower.

He wraps it around his waist and staggers into the bedroom, collapsing onto the bed. His breathing is labored, and another coughing fit hits him.

I rush over to where he's hunched over and shake his shoulders, my desperation rising. Tears brim in his eyes as he continues coughing, and soon, blood spatters my face.

"Oh my gods," I gasp, not understanding what is happening. "Jax, what's wrong?"

His bloodshot eyes meet mine, and he takes a shaky breath. "I'm sorry, Rose. I didn't want you to know."

Fear strangles me as I leap for my phone. "I'm calling for help."

Jax takes my hand in his and shakes his head, his eyes begging me not to.

"I'm so sorry," he gasps. "I fucked up, Rose."

Holding his face in my hands, I gaze into his cobalt blues, filled with an intensity I've never felt before. He needs me and I will move the stars for this man.

"Don't be sorry," I whisper. "I'll help you, but first you have to tell me what's going on."

"I broke a fae promise."

"What?!" I shriek. "No. No, no, no. Tell me who?!" I grip onto his shoulders. "Now, Jax!" Tears pour down my cheeks as the panic sets in.

He closes his eyes and exhales slowly, seeming resigned to his fate. "I promised Dean Fallgren I'd keep her updated about your whereabouts and any incidents you were involved in, and I broke it."

My heart stops, and cold dread creeps over my body. "Why?" I whisper, barely able to breathe through the hysteria and betrayal slicing through me.

I don't wait for a response as I dial Dean Fallgren's number. She doesn't answer. I re-dial it again, my hands trembling so badly I can barely hold onto the phone, let alone dial her number. Desperation fills my lungs and fear sits heavy in my throat. Her voicemail picks up, and I shove it into Jax's face.

"Tell her, now!" I shriek as his breathing grows labored. "Everywhere I was! November second, one p.m. to five p.m., surfing just North of the lighthouse, repeat after me!"

"November second, surfing by lighthouse, one to five p.m.," he chokes, blood sputtering from his lips.

"November second, eight a.m. to one p.m., classes," I bellow. "Now say it!"

"November second, eight a.m. to one p.m, classes," he repeats, finishing in a ragged breath.

My limbs shiver uncontrollably as the voicemail clicks off, my heart racing as all hope fades. I fall into Jax's arms, my soul broken and in despair, and he lays a hand on my cheek. He whispers *sorry*, but I know it won't do any good. I pull away, tears streaming down my face, and grab the phone to redial. "You tell her, Jax," I utter in a voice barely above a whisper, "and you tell her everything! Don't you dare leave me."

I need to find her. I jump up, frantically pulling my clothes on, not even taking the time to put on shoes. I burst out of the dorm, careening down the four flights of stairs and tearing through the front door. My feet fly across the ground as if driven by a force of its own, until I reach the door to the staff dorms and throw them open.

"Where is she!" I scream at the top of my lungs, my voice echoing through the halls. "Where is the Dean!"

Staff pop their heads out as I try for the knob on the dean's door, finding it locked. I slam my fists into it, pounding it until my hands are bloody and bruised.

Suddenly I hear the locks click and the door swings open. Dean Fallgren stands in the doorway, her eyes aglow with worry. "What's going on?"

I shove past her, eyes wild as I search for her phone. "Where is it?!"

"What is the matter with you? And why are you covered in blood?"

"Your fucking phone!" I finally spot it on her desk and lunge for it. I shove it in her face. "Check your voicemail, now!"

My hands are shaking as she takes the phone from me and dials in her pin. After a few moments, a voice floats through the speakers.

The voicemail plays, and Dean Fallgren's face leaches of all color. "Where is he?"

"He's dying in his fucking bed! Now release him from his fae promise!"

She gapes at me, her face a mixture of shock and terror.

"Please," I beg, crashing to my knees.

Finally, her resolve seems to snap into place, and she lurches forward. "Come with me," she commands.

She sifts us to our dorm room, landing in the center of the bedroom. Dean Fallgren kneels beside the bed, forming a triangle with her hands. I climb in on the other side, cradling him in my arms. She begins to speak in a strange, ancient language—words that fill the air with a heavy weight. With each word, my senses seem to become alive—sparks of energy floating around the room like electricity.

The ritual drums on, swathing us in a surreal spell. Without warning, an eerie ticking echoes through the room, crushing the energy.

We freeze, fingers of silence clawing at us until Dean Fallgren stands, her face ashen.

"It's done," she croaks.

I check Jax's forehead. It's cool to the touch as he blinks up at me, shame weighing heavy in his gaze.

Whipping around to face the dean, I stalk towards her, baring my teeth. "If you ever use anyone else as a pawn in your little vendetta you have against me, it will not be them on their deathbed, but you."

She stares, her mouth slightly agape. "You don't understand. I did this to protect you."

"At whose expense?! Since when does my life trump that of his? Anyone's?" I throw my hands up in frustration. "You want to know where I am? Ask *me*." My voice is brittle, bordering on hysteria as spittle flies out my mouth.

She faces Jax, coming to his side. "I made a grave miscalculation, please forgive me."

Jax nods and wraps his arms around her in a tender embrace.

The Dean turns to me, her face somber. "Do not think I don't understand the gravity of my mistake."

She sifts out without another word, the silence in the room a heavy weight. I approach the bed, and sit at the foot of it, facing the window overlooking the lighthouse.

My voice comes out haunted. Broken. "I wish you'd told me."

Jax's words are almost too quiet to hear. "I was trying to protect you."

"I know," I breathe, tears in my eyes. "I understand why you did it, but it doesn't mean I'm not angry."

Leaning forward, I place my head against his chest. He wraps his strong arms around me as I finally let go of the tears and emotion I'd been suppressing.

For a long while we just lay there, together in our shared grief. Finally, he speaks. "Come on, let's get some sleep."

CHAPTER FIFTEEN

ROSE

My thumbs fly across my touchscreen, responding to all the missed messages from last night. The first is Mekhi. Bennett had told him about the bracelet and necklace, and he's worried. Lopey heard from another student about me losing my shit in the staff dorms and wanted to know if everything was okay. Theo asks if I can join him for lunch today since he'll be on campus for a bit, but I tell him I can't, but will connect with him later. My mom is planning on stopping by for lunch in disguise.

In my elemental arts class, I pair with Deakan again, filling him in on the drama from last night after he'd gone to his room. He said he'd passed out soon after he got back after his contact high from Kieran smoking something potent.

"I can't believe Dean Fallgren did that," he whispers as we place our hands together, sparks dancing above our hands.

"Not so sure I agree with you there," I grumble under my breath, and the sparks surge. Snapping my hands back, I check the handout again. "Freestyle?"

Deakan stands over my shoulder, peering at the paper. "Huh. Alright."

Professor Rowan approaches us, keeping a watchful eye as Deakan and I face each other and intertwine our hands. His are hot after our last step, and he stares in my eyes, his gaze just as electric.

A small spark ignites between our palms as I concentrate on the fire element. Deakan's awed expression is infectious as a small flame dances above our conjoined hands. As easily as the wind whispers through the trees, our magic dances together.

Professor Rowan holds out a cautious arm to keep the other students back as he coaches us, his voice low and gentle.

The flame in the middle of the room roars with intense energy, sparks shooting from its core like little stars, the smell of sulphur permeating the room. It seems to be alive, thrashing and fighting against us as we try to contain it. Suddenly, a stray gust of air magic hits the flame from a student's errant spell, sending it into a wild frenzy, sparks flicking out into the air.

My clothes go up in flames, burning everything in its path. Panic takes over the room and screams echo off the walls. Deakan races toward me and wraps his arms around me, smothering the flames before they consume him too. But it's too late—his clothes catch fire as well.

Professor Rowan steps in, sending a downpour of water over us to put out the flames. As we stand there in the pouring rain, Deakan still has his arms around me. A powerful energy pulls us together and my skin glows a steady bright blue, a sign that my Luna order is keeping us safe from the flame. The only sound in the room is our heavy breathing and I realize that my magic has reached out to protect us both from the fire. I've never seen my magic race to protect someone else like this.

Not even when it would've saved Bennett's life.

The implication of it is something I don't even want to think about.

We just stand there, quiet, until Professor Rowan clears his throat. "Well done," he says, his voice a bit hoarse.

Over my shoulder, a petite witch bursts into tears, and a friend consoles her as she chants, "It was an accident! An accident!"

It distracts me enough to realize Deakan and I are still naked, pressed tight against each other when some of the guys begin to whistle and catcall. I cloak myself and take a step back, my face heating up from the embarrassment.

"How do you go invisible?!" Deakan panics.

Shit. He's brand new to magic, and this takes a while to perfect. Instead of letting him stand there without clothes in front of an entire classroom, I pull him to me again, sharing my cloak so he's invisible, too.

"If you wanted me naked, Rose, you only had to ask," he teases, his voice low enough only I hear. Though I'm not so sure he's joking. The warmth of his breath cascades down my neck, igniting a trail of shivers.

"We're going to go back to our dorm for some clothes, I'll stop back in a little bit," I call out to the professor, whose attention is about half a foot off from where we actually stand because we're still invisible.

"Alright. Good work," he says as we slip away and make our way to the dorms.

The air is different now, filled with unspoken words and barely concealed secrets. We walk in silence, and I can't help but wonder if this is the start of something new. It's odd to stroll through campus naked and holding onto someone else, all while everyone is oblivious to what we're doing.

Seeming to echo my thoughts, Deakan stops walking in the middle of the path at the center of campus. "Wait." He brings a hand up to my face, running his thumb along my jawline.

"What?" I squeak.

He brings his forehead to mine, our skin pressed together. It's as though the world around us ceases to exist at this moment. "No one can see us?"

"No," I breathe, my voice shaky.

His gaze heats, and my pulse and breathing increase. He brushes his lips to my ear and whispers, "Truth or dare, little Rose?"

I BITE my lip and grin, a thrill running through me. Most people consider a dare as the most 'daring,' exciting option there is—but when it comes to feelings, truth is the most dangerous. I take a deep breath and whisper back, "Truth."

"True or false; you want to kiss me?" His thumb drags across my bottom lip, tugging it out of my teeth.

I suck in a breath. "True." My skin glows bright between us, and the evidence of his desire presses against my stomach. "Truth or dare?" I counter.

"Dare," he whispers.

I stand on my tiptoes. "Kiss me."

He doesn't need to be asked twice. He presses his lips to mine, and a bolt of electricity passes through me as I fall into him. His hands are in my hair; his taste a mix of honey and spice. Panting, we draw back but still cling to one another so we're both still cloaked. Beneath my palms, his heart races.

"Let's get back," I whisper, a grin still on my lips.

"My room. You can borrow my clothes." He takes my hand and together, we rush to his room.

Checking that no one is in the hallway while we stand in front of his room, I let go of him so he can scan his irises with the scanner that unlocks his door. His roommate isn't home, and I watch as he struts to his bed, his bare skin looking like a canvas as the light streams through his window.

We don't need words, but I hear them in my head, nonetheless. I want to be like my mother, the queen of all fae. I need to prove that I'm ready for more than just flings and casual hookups, that I can have the relationships she has—the ones with power and a future. And if someone is interested in sharing, who am I to deny him?

After a deep sigh, I shut the door and lean against it, so I face the room. The cloak is no longer covering me.

Deakan flings himself backwards onto his bed, his eyes heavy as he watches me. In that moment, something shifts in me. For the first time, I'm not scared of what could happen next—instead, I'm curious to see what will.

Stalking towards him, I pause in front of the bed. "Truth or dare?"

"Truth," his hoarse voice grinds out. His attention catalogs my entire body.

"How well do you share?"

He gulps. "Share?"

My lips curl into a smirk, and I lower myself so that we're face to face. "Share."

He searches my eyes for a moment before he finally answers. "Very well."

I lean in, our noses almost touching as I whisper, "Good."

And with that, I press my lips to his. His hands come up to cradle my face as we slip off the bed and onto the floor, uncaring we've fallen. Our mouths explore each other, losing ourselves in desire, our passion. My hands tug at his hair, desperate to feel more of his skin against me. We're frantic, mad with hunger, and fueled by need.

"Protection?" Deakan pulls back to look at me.

"Please." I smile, and his lips curl into a smirk.

He pulls out the drawer beside him, handing me a foil packet before he slides the drawer back in.

"Are you sure about this?" His whisper is barely audible, yet to me it's like an earthquake that brings with it an entire world of possibilities.

"I'm not certain you've done enough groveling for me to have forgiven you, but you can make it up to me," I tease, and he laughs softly before his hands tangle in my hair, pulling me closer as I press against him.

"Maybe I just need more practice," he murmurs against my lips, and I giggle, falling deeper into him as I forget the world around us.

His arousal presses against my stomach, both of us moaning softly as our tongues dance together.

He settles in front of me, resting on his heels as he rolls the condom over his length. I watch, mouth wet with want, and spread my legs for him. Shifting so he's over me, his eyes hold a reverence that wasn't there before. With a gentle thrust, he slides into me, the two of us moaning in pleasure.

The fit is tight, but less pain and more like a snug glove. We move together, our bodies slick with sweat as he drives into me like we're two ravenous wolves, eager to slake our hunger. His hand comes between us, pressing his thumb against my clit, rubbing in a steady, smooth rhythm. Each ministration brings me closer to orgasm. I cry out in pleasure just as the door to his room opens.

Deakan throws a palm over my mouth to keep me quiet as our eyes train on the floor in front of the door. My body still reels from my intense orgasm, and he's still hard inside me. We're on the side of the bed away from the door, so we can't be seen from where he's at. I've cloaked us just to be on the safe side. Deakan grins down at me, his eyes dancing with mischief as his roommate steps into the room.

"Practice is tough, man," Kieran speaks, and my heart rate spikes in fear.

Is he ... who is he talking to?

"You know why," Jax's voice follows as he steps into the room behind Kieran.

"It's that fucking princess," Kieran hisses.

Me? My stomach bottoms out. What do I have to do with practice?

"She's good for you." Jax stands up for me. He stalks to Deakan's bed, and we scramble under it, so he doesn't bump into us where we're still joined at the hip. With both of us under the bed, it's a tight fit, even with taller bed frames that can store full-sized trunks under them.

It's even tighter when Jax plops down on the bed, causing the mattress to dip. This presses us even closer together. Deakan grins, using the position to drag his pelvis across my clit with every thrust. I'm too lost in the throes of pleasure to protest. I hadn't known about my voyeuristic kink until now.

"The hell she is." Kieran tosses his bag onto the floor next to his own bed before laying down with his back against the headboard.

"Who cares if she's a princess?" The mattress squeaks as Jax moves on it. "I saw the way you looked at her when you walked in on us. You're attracted to her. You wished it were you."

"She's the hottest girl on campus," Kieran chuffs. *Why thank you, asshole.* "Of course, I'm attracted to her. But she's not the only warm hole here, and others come with way less baggage."

They're quiet for a moment before Jax speaks. "Is that why it smells like sex in here?" Does it? Do I care?

"What? I haven't fucked anyone," Kieran scoffs. "One-hundred bucks it's Deakan."

"No, he's got it bad for Rose. He's not going to fuck some rando."

"Then why is there a condom wrapper on the floor next to the bed?"

Shit.

The mattress squeaks, and Jax's hand comes down to collect it from the floor. "Leviathan: Thin and Ribbed?"

I'm so close to another orgasm, I hear nothing but the roaring static in my ear and Deakan's heavy breathing. Why my vision and hearing dims when I orgasm is a mystery to me.

My abs tighten and my body convulses as pleasure rips through me. I chomp down on Deakan's shoulder to keep from crying out, and this triggers his own release. My jaw locks as I do everything I can to hold out through the fire blazing through me. A metallic tang coats my tongue when I free his marred skin.

"Did you hear that?"

The two listen quietly for a moment before Jax responds. "Yeah." They both place their feet on the ground. Jax's boots tap right next to our heads.

"Is that ... breathing?"

Peeking my head out from under the bed, I watch as Kieran's eyes turn serpentine. I've never been so thankful that this cloaking spell blocks our heat signatures so we're undetectable from his magic-tracking order. It's not Jax I'm worried about seeing us.

What I hadn't counted on was Kieran's acute sense of smell. He can't scent us through the cloak, but he can definitely smell where we've been. Together.

His nostrils flaring, he walks over to Deakan's bed. My adrenaline and fear levels skyrocket as he inhales right where we landed on the floor.

"I smell Rose." Crouched on the floor, Kieran's eyes land right where we're hiding under the bed. He can't see us.

"What?" Jax brings his own nose to the floor.

"See? Deakan *is* fucking her. I told you we can't trust her. She's already fucking around behind your back."

"I told Rose I'd share her." Jax rests his arms on his knees, glancing up. "She can sleep with whomever she wants."

"What the hell is the matter with you? You want to share her? Are you fucking Deakan, too? You said weren't going to sleep with either of us."

While I don't like labels—like most fae—it's always been an unwritten rule my best friends are off limits, even to me. "What? No. It's not like that at all—"

"That's some magical fucking pussy. Just be careful she doesn't give you fae herp—OOPMH."

Jax tackles Kieran, his fists slamming into his face as soon as he gets him on his back, the motion rattling the floor. Blood and saliva fly, splattering on my face, and I have to hold in a shriek. The sound of angry grunts and skin slapping skin fill the room. Bones crunch, and I shove Deakan off me and scoot out from under the bed. None of them notice me.

Somewhere along the way, a shirtless Kieran maneuvered on top of Jax. I tackle him. He never sees it coming and is knocked off Jax, landing on his back. For so many unkind words, I pummel him. He's too stunned to find a naked me on top of him to fight back until I've got a few good hooks in. That's when he turns to some of the maneuvers we've learned in practice, and I work to deflect them blow-by-blow.

He scoops my leg, knocking me off top so he can scramble me into an Earth move I taught the team called a full nelson. He has me pinned to his front while he lies on his back.

"Fuck, that's hot."

Kieran and I pause, turning our heads towards where Jax and Deakan sit on the bed, eyes heated as they watch me wrestle naked. I use this moment to break Kieran's hold, and shove off him. Stalking over to a dresser—I'm not sure whose—I yank open the top drawer and pull out a pair of boxers and slip them on before finding a t-shirt in the next drawer to put on.

Kieran peels off his shirt and presses it to the cut on his lip. Miraculously, all his piercings remain intact.

Crossing my arms, I stare him down. "Fuck you," I hiss. "You know damn well Jax took my virginity. You were there to witness it, you overgrown, lizard-brained shit stain. What is your fucking problem with me?!" I shove him, and he catches my wrist to spin my around and yank me to his chest. Despite all of Dean Fallgren's bullshit, I genuinely believe she thought she was protecting me. Kieran's animosity for me is too much to ignore, and I'm convinced now more than anything, he's behind my threats—on campus at least.

"Is that what you want, Rose?" His words end in a serpentine hiss, and the flicker of his tongue brushes my ear. "You want me to fuck you?"

"I didn't say that!"

"You just offered." He presses his pelvis against me, his erection firm against my ass.

"Control your roommate!"

Deakan thrusts an elbow into Kieran's abdomen, and he releases me.

I storm across the room and throw open the door, swiveling my head around to look at the three boneheads.

"I would've, you know," Kieran calls out to me. All three have hooded gazes as I slam the door shut and stalk down the hall to my room.

∽

JAX

"What the hell just happened?"

All three of us stand in stunned silence after I've sprayed the hell out of the room with Kieran's cologne to get the smell of sex out of the air before it causes me to chase Rose down when she just needs some space. Turning to face Kieran, I put a hand on his shoulder and squeeze harder than necessary to get my point across.

Before I can say a word, Deakan shoves Kieran. "You ever lay a hand on her, or utter another bad word about her again, I'll kill you."

"What the hell, man?" Kieran shoves him back.

Deakan falls backwards, but before he hits the ground, he shifts into his lion form, his hind legs pushing off the ground as soon as he lands. He leaps after Kieran with a vicious roar that rattles the windows.

Kieran's eyes widen, and at the last moment, he shifts into his serpent form. I don't know what's gotten into Deakan, but he's got the overgrown snake pinned to the floor and his maw bared in his face.

Shifting into my dragon, I blow a plume of ice, freezing them both. Their faces tangle into snarls, but they can't hurt each other. Together, our shifted forms take up most of the place.

A professor I don't recognize bursts into the room, hands up and ready to dismantle any spell. The door clicks shut behind him. His eyes dart from me to the two frozen fae, brows furrowed in confusion.

I shift back to my fae form and explain the situation. He takes a contraption out of his pocket, tossing it onto the ground in front of them. Slowly, they thaw and shift back.

"Now, are you going to tell me why you shifted on your roommate and attacked him?" The professor, dressed in a business suit, turns to Deakan.

"He insulted my girl."

"So, you thought killing him would be a good idea?" He scowls. "And put on some damn clothes. This is why I don't come to campus," he mutters under his breath.

Deakan climbs to his feet, glaring at Kieran as he opens his drawer and pulls out a pair of sweats. "Yeah, and it still seems like a pretty good idea to me."

The professor storms over to Deakan and spins him around. It's then we both notice he's bleeding.

"Did you bite him?" The alarmed professor whips his head towards Kieran. Serpent venom can kill a full grown fae in minutes. If they're lucky enough to have feathers, they can be brought back to life. Otherwise, they're screwed unless they get antivenom in time.

"No."

Deakan brings his hand up and winces as he touches the wound at the junction where his shoulder meets his neck. "It's fine, my girl bit me."

The professor sighs. "Well, that explains it. You really ought to keep your mate in your den for at least the first week without any other males around. Didn't your parents teach you that you're bound to kill any that get close to her, save for the few minutes immediately after intercourse when your beast is temporarily sated?"

My eyes narrow in rage, and I snarl, "What the hell did you do?!" I shove Deakan with all my might, and I can see the possessive glint burning in his eyes.

His voice is like a deathly hiss as he utters his repulsive confession, "She marked *me*." The phrase echoes in my head like thunder, and a seething agony consumes my entire being.

"Did she mean to?" Kieran stands, brushing off the back of his pants. Is he ... jealous?

I am.

I'd like to know the answer to that question, too.

"She's mine. She wanted me, so she mated me."

"That doesn't answer the fucking question, Simba."

Deakan retaliates by extending his claws and raking them across Kieran's chest. Blood pools like tiny, crimson rivers.

The professor jumps in-between them and does some weird mind control thing with his eyes. "*Back down*," he growls. Deakan averts his eyes, taking a few steps back. "You can't mate someone without both of them being open to the idea. Whether subconsciously or consciously, *your girl wanted you.*"

Well, fuck. A stab of misery consumes me.

Deakan's triumphant stance wilts my own. Rose might not even know what she did, otherwise she'd probably be in here.

"Thanks, Professor ...?"

"Pyxis."

Ahh, Astronomy. He's new this year.

Leaving their squabbling to themselves, I chase after Rose, finding her crying in the shower, Kieran's clothes discarded on the floor near the door. I shed my own and step into the shower with her, taking her into my arms.

"Hey now," I press my lips against her hair and cup her cheeks in my hands.

"Why?"

"Why what?"

"Why do men cheer their friends on for sleeping with lots of people and, in the next breath, imply a woman is dirty for doing the same? I was a virgin before sleeping with you!" Her voice breaks.

"Broken men hurt women. He's punishing himself for wanting you and is doing what he can to make you seem undesirable."

"It's fucked up, Jax."

"I know."

"Even good men hurt women," she whispers, and I know she's talking about my betrayal. Things have been strained between us since.

That's not the heaviest thing weighing on my mind. My whole being burns with the question: *did you mean to mate Deakan?* But I don't ask her. I can't bear to know, because my next question would be if she wants to mate me. And if the answer is, no? Well, I might not survive it. We've grown close, and the thought of her not choosing me makes me feel ill.

We let the water run, not bothering to wash our hair or body. Just let the water carry our burdens and tears and wash them down the drain. When the hot water runs out, I wrap her in a fluffy white towel and lead her to the bedroom. Her fingers run through my hair first, using her magic to dry me when I place my hand on her wrist to stop her.

"Don't use your magic. You don't want to get in any more trouble."

Rose takes a deep breath and lets it out through puffed cheeks. "I should go get my necklace from the North Woods, anyway. I'm half tempted to feed it to the Caspari."

I frown, already missing her closeness. "We could, and then you'll never have to wear it again. Do you want me to come with you?"

"No." She shakes her head. "I'll meet you at practice. If Dean Fallgren catches me without it, she'll probably expel me. I can't risk it."

She dresses and leaves, giving me an apologetic look as she slips out the door. The cavern between us is massive. I'm left in silence, my thoughts already turning to what I need to do.

CHAPTER SIXTEEN

ROSE

In the locker room, the thunderous roars of the crowd rise to a deafening crescendo, like the sound of a foaming ocean. Waves of sound crash and each wave is bigger than the last. My hands shake as I lace up my shoes, trying to ignore the rising panic inside of me. I need to focus, keep my head in the game. Last night, I hardly slept. It took everything in me to not march down to Deakan's room and demand he hold me and kiss me and whisper sweet nothings into my ear and fuck me until I begged for mercy and then do it all over again. I can't get him off my mind. It's only been half a day since we gave into the attraction we feel to one another, but damn. I've got it bad. He sits right there in my mind space with Theo, who bears a similar aura, all golden and majestic-like, only Theo has darker hair.

This game is with Moonfire Academy. Their school has some of the most formidable competitors, but I know that Bedlam Academy is no pushover. We have our own set of skills and we're determined to show them off.

I stand and check my necklace. I'm competing in the unarmed combat bout, which takes place after non-lethal magic and before strategy. After those three bouts, each team picks a champion to run through a round of all three games. As Luna fae, I have an unfair advantage in combat because of my ability to regenerate magic through healing and hurting, which is why I must wear my magic suppression necklace.

I take a deep breath and enter the arena. I'm met with an ear-shattering roar from thousands of people, my family's faces among them. My parents, grandparents, and siblings are just specks in the crowd, but I feel an inner warmth knowing they're there to support me. Mekhi and Deakan might be here, too; I don't know for sure. The energy is contagious and empowering.

Penelope gives me a playful bump of her shoulder, her brown eyes twinkling with anticipation. "Let's show them what we've got," she says, a smirk on her face. She and Corson are our third leg, while Kieran and I take the second. Jax and Basher are first.

Now that Kieran knows about Jax and me, I've got no problem showing him affection out in the open, but I'm still a little broken over his betrayal. For the sake of keeping positive energy for the game, I swallow the hurt and wrap my arms around his neck and give him a big kiss. He lifts me, nipping my lip before setting me down. Coach raises a brow at me as I pass him by to sit at the end of the bench. Jax and Basher approach the field to join the two non-lethal magic players from Moonfire Academy.

A large wooden pillar stands in the center of the playing field, and when lightning strikes it, the stadium lights shut off, signaling the beginning of the game. Bedlam players throw spells at each other in the dark while Moonfire players dodge and weave to avoid being hit. With each spell, a different color light fills the stadium.

Kieran takes his place next to me, giving me a few words of encouragement. I do a double take at the kindness he displays but thank him anyway.

Jax runs past Basher, the two tag-teaming on the field. "Pass!" he shouts as he slides into a tumble that ends with a roll that carries him back onto his feet. The crowd erupts in cheers as he launches a wall of water at the red-armored warrior on the field. It doesn't last long, though. The seven points he just earned for Bedlam are soon overshadowed when the stout, beefed-up Moonfire champion makes a run for the pillar.

"Go, go, go!" I yell at Jax as he sprints towards the pillar. On it are supplemental ingredients players can use to enhance or amplify their spells. Jax's opponent reaches it first, nabs the ingredients, and turns around to battle.

The crowd's roar grows louder as the fight continues. It's too close to call. The cheers turn into screams of victory as Jax surprises his opponent by shooting a fireball right out of his mouth. The heat of the blast reaches the bench, causing everyone to jump back. With a magical barrier in place, nothing can hurt us or the crowd, though. Twenty points join the scoreboard, marking Jax victorious in his individual match.

Representatives from both teams line up on the field, ten male and five female, divided by color and division. Symbols hover over their heads, indicating which order they belong to. The crowd cheers and calls out encouragement to those who fight, screaming Basher's name. Music and drumming fill the air like an invisible force in the clouds. The referee throws her arms up and shouts for quiet, then turns to Basher and nods.

He flings his arm toward the sky and lets out a roar as Earth magic surges from his body and shoots into the air toward a boulder half-buried in the ground. The temperature drops ten degrees in a second as the dirt turns rock-solid, frozen in place for two minutes for Basher's opponent to break free. She doesn't seem phased or surprised by his near match-winning move. As soon as she can move it again, she stomps over to him, while he makes his way back to our side of the field. Moonfire roots for her as she begins her attack on him. Basher still battles, firing Earth magic at his opponent. He wins a few seconds later, making us all cheer in celebration.

Jax and Basher run off the field to get patched up by the medics while Kieran and I take our places. He gives me a fist bump while we separate into our individual circles on the field. The pitch resembles a wrestling mat, though it's made of dirt and grass. Each circle is tinted a different color, complementary to each team's flag.

The referee throws a coin into the air, and it lands on Moonfire's side. For unarmed combat, I'm paired with a guy named Oleander. He's got yellowed-dyed hair braided flat against his scalp, and a swimmer's body.

I don't know what to expect, so I try and stay loose. The referee gives the signal, and we come together in a clash. My fists fly and dodge in tandem, as I try to fend off Oleander's blows. He moves with a swiftness that surprises me for someone so tall and lanky. I try my best to stay conscious of my movements and not let him get the better of me.

He tackles me at the waist, and we fall to the ground, knocking the wind out of me. He grins, obviously thinking he's won this round as he's got me pinned, but with one last burst of energy, I manage to kick him off and scramble to my feet. That's when I notice Kieran has already won his match against a short witch with a thick beard and gauged ears.

The crowd erupts into a roar as I back away, regrouping. My heel catches on a raised part of the dirt, the sound of a wire snapping loud enough for only my ears. As if it's been activated, the ground springs to life, sending a trail of dirt straight for the giant, flaming goal post just yards away from me. It reaches the base, exploding and sending the post careening towards me. Without the use of my magic, I can't move fast enough, and I'm hit with the full force of ...

Coach Thorn? He plows into me, knocking me out of the way of the flaming post and onto the ground, taking the full brunt of the impact. The crowd gasps in horror as he is engulfed in flames and convulses in pain. Ignoring my own safety, I rush over, grabbing onto the burning wood, my hands blistering from the heat as I yank with all my might. Oleander, Kieran, and Jax are the first to make it to us, helping me drag the burning structure off Coach. The referees rush to the scene, working to heal coach with their magic, but not before every inch of his body has been scorched by the flames.

Coach's face is ash colored, his body shaking violently as he manages to pull himself up to sitting. His skin is pasty, his eyes are unfocused and the veins in his neck stand out in sharp relief. The reek of scorched hair and body fills my nostrils. His voice is raspy and strained, but the words echo in my ears, nonetheless. He begins to speak in a slow, measured cadence, as if each word is drawn from a deep well that's nearly gone dry.

"The necklace, Rose. You have to remove it."

I kneel by his side as he takes the key hanging from a metal chain around his neck, the entire stadium still as he uses it on my suppressant necklace. As soon as it springs free, my skin flares a brilliant blue, and I let out a groan as magic floods my system, relieved when it starts to heal my injuries. I place my hands on his, grasping them tight as I heal him, too.

"Thank you," I whisper.

"Don't let them win, Rose."

Whether he's talking about Moonfire Academy, or whoever just tried to kill me, I don't know. Jax and I help coach to his feet, escorting him to the benches while the team works to clear the field.

The unbreakable glass sphere surrounding the pitch remains intact, preventing anyone from entering or exiting the arena, but that doesn't mean someone couldn't have placed the trap before the match.

After a short intermission to ensure everyone that coach is healed and the turf is cleared, my opponent and I approach the pitch. We meet, and he shakes my hand, whispering a word of apology about my almost getting hurt.

Coach shouts from the bench for me to clip this guy's wings, and I launch forward. We battle for another few minutes until I'm able to pin him down. I'm straddling his neck, resting my butt on his chest and cutting off his air supply. I feel his heartbeat against my thighs, like a wild animal that I've cornered with nowhere to run. He taps the mat in submission, and I pop up, giving him a hand.

The crowd rewards me with thunderous applause, and I smile as I look towards the bench. Coach is already standing up, motioning for me to join the others. As I run off the field, a rush of adrenaline courses through my veins. This is what Spar Games is all about. If we forget the attempt on my life, the camaraderie and teamwork displayed by my teammates has made this day one of the most thrilling experiences of my life, and it's not even half-way over.

Jax inspects my skin, ensuring I'm okay before handing me a water. Kieran pauses in front of me with an easy smile. Could it have been him? Is that why he's being so nice to me, to get me to let my guard down?

"Good work out there." He peels his shirt off and I get to work on his cuts and bruises.

My order requires me to touch the injury rather than do it from afar, but he doesn't seem to mind. When I finish, my eye catches on a crow circling the stadium overhead, its bright silver eyes visible from here.

A smile crosses my face when I see it, happy that my little friend is watching the game. He's got the best view in the house.

We take our seats on the bench to watch Penelope and Corson in their strategy match. This is the hardest to train for because each competitor must think on their feet and adapt to the other's moves.

In this round, players face a real-life puzzle. Not one with jagged pieces and colorful illustrations like the ones I used to work on as a kid, but one that requires tactic and calculation. This one is about war strategy.

On the field is a hologram of a real-life ancient battlefield, complete with trees and rivers. Penelope and her opponent move holograms of soldiers around the board, trying to outsmart each other. It's mesmerizing to watch, and both have insane talent. As soon as one of them gains the lead, the other steals it back right away, and this goes on for a while.

The game ends in a tie, with neither of them able to gain a significant advantage over the other by the time the timer hit fifteen minutes, signaling the end of the round.

They jog back to the bench, both of them grinning from ear to ear. While Penelope didn't win or lose, Corson came away victorious.

I give Lopey a hug, proud of her accomplishment, and then it's on to the next game.

The sun has started to dip below the horizon and fae flies take flight, igniting the stadium in a sparkle of magical energy. The night has only just begun.

We vote for Jax to be our champion, while Moonfire chooses Lopey's opponent as theirs. The two of them head to the center of the field, and I watch with bated breath as they face off against each other.

The combat is fast and furious, with Jax gaining the upper hand. He dodges Moonfire's most powerful spells and ends the round in spectacular fashion. Instead of breathing fire, he breathes ice this time, freezing his adversary. The crowd erupts into a frenzied cheer, and I jump up, screaming until my voice grows hoarse.

With the final two rounds, Jax sweeps the competition and claims the top spot, finishing the game 126 to 118. We storm the field, and I tackle Jax, giving him the biggest, sloppiest kiss ever.

My team is victorious, and it feels fantastic. I know that all of us worked hard, and this victory is the result of our combined efforts and dedication. The only thing that would make it even better is if Deakan was on our team, too. But he's somewhere in the stands. Hopefully.

It's customary for the winning team to say a few words, and before Jax can take the mic from coach, Kieran does. Jax doesn't fight him on it.

"We may not have won all the games today, but we put up a good fight. And that's what matters." He beams. "Bedlam Academy doesn't let threats stop our victory." The crowd cheers, and I smile up at the crow still circling overhead.

It's been a long, hard game, but success has never tasted so sweet.

Until everything goes wrong, that is.

CHAPTER SEVENTEEN

ROSE

"We wouldn't have been able to do this without all the great moves my teammate brought to us from Earth." Kieran claps a hand on my back, and my face shows on the jumbo screen near the scoreboard. I've got a giant smile on my face, and everyone in the stadium roars with cheers. Maybe he feels bad for the way he's treated me, and isn't behind the attacks? But then who could …

My half-formed thought leaves me as the team lifts me off my feet, and I'm floating on cloud nine. This is the moment I've been waiting for ever since I first stepped foot onto the Spar Games practice field.

"High Princess Rose Drake, would you care to share any words?" Kieran levels me with a smug look.

The crowd collectively sucks in a breath, murmuring as I watch the blood drain from my face on the jumbo screen. My team looks on in confusion and shock, but I'm too terrified to put two words together.

How could he?

Why?

Does he hate me so much that he'd reveal my secret to the whole realm? Doesn't he know this only puts me, and anyone close to me, at risk? After everything that happened today?

Suddenly, everywhere I look, there are walls, trapping me in a world where I'm alone and exposed. In the distance, I can hear the deafening silence of the stadium, and all my anxieties bubble up in me. Seconds away from a complete mental breakdown in front of thousands of people, a pair of strong arms surround me. Slowly, I look up, and what I see almost makes me forget why I'm there, in the middle of a panic attack—Jax's face, so close to mine that I can feel his breath on my skin.

"It doesn't matter who you are, Rose. You're one of us and that's all that matters." He presses his lips to mine, squeezing me before letting go.

The crowd roars in approval, and a wave of relief washes over me. He just saved me from the biggest embarrassment of my life. I'm speechless, and I don't know what to say or do, so he takes the stage.

"We've come here today to win, and that's exactly what we did." More deafening cheering ensues. He points to me, "And yeah, Rose's full nelson lessons helped all of us." He winks at me, and my cheeks heat. "None of this would've been possible without our brave Coach Thorn, so I'll let him share a few words."

Jax wraps an arm around my shoulder and escorts me to the locker room, and I'm filled with gratitude. He didn't have to do that, but he did anyway.

As we walk away, I turn to him and whisper, "Thank you."

He smiles at me, his eyes filled with admiration. I pull up short when we encounter a female fae tossing a ball of water in the air just outside the double doors. Long blonde hair cascades down her back, and bright green eyes meet mine.

She smirks at me and winks. Breaking away from Jax, I tackle her.

"Mom," I cry. She's disguised quite well, but I'd recognize her aura anywhere. She's really a tall brunette with blue eyes, and just on this side of thick. Mom is easily the most beautiful fae in the entire realm.

We hug for a few moments before she pulls away. "Your dads are looking into what happened on the field. Whether it was an accident

KATHY HAAN

or a part of the strategies game, we're not sure. Either way, I'm so proud of you." She glances behind me. "Jax, is it?"

His eyes widen in surprise as he nods. "Yes, ma'am."

"Call me Astrid." She grins and turns toward me. "At least when I look like this." She winks. Her name is really Lana.

"Apologies, Astrid. It's great to meet you." Jax shakes her hand, and she pulls him into a hug.

"Just thank you for helping Rose out today." She steps back and places a warm hand on my forearm. "I'll let you two get cleaned up." She glances over our shoulders to see the rest of the team heading in. "We'll meet you back at your dorm."

Mom gives me one last hug before leaving, and Jax and I head to the locker room for a post-game shower. On the way, I glance up at him, noticing his sweat-dampened hair resting on his forehead, and how handsome he is with his post-game glow.

"You saved me," I whisper.

He squeezes my hand. "Always."

The team showers and changes before meeting Coach in his field office. Kieran is already there when Jax and I arrive, avoiding my eyes. The others aren't quite sure how to approach me, so they don't. Are they afraid to talk to me now?

Coach levels a glare around the room, his gaze finally settling on Kieran. "I trust you all know why we're here," he begins, and Kieran's eyes snap to mine. He knows he's in trouble.

For the next few minutes, Coach lays into Kieran about the importance of keeping secrets and respecting privacy. Kieran studies his feet, clearly ashamed and embarrassed. Apparently, the entire coach-almost-dying-thing forgotten in the wake of Kieran's bullshit.

When Coach finishes, he turns to me and gives me a knowing look. He knows I'm brave enough to handle this moment, so he leaves it to me to speak. I take a deep breath and muster up all the strength in my body.

"Surprise," I say, my voice strong and steady. "I'm a princess, and I'd appreciate it if you treated me as though I'm not. And also, thank you. All of you for your help on the field today."

Penelope wrings her hands, glancing nervously at the others before mustering the courage to speak. "You all know Rose. She's still just Rose, guys."

"She's one of us." Eli stretches.

The others murmur their agreement, and my heart swells with gratitude. I catch Jax's eye, and he grins.

After the meeting finishes, I snag Penelope.

"Thank you for sticking up for me." I glance around. "I'll make it up to you, but first, I've got a huge favor to ask."

"Not necessary, but what's up?" She inspects the charred ends of my braid. "I think I know of a spell that can repair this."

"Can you pretend you're my roommate, just until my parents leave?"

Her head snaps up. "Y-you want me to m-meet your royal p-parents?" Her voice shakes, and a line forms between her brows.

I place a hand on her shoulder. "It's okay, Lopey. You don't have to if you don't want to."

"I want to help you." She winces. "I do. But they're scary."

"What!" I laugh. "No, my parents will freaking *love* you. They're basically me, in imposing form."

I shoot her a wink, and she breaks into a smile.

"Alright, I'll do it," she agrees.

Jax heads off to Deakan and Kieran's room for the time being and the two of us head to my room down the hall. Penelope will wait for all clear before joining us, though, on account of my baby sister I don't want *anyone* to know about.

CHAPTER EIGHTEEN

ROSE

In my room, disguises have disappeared, and I hardly know who to attack with hugs first. Bennett is the first to reach me, and he throws his arms around me before my sisters, Mom, and Dads join the group hug.

They all talk at once.

Finn growls, "If this wasn't an accident, I'll kill 'em."

"I still think you should come home." Mom wipes a tear from her eye.

"Glad you used that full nelson I taught you as a toddler." Auguste beams.

"Who was that boy you were kissing and where is his room?" Gideon interjects.

Oz answers Gideon with an affirmative that he'll find out and make sure it's nowhere near my room.

My other dads, Casimir, Penn, and Grimm, regale me with their own Spar Games days.

"Hi, beautiful," says Mekhi from where he's seated on the trunk in front of my bed.

I move towards him, and he stands to give me a hug. "I'm so glad you're okay." Mekhi lifts me off the floor, spinning me around until we both fall into a fit of laughter.

Novaleigh begs for me to show her my collection of clothes, and I promise to show her later. In her arms is Bee, who's grown so much in the time I've been away. I take her from Nova and press a kiss to her chubby cheeks. She squeals and claps her hands, and I'm reminded of why I love babies, and plan on having a small army of my own someday.

"My roommate is outside," I tell my mom. She nods in understanding.

"Finn will sift home with Bee, and Pierce is going to watch her tonight." Pierce is my mom's personal guard, and one of our most trusted friends.

"Where are Grandma and Grandpa?" I try to keep the hurt out of my voice.

"Oh, they watched the whole game! They've just been caught up checking out the academy gardens with Professor Blush. They'll be up shortly," Mom reassures me before she lowers herself to sit on my trunk. "Is that kid going to be any more trouble?"

"Who?"

"The one who told the entire stadium who you are." Finn's eyes sparkle with mischief as he gets up and hovers over Bee, making airplane noises as he rumbles over her tummy. He glances up at me, and his expression changes from playful to serious.

I sigh. "Nothing I can't handle."

"I don't feel good about leaving you here by yourself." Mom smooths Bee's hair in a nervous gesture.

"I'm not by myself, Mom. I've got friends."

She raises a brow. "Can they use magic?"

I nod. "Most of my friends are second years."

"Maybe you should transfer to Solstice Academy, where they don't know who you are." Finn crouches so he's at Bee's level and blows a raspberry on her tummy. "Or we could kill him." He glances back at me and winks.

I feel my cheeks burn. "Wh-what? How would that solve

anything?" I don't even want to address how uneasy that makes me. Kieran may be an asshole, and he's ruined everything for me, but I don't want him dead.

"It won't. But it'll make me feel better." Gideon chuckles.

"Technically, he did commit treason," Penn grumbles, opening a bottle of water with a sharp snap when everyone looks at him.

The rest of my dads grunt in a unified front, as though they're considering killing Kieran.

"No!" I whisper-shout, eyeing the wall. This is probably where I should tell them Kieran's room is right next door, but I don't. "We're not killing anyone."

I give Bee more hugs and kisses before Finn takes her from me and sifts out. He's back in minutes, and I crack the door open to let Penelope in. Her eyes widen at the chaos that is my family.

"Don't worry," I whisper. "They're all bark, no bite." *Unless they're plotting to murder Kieran.*

Penelope pastes a smile on her face and curtsies.

"Everyone, this is Penelope." I introduce her. "My roommate."

Mom steps forward and embraces her. "It's lovely to meet you, Penelope. We are so glad Rose has a friend like you. Excellent strategy work, too." She winks.

Penelope's smile turns into an actual one.

My dads take turn shaking her hand while I introduce them. After Mekhi shakes her hand, Novaleigh hugs her and compliments her on her pretty shoes. They've got a band of glitter along the soles.

Before Lopey can thank my sister, Gideon speaks up. "No bathroom door?"

I laugh and launch a pillow at him. "C'mon, Gideon, give the woman a break. She just helped win us a tournament, with a nearly impossible strategy leg."

Gideon grins. "She's definitely family material, then."

I've never seen Lopey's smile so wide, so authentic.

And just like that, my family has won her over.

By the time my family leaves, I'm dragging my feet and am so tired. I'm about to curl up on the bed with Jax when I remember Kieran.

"Did you leave him in one piece?" I tilt my head to ask him.

He shrugs, "More or less. Deakan helped."

"Sounds like you two both deserve some extra attention tonight."

"Oh?" His gaze grows heavy. "Should I call him over? He's been dying to see you, but Kieran's blackmailing him with something to keep him away, I think."

I stand on my tiptoes, and tug at his dark curls before pressing my lips to his.

"Only if you two can share nicely," I whisper against him.

And that's how we end up dragging our two beds together before Jax shoots off a text to Deakan. A knock sounds at the door seconds later, and Jax hops up to answer it.

He cracks the door open and yanks Deakan inside. Deakan finds me in the center of our giant bed, completely naked, and his eyes go hooded with desire. He stalks forward, cupping my face in one hand and tugging at the back of my neck.

"Hello, little Rose," he whispers against my lips.

My body sags against his with relief, happy to just be near him again. The ache I've felt since we parted is sated. I smile into his kiss as Jax moves to climb into bed beside us. "Truth or dare," I smirk.

Deakan chuckles, tugging me closer to him. "Truth."

"How do you want me?"

Deakan's eyes darken. "In every way."

Licking my lips, I turn to Jax. "Truth or dare?"

"Truth."

"Do you prefer to watch or are you okay with joining in?"

Jax grins, looking between Deakan and me. "I'm always ready to join in."

Deakan's lips curl into a wicked grin, and he tugs me closer. "Let's do this, little Rose."

As fae, I'm not a petite creature like a human woman. We're tall, have softer hair and more vibrant eyes, full lips, pointed ears, and naturally curvy bodies. Being caged between two male fae who are even larger, more muscular, and more dangerous makes me feel like a dainty treat being devoured by two predators.

Catching a glance between the two, they seem to communicate without words about how this will work between the three of us as they strip out of their clothes. I don't miss the uptick in their heart rates. Pale moonlight streams in through the window, casting stark shadows on the bed. Their eyes burn, and the magic that radiates off them mingles with mine, luring it out to play. They trail along my skin, my glow dancing in its wake. Teasing fingers give way to lips and tongues and then to teeth, all grazing and nipping.

They've got me so on edge, and I'm desperate for the release they keep denying me. My hips chase their touch, trying to get my own hands where I need them most.

"Truth or dare?" Deakan settles between my thighs, his breath warm on my already overheated skin. He traces a teasing circle around my swollen clit and teases me with the threat of contact.

"Fucking dare!" I whine.

The best friends chuckle and share another look.

"Remember how we've shared so many firsts?" Jax whispers in my ear. "What do you say we share another?"

My hand cups the back of his neck, and I arch into him. "Tell me already."

Deakan drags a finger from my clit to the puckered hole below. "I dare you to let Jax take this tight little ass."

"Is that what you want?" I turn to Jax.

He smirks. "I want all your holes, Rose."

Licking my lips, I rise to my elbows so I can get a better look at Deakan. "Want to double down on that dare?"

"What did you have in mind?" Deakan massages the insides of my thighs.

"He takes yours first." It's an asshole thing of me to ask, and I regret the words as soon as they fly out of my mouth. Other than a heated glance, neither of them have given me any indication they'd ever thought about fooling around with each other.

It takes a moment for them to understand what I'm implying. "You want me to fuck Deakan?" He considers his best friend.

The thought of watching the two of them together makes me hot as hell. "I want to watch," I correct.

"How about this." Jax shakes his head and kneads my breast, tugging on the nipple with his giant fingers, pulling until it's hard, making me arch my back. "That wouldn't be us sharing our first, now, would it?"

Is he implying he'd do it another time? Color me intrigued.

"No." I pout.

"How about Deakan and I take you at the same time? I could have your ass while he has this pussy." He emphasizes his point by cupping it with his free hand.

"Deal." Though as soon as I say the words, the reality of what I've just agreed to sets in. I trust both of these males implicitly. But this is a big first.

Deakan crawls over me, securing his arms under my body, and flips us so I'm on top of him. He's already got a condom rolled up for me to slide on, and I press my mouth down on his, tasting him as he groans, taking over the kiss as I lower myself.

I roll my hips, dragging my pussy up and down his shaft, but his grip tightens, and we sync into the same rhythm. It's slow and tortuous, driving me crazy and not allowing me to take charge, which is what I really want. But when the heat of Jax's body brushes behind mine, I surrender.

He drags his tongue from where Deakan fucks me to my ass before he spits, rubbing a lubed finger along my crack. We slow our movements, and the sensation is foreign as Jax works his finger against my rim, massaging it. This feels so dirty, but so right with them.

A moan escapes me when his finger presses into my hole, pushing past my tight ring and filling me so deliciously. I bite down on Deakan, and he lets out a groan.

"Fuck, I love when you bite me," he grunts. A hand reaches around and grabs my hair, pulling my head back as his lips find my neck.

His teeth break skin just as Jax inserts another finger inside of me, moving with agonizing slowness. He scissors his fingers around inside of me as I ride his hand and Deakan's cock, my orgasm building higher and higher. It bulldozes me as Jax eases into my tight channel; the sensation of having both of them inside of me is too much for my senses to take.

I rip my mouth from Deakan's skin, a low, keening moan tearing from my throat as they work in tandem to please me. With Jax settled between Deakan's thighs, I'm surrounded, the two men taking me in their arms, riding the waves of pleasure with me.

The three of us spend the rest of the night exploring each other, taking turns with truth or dare until we collapse into an exhausted heap.

CHAPTER NINETEEN

ROSE

As there's just a few days left of winter break, Mekhi will spend it with me. It's not our first time sleeping in the same room, but it'll be our first time doing so as boyfriend and girlfriend.

"You remember Jax and Deakan?" I gesture towards the two fae lounging on my bed, their presence intimidating even to me, but Mekhi doesn't seem fazed. Over the last couple months, he's had plenty of opportunity to get used to the idea of sharing me.

"How could I forget?" He drops his bag at the door before slipping off his shoes.

I threatened to withhold sex from Jax and Deakan if they're mean to Mekhi, so they're behaving.

"Hey." Deakan approaches my boyfriend, extending his hand. "Sorry about the photo thing."

Mekhi raises a tentative hand. "And the text?"

"That, too." He grins, and their hands clasp, both of them wincing at the enormous amount of power they both put into the handshake.

Testosterone brews in the air, and while I can't stop thinking about Theo, a small part of me is glad I'm not introducing everyone at once. I motion to the couch Jax and I put in along the wall, and Mekhi takes a seat, pulling me onto his lap.

He puts a possessive arm around my waist before he stiffens. I turn to face him just as his nostrils flare; no doubt the massive amount of sex Deakan, Jax, and I have had permeates the air. Hurt flashes across his face before he schools his expression, and I grab his hand in mine.

"I gave Jax my virginity," I confess, staring into the deep well of his hazel eyes. "But that doesn't mean I don't love you or that I don't want to be with you."

Mekhi sucks in a deep breath, letting it out slowly before speaking. "I figured as much. He's here, and I'm there." He shrugs, glancing at Jax. "Lucky guy."

Jax says nothing, as he knows it isn't a conversation for him, but for Mekhi and me.

Mekhi holds my gaze, his emotions painted across his face. He cradles my face in his hands and kisses me with a tenderness that almost makes me forget the heartbreak of my confession. Almost. He pulls away and looks at the two fae before turning back to me.

"It's why I've asked for a transfer," he says, and my heart soars. "They've already approved it, but I can't start until January 5th."

I reel back with disbelief. "Are you serious?!" I leap from his lap, grabbing onto his hands. "You better not be fucking with me!"

He grins, the sight taking up his entire face. "Bennett got approval for transfer, too, but your parents are holding out on it until the threat clears."

I sink to my knees, and relief in the form of tears pour down my cheeks. "But how?"

He swipes the tears from my eyes, his touch holding so much reverence and love. "I called the Dean myself and asked."

Mekhi helps me to my feet, and I wrap my arms around his neck. "This is the best Christmas present you could've ever given me." To have both Bennett and Mekhi on campus with me? That'll solve half of my heartache. Maybe Dean Fallgren isn't as terrible as I thought she was.

Deakan's phone goes off, signaling the alarm he set for us to head to the Witches Woods. Earlier today, we'd started on a protection spell, that when cast, will protect all of us from any supernatural threats. It's dark magic, and something we shouldn't be dabbling in, but my parents agreed we should try it.

After the game, I had to put my suppression necklace back on, so I won't be able to use any of my magic, but I can use my blood.

Clasping his hand in mine, Mekhi and I lead the four of us out of the dorm. We march forward as a group and enter the heart of the jungle, just off the grounds in an ancient clearing filled with thick boles of giant trees.

"Where will you sleep?" Jax asks Mekhi.

"Well, Bennett will need a roommate once he gets here—" Mekhi begins, but I interrupt him.

"I might know of a place off-campus, but I'll have to clear it with him first. For all of us."

"Off campus?"

"I don't want to say anything until I talk to him. But yes, off campus."

Having us all under one roof would be great, though it may take time to integrate everyone together.

We stop at the center of the clearing, the ring of stones around us alive with energy, and the only other being is a giant black bird in the sky. I survey the faces of my group: Mekhi, Jax, Deakan. We each pick up a black candle, and I light mine before Mekhi uses mine to light his before tilting his to Jax, then Jax to Deakan. We kneel at the center as we stick the ends of the candles into the earth. Taking a blade from my bag, I make the first cut across my palm, a crimson line welling in its wake.

The spell shakes the ground beneath us, the trees bending inward slightly in response from the offering. One by one, each of us adds our own blood to the pile in the center, and I can feel the spell we're about to perform taking shape. We grip one another's hands, forming a tight circle as we chant a binding spell that will protect us from any and all supernatural threats.

"Forever bound, we will be,
All enemies whose sight we see,
From the dark and from the light

Our protection will bring us might," we chant in unison.

The energy from the spell ripples through the night sky, washing over us in a gentle embrace. We all stand in unison, our palms held out to each other, and the candles snuffed out.

"It's done," I say, my voice barely more than a whisper.

The energy swirls around us like a cloud of snowflakes, then settles in the earth. The smell of damp palms and moss floods through me until I am surrounded by it. The earth sighs, like a paramour returning at last to his lover's arms.

"I don't understand why so many people fear the dark arts." Deakan helps me pack up the candles while Mekhi and Jax work to restore the evidence of our ritual.

"Too many scorned lovers, probably," Mekhi volunteers, and I freeze before turning my attention to him. "Kidding." He grins.

Because the dark arts are about balance and justice, not about evil and fear. I playfully check him with my shoulder, and he snags me around the waist to sear me with a kiss.

We head back, shoulder-to-shoulder under an oppressive night sky. Maybe it's the spell we just cast, but I feel more secure than ever.

"What are you studying?" Deakan leans forward to look at Mekhi.

"Cooking," he deadpans.

"He is not." I laugh.

"Sure, I am." He drapes his arm around my shoulder, grinning and with mischief dancing in his eyes. "I'm looking forward to a new recipe I've been dying to try. Spit-roasted Luna." He coughs.

I squeak, nearly choking on my own spit. I spin around, walking backwards to face them, leveling them with my finger. "Nope, you three are not going to do this bro thing and gang up on me."

Deakan throws his arms around Jax and Mekhi, leaning towards my boyfriend with a smirk. "Lucky for you, that's our specialty."

CHAPTER TWENTY

THEO

By the time Sunday rolls around, I've got everything ready for tomorrow. But tonight, I want to spend some time with Rose at Sanctuary. She's busy until supper with the other guys, but she's right on time when the door to the room clicks open.

Rose wears a small, satisfied smile on her lips as she crosses the room to me, her dimples on full display. Heat radiates from her body in this chilly room, and all my own worries seem to melt away now that she's near.

"Hey there," I murmur, wrapping her up in a hug and pressing my lips against her temple.

Rose's arms encircle my neck, and she leans into me, her breath tickling my ear. "What have you got planned for tonight?"

I laugh, my chest rumbling beneath her. "Oh, I think you already know," I whisper, trailing my lips down her neck.

Rose shivers in response, her fingers tangling in my hair. I step back and take her hand to lead her to the table I've got set with all her favorite dishes. We've talked about this for a while now, how she missed some Earth food she can't easily get here. I spent a small fortune gathering supplies at Shatterlee Market to make these dishes for her.

On the table are lasagna, garlic bread, French fries, and a strawberry shake with real strawberries. When we discussed the finer desserts of the Earth realm, she spent at least ten minutes lecturing me on the importance of real strawberries, and none of that fake syrup shit some restaurants use. I pull out her chair and motion for her to take a seat.

Rose gushes, taking a fry and dipping it into her shake. I watch in horror as she puts it in her mouth.

"What traitorous thing did you just do?" I tease.

Rose just laughs and takes another bite. "It's so freaking good. Here." She dips a fry and holds it out for me. "Try it."

Fat, sugar, *and* salt? No wonder humans are a dying breed. But this is Rose, so I do what I can to appease her.

I close my eyes because who can look at this nauseatingly—

Delicious marvel of the human world. I groan at the flavors bursting on my tongue. "Where has this been my whole life?"

"See? Now you can't ever doubt me ever again." She tosses a fry at me.

I raise my hands in surrender. "Never," I joke, leaning forward to press a kiss to her forehead before heading off to take the popcorn out of the oven.

"Did you just make popcorn in the oven?"

"How else would you make it?"

"The stovetop ... or a microwave?" Confusion mars her pretty little face.

I scoff. "Why, when it's so much easier to use the oven?" She's so adorable, I could eat her. Everyone knows you make popcorn in a dutch oven, which only fits in the *oven*. It's far too big to fit on the stovetop, and definitely won't fit in the microwave. You never put iron in the microwave. I'll have to watch her closely so she doesn't hurt herself, or burn our house down.

"Not so sure about that, but alright." She hums, scarfing down the giant pot I set in front of her.

Peculiar little creature.

Rose enjoys the rest of the food I place in front of her until she's too full to appreciate herself anymore. We both lie on our backs on the bed, pants unbuttoned, stomachs full.

"It's moments like these that make me grateful for being here," Rose mutters, her voice barely audible over the crackling of the fire.

"Me too." I slip my hand into hers and lean over to press a kiss to her forehead. "Want me to show you a neat little magic trick?"

"Sure." She sits up on her elbows.

Placing my palm against her abdomen, I envision the food absorbing into her system, fueling her with energy and nourishment. It churns beneath my hand, almost as though it were a sentient being.

Rose eyes widen, and I grin at the awe on her face. "I'm not uncomfortably full anymore!" She rolls over.

"That's the beauty of magic." I press a kiss to her temple.

Before I can roll back over to my side, she stops me. "Theo," she whispers.

"Yeah?" My eyes search hers.

"Will you give me a proper kiss?"

My heart slams against my ribcage as I can scarcely breathe. I've been waiting for her to ask, and as soon as she does I'm lost, pulled into a whirlwind of sensation. Her lips part against mine, a soft sigh escaping her as our embrace grows more passionate. I feel like time stops, frozen in this moment, we are the only two people in the world — no past, no future, just our joined souls. I reluctantly pull away, savoring the taste of her on my lips.

Coming up for air, I cradle her face in my hands, nuzzling against her.

"Rose?" I whisper against her ear.

"Mmm?" she mumbles against my cheek, the warmth of her breath tickling my skin.

I pull away, my eyes searching hers. The silver flecks, only visible to my kind, dance and swirl in a mesmerizing pattern.

"Do you think I could meet your boyfriends, see if we can all get along? You're so special to me, and I want to do whatever I can to make things work between us." *Desperate to make things work between us.*

The corner of Rose's lips curl up, softening her features. "That would mean a lot to me." She stretches up, placing a gentle peck on my lips.

"Consider it done," I whisper, my heart fluttering in anticipation.

Rose has opened a part of herself to me that she never has before. She's still cagey about who she is, and I'm determined to break down these walls, even if it takes a wrecking ball. I'll do whatever it takes to protect her, which means I've got to know her.

Her head rests on my chest, her breaths slowing as she drifts off to sleep. I look down, a small smile tugging at my lips. She knows she's safe with me here. Just as I'm called to her, she's called to me. *How it's meant to be.*

Sometime hours later, Rose's skin glows a beautiful blue, the light waking me. She stirs in her sleep, and I'd wake her if it were a bad dream, but the whimper and small grin on her face tell me she's enjoying it. I smirk and tug the blanket up to her chin, then press a light kiss on her forehead because I can't help myself. I can hardly believe I've found her after just six years.

Her hand clenches my shirt, and I know she's awake now. She peers up at me, her eyes glimmering in the dimly lit room.

"How long was I asleep?" Rose asks, her voice barely a whisper.

"Couple hours."

She stretches, her back arching, and I move to sit up. She pouts and grabs my arm, pulling me back down.

"Stay," she whispers against my chest, her breath warm.

I chuckle and place a kiss at the top of her head. "As you wish."

"Do I get everything I wish for?" She raises an eyebrow, and I can't miss the seductive tone of her question. The glow hasn't gone away from her skin.

"No." I laugh, nudging her away from me so I can look into her eyes. "But I'll do my best to make sure that you get whatever it is your heart desires." My voice ends with far more emotion than I intended, and her eyes widen.

"And ..." Her fingers dance along the planes of my neck, tracing the patterns of my tattoos. "What if you're what I desire, Theo?" Her pupils flare when her eyes meet mine.

I still her hand. "Do you?" I ask, my voice low.

Rose swallows and nods, her gaze never leaving mine. "Yes," she whispers, her voice barely audible, but resolute in its conviction.

A wave of emotion washes over me, so strong and unexpected that I'm left speechless. My arms wrap around her waist, hoisting her close, and she swings a leg over me, so she straddles me. I can feel the wet warmth between her legs and the softness of her breasts, rising and falling to the rhythm of my breathing. Her lips press to mine, eager.

She breaks away, her lips swollen. "Please tell me you have protection."

I fumble for my wallet in my back pocket and hand her the lone condom I have. Fae don't have many communicable diseases, but pregnancy is a concern now that birth rates are on the rise again. I've carried that damn thing around since I matured.

"Better check the expiration date." I wince.

Giving me a wry smile, she inspects the condom and breathes a sigh of relief. Tossing it onto her vacated side of the bed, she hooks her thumbs into her tank top and pulls it over her head. It lands on the floor without a sound, and my eyes trace the line of her smooth, tanned shoulders as she starts to pull off her nude bra. She mumbles something under her breath, seeming to struggle with removing it.

I sit up, leaning forward to ask if I can do it for her. My fingers itch to feel the soft skin of her back, and I swallow hard as I try to find the words to tell her how special this is to me and how perfect she is, but the words die in my mouth as I unclasp her bra. Her breasts spill out as she slides the bra straps down her arms, flinging the bra behind her.

Flawless, dusky rosebuds sit atop my favorite shade of olive-toned skin. My fingers trail the valley between them and up to the hard peaks. Her breath clips when my thumb catches the flesh of her peak, tugging on it gently. She helps me out of my t-shirt, returning the favor by going straight for one of my own nipples, pulling on it and kneading my flesh between her fingers. She leans down, nibbling it between her teeth before taking it between her lips, flicking it back and forth before sitting back with a grin.

Her hands make quick work of my belt as she pulls it from the loops of my pants, eager to free me from them. Long, dark locks brush my stomach and sides as she kisses her way down my body, stopping to kiss and suck my left nipple again before doing the same with the other. She helps me shimmy out of my pants before tossing them carelessly behind her, and I lift my ass off the bed so she can push my boxers down. My erection springs free, thick, and weeping.

Her hand closes around it, as though marveling at the texture, and her fingers pump my cock. My breathing shallows, the feel of her is almost too much to handle. My whole life I've waited for this. For her.

Eyes meeting mine, she leans forward and licks my pre-cum from the tip, then takes me into her mouth. "Fuck," I groan. She licks around the head and base of my cock, working her tongue up and down the shaft, paying attention to the way my body responds to each little thing she does.

My fingers slide into her hair, tangling in it as I guide her with a gentle push and pull. Never in my life have I ever felt something so good. My stomach begins to tighten.

"I'll die if I don't get to come between those pretty thighs." I ease her off me, and she rolls onto her back. "But I want to feast before I feel that tight pussy on my cock." Sliding her shorts down, I discover she came here without panties, and I whip my head up, gaze heated. "Did you do that for me?"

She grins as I smooth a hand down the soft tuft of dark hair between her thighs. She kicks off the shorts and lets her knees fall open, revealing the glistening pink lips of her pussy. Like a man starved, I lower my mouth between her legs, lapping at her with a rough hunger I don't even try to control. Little mews escape her throat, and I can feel her trembling as she peers down at me when I focus on her little bundle of nerves buried in the most sensitive spot at the top of her slit.

Her back arches and her fingers curl around the top of my head;

she has no hesitation about riding my face to chase her pleasure. I lick and suckle on the little bud and slowly piston my fingers in her until I find the place that makes her buck off the bed with a cry. She throws her head back, soft thighs quaking around my ears as she climaxes, and a puddle of warmth spreads around my tongue.

The taste of her is like ambrosia, and I lap at her cunt with relish, savoring the warm honey that pours out of her onto my lips.

"You are a talented man." She collapses onto the bed, breathless.

A grin tugs at my lips as I settle between her thighs. "Only for you."

I lean over her to reach for the condom, and my cock brushes against her wet heat, causing her to moan. My fingers close around the foil, but I don't sit up. Instead, I buck my hips, grinding the head against her swollen bud.

∽

ROSE

If this man doesn't spear me with his cock right now, I'm going to do it myself. He teases me with the fat head of his cock, sandwiching it between my folds. Sliding up and down, up and down. An orgasm rips through me, and I cling to him for dear life as I come down from my high. My hands fumble for the condom he dropped next to my head, and I tear it open with my teeth.

He brings his mouth to mine, enjoying drawing this out for me. Tearing my mouth away from his, I roll the condom down his shaft, taking great pleasure in the sensation of his velvet skin on my fingertips. He notches his hand under my knee, and as he enters me, his eyes meet mine.

Pooling in the depths of his irises, I see the flicker of a hundred thousand stars and all the love he can give me. Tears prick at the backs of my eyes, and I shutter them, afraid of the strong emotion bubbling inside of me.

"Don't." Theo cups my cheek as he stills.

I peer up at him to find his eyes swimming with emotion, too. He brings his forehead to mine and whispers in my ear, "Can you feel it?"

Our bodies ride together like they've been doing it for millennia, moving together in a natural rhythm as old as time itself.

What am I feeling?

Every cell in my body lights, infused with electricity and a deep sense of knowing that my life is about to change forever. Who is this man? And why do I feel him soul-deep?

His magic dances with mine, as though greeting an old friend—not a *hello* but a *welcome back*. Nostalgia. At our lips, I have a feeling as though we share something deep within us—that while on the outside, we appear different; on the inside, we're connected at a level only felt within our souls, the very marrow of our bones. Though there is no single word that captures his essence, I know—I feel it in the depths of me—that he is no ordinary man. No ordinary lover.

Mine.

CHAPTER TWENTY-ONE

JAX

"Where is she?" Deakan paces the space in front of Rose's bed, the same spot he paced a thousand times since he returned from classes.

"She texted to say she's likely going to stay the night with Theo." I frown at my phone. I've yet to meet him, but we've got plans for an official meetup with every one of us next weekend. I'm not sure what to expect, and I feel a wave of jealousy, but it subsides quickly. If her subconscious chose to mate Deakan—whom she didn't outwardly want—she'd definitely want to mate with me. *Right?*

"Is she rejecting me?" Deakan tugs at his hair. "Isn't she losing her mind being away from me right now?"

Deakan had been adopted by a pair of faun fae. Imagine their surprise when his magic came in. They had no idea how to handle a lion shifter, which means he's not as informed as he should be about mating rituals among his kind. Good thing I researched the crap out of Luna orders when I found out Rose was one.

"Dude, chill. If her magic is fully charged, she might not feel the draw as much. You know she constantly regenerates, especially during a Bedlam Moon." I peek out the window, spotting the crimson orb just beginning to rise alongside the others. Even with her necklace on, the Bedlam Moon might be enough to take the edge off, even without her full powers.

"I don't know, man, something isn't right. Give me her number," he demands.

"Get it yourself! If she wanted you to have it, she would've given it to you." *Okay, that was a low blow.* I might be more than a little jaded she mated him and hasn't asked to mate me yet.

Deakan clutches his chest, rubbing at the center. He thrashes his head as though he's trying to shoo a fly off him like horses do. A low growl sounds in his throat and he turns to face me, his body pulsing with a strange energy.

"I'm going after her," he growls out. "I need—" his last word is cut off as he shifts, his body morphing from fae to large lion in one swift move. As the transformation continues, his golden fur sparkles in the dim light. There's a sheen to it I've never seen before, and then the air behind him sparks and ignites, a single flame flickering in the darkness. He roars, tearing into the enormous door to his room, leaving deep gouges in the woodwork. When his claws won't open it, he rams it with his giant lion shoulders, but it still doesn't budge.

His head thrashes before he whips his attention to the window.

I see it in my mind before he does it, and with two tremendous bounds, he launches himself at it. I've already leaped in front of the window to prevent him from hurting himself, but my fae form is no match for his shifted one, and he crashes into me. The window shatters as we careen into it, and a cascade of glass rains down on us.

I try to shift into my dragon as we fall out of a fourth story window, but a large shard of glass protrudes from my chest from where it entered my shoulder blade. The coppery scent of blood invades my nostrils, and I can feel it trickling down my back before we hit the ground with a painful amount of force. The glass saws into my chest as Deakan's lion form slams into me. Blood fills my mouth as I try to breathe and shift into my dragon form to heal, but nothing happens.

"Help." I grunt through the burning, stabbing agony. But my voice is quiet as I try, in desperation, to take in air. I attempt to sit up, but the darkness threatens to take me under. The simple act of turning my head is excruciating, but I do it anyway, looking for help. But our dorm windows face the sea, and the only thing between here and the lighthouse is tall grass and sand.

You'd think that as I lay here dying, my thoughts would turn to all the fond memories I had with my parents as a kid, but it's thoughts of Rose that consume me. Is it too soon to fall in love? Probably. Am I crazy? Undeniably.

One word plagues me: regret.

Why didn't I tell her?

My vision swims, and the last thing I see is a lion bounding off into the night.

CHAPTER TWENTY-TWO

THEO

So, this god-touched Luna fae is my soul-bonded mate. I knew as a griffin I'd be driven to protect her, but to have a soul bond on top of that? No matter who else she mates, all our bonds will remain intact. This is fate, destined by the gods themselves.

Rose lies nestled within my arms, but her heartbeat grows stronger, as if it has increased in volume. Like the cords of a marionette, she and I are both being pulled by forces outside of our control. But there's something else here. I can feel it in the bond, the presence of more. When did she mate with Mekhi and her other boyfriend?

"I can feel you," she whispers.

"I can feel you, too." I smile down at her.

Her sleepy gaze, unwavering, takes me in from head to toe. Delicate fingers explore the softness of my hair, trace the shape of my mouth, run over the contours of my cheeks, and then reach the planes of my muscles. For hours, we've cataloged everything from the ridges in my fingerprint to the light shining through her pores when she's turned on. We discuss our thoughts and fears, as I gaze at every detail; her makeup and jewelry, the indention of her waist, and the movement of her neck as she drinks. A fierce possessiveness consumes me, from the roots of my hair to my marrow. Just as I am hers, she is mine. Forever.

"Your other mates don't mind you being away from them right now?" I can't be certain, but I don't think she had a bond with them when she was last here.

She sits up. "I'm not mated to anyone else."

I laugh. "You don't have to pretend I'm the only man in your life, Rose," I tease. We've already discussed me sharing her. It isn't ideal, but what's the alternative? Being without her? I'd rather die. "But really, they're okay with it? Do you need to bring them here?"

New mating bonds bring out some pretty crazy emotions in males. I've built this place as my griffin nest, and I knew I'd someday have a family here.

"What are you talking about?"

"You don't feel them?"

"Feel who?!"

"Your other mates."

Her chest rises and falls in a mild panic, brows furrowed. Closing her eyes, she goes preternaturally still. "What the fuck?" she scrambles away. "Who are they?!"

"Your boyfriends?"

She shakes her head. "I didn't mate with anyone else, Theo."

This is the second instance I've heard of this in mere days. Rose reaches over my lap for her purse. Her hand grazes my leg as she digs into her bag for her cell phone. "It's already seven a.m.," she says, settling onto her heels where she kneels on the bed. "I've got class soon. Don't you?"

"Not until tonight." I tug her closer to me. "Are you sure you want to go? This is kind of a big deal."

"I think I need the time to get my head around it." Her legs wrap around my torso, her wet heat pressing against me.

"Rose ..." I growl. "You can't tease me like this and take off."

She grins. "Sure I can. Save me some of this—" she grazes her pussy against the head of my erection, "—for tonight."

Groaning, I try to scramble after her as she bounces off the bed, laughter tinkling above my protests. She dresses, and I plop back onto the bed in invitation, but she stands before me with a wicked glint in her eyes and begins to open the door. "Save some of that for tonight?"

"You know it," I call from my position against the headboard, and she turns with a shrug and a grin. The door snicks closed behind her, and I'm left with a case of some serious blue balls.

∼

ROSE

Taking the path through the woods, I have time to reflect on what I know:

- I have a soul bonded mate.
- And, apparently, I have two *other* mates.

My heart does something funny in my chest when I think about that. It's at war with my mind: yay for multiple mates because I've always wanted what my mom has with my dads, and the other part of me is wondering if Jax or Deakan mated me without my knowledge. If so, how do I feel about that? You can't mate anyone without both parties wanting it, so that makes me feel a little better. Maybe my heart knew something I didn't when it happened. I'll ask them about it with the understanding that, either way, it was inevitable.

A thought strikes me once I reach the campus courtyard. *My dads are going to kill them.* I've only just reached maturity, and I'm lucky enough to have three mates—everything I've always wanted, but now they'll get taken from me. Maybe I can hide it from them.

The Bedlam Moon casts a crimson glow over the university. A guy brushes past me, nearly barreling me over. A group of witches jog in the same direction, and a trio of professors run. Why is everyone in a hurry as they pass me by? Did I miss an assembly? Where exactly are they trying to go? I stop a woman coming from that direction to ask what's going on.

"There's a lion shifter stuck in his beast form, and they're trying to lure him out of the student union building. He's hurt, judging by all the blood and the way he's roaring." Her lips turn down in a frown.

"Poor thing." I hug my midsection, suddenly feeling unsettled.

Deciding the shifter doesn't need any more witnesses to his obvious distress, I head to the gym for a quick workout and shower before class. The weight room is empty when I arrive. Sometimes Jax and I get a workout in before classes, but he must've skipped out this morning on account of my being with Theo.

I'm just pulling on a t-shirt after my shower when someone pounds on the door I've locked to the changing room. It's kind of an asshole move of me, but if I can avoid others seeing my suppression necklace, I'm less likely to get questioned about it. I throw on a hoodie to help hide it. "One second!" I shout while I pull on a pair of shorts. More pounding ensues as I rush to the door. "Jesus, I said one second!" I shrink back when I find the dean on the other side.

She cries out, "Rose," and her voice chokes with emotion.

My stomach drops. The dread is so intense that I'm nauseous with it. My trembling fingers grip the door handle to keep from dropping to my knees. "What is it?"

"Come with me," she says. Her arm links around mine as she escorts me across the sand-covered court to the periphery, past ancient hedges of wild roses and over a knoll that culminates in a pile of old rocks gathered in the shape of a chimney.

"Is my family alright?" Gods, *not any of my sisters. Or my brother. My parents?* My wet hair drips down my back, giving me a chill despite the heat of the morning.

She gives my hand a squeeze. "They're fine," she breathes.

Sweet relief sinks into my bones, and I walk a little lighter. "Where are you taking me?"

"The medical bay." We pass by students who give me a peculiar look. "There are some investigators who'd like to ask you a few questions."

INVESTIGATORS? Shit. I know that with the Bedlam Moon my magic is at its all-time highest. The necklace still works, but last night, while Theo and I mated, my magic flared. *Gods.* Can they know when I'm having sex with this thing on? Heat creeps up my cheeks. My dads are going to kill me *after* they kill my mates.

Is the academy kicking me out for this? "I didn't mean to!" I blurt.

The Dean's horrified look is a little gratifying, but I still feel mortified that my parents are going to find out about this. I'm an adult, though, so maybe they won't.

She looks really sad, so maybe they *are* expelling me. I've already been warned plenty of times.

A group of official royal investigators meet us at the entrance to the sick bay, their faces expressing various degrees of alarm. The head honcho, judging by her blue sash, a first-aid badge, and a stethoscope around her neck—she's wearing it as a necklace—steps forward, hands on hips.

"I've got to go call her parents." The Dean hands me off. "She just admitted her involvement in the incident."

Wait. Incident? They must mean my mating with Theo. Or maybe they're talking about my mating with Jax and Deakan?

"Wait, please." I reach for her. "Which one are we talking about? Jax and Deakan? Because I didn't even know—"

"Just how many are there?!" Her horrified voice is almost a shriek.

I wince. "Three?"

The stethoscope lady calls over her shoulder, and one of her subordinates steps forward. He wears a similar outfit, though his sash is forest green instead of royal blue, similar to the uniform officers wear at Bedlam Penitentiary. My attention goes to where he reaches for a pair of handcuffs clipped to his belt, and he removes them as though he already has plans for their use.

These are magical cuffs and judging by the thick band of grey metal similar to my necklace, which is formed into two circles joined by a bar, the cuffs seem more capable of restraining a troll than a human being. *Suppression handcuffs.* Great.

"Since when is sex a crime?" I spit as he spins me around, cuffing my hands behind my back. "A misogynistic pig is what you are."

"High Princess Rose Ankida Drake, you are under arrest for the murder of Jax Cavë—"

"What?" My voice comes out strangled, hysterical. "What did you just say?!"

"The body of your roommate, Jax Cavë was found at approximately 6:32 this morning under suspicious circumstances. You shoved him out of a fourth story window."

CHAPTER TWENTY-THREE

ROSE

My legs crumple beneath me, and I fall to my knees, a keening wail stripping my vocal cords, causing me to throw back my head and let it rip. The shrieks coming from my throat sound inhuman, like the howls of a wild animal. My lament echoes off the surrounding buildings and penetrate the Bedlam Moon sky. The cuffs tear at my skin, and my flesh becomes grotesque as I rock back and forth on the ground, feeling as though my whole being is split into two.

The officer hauls me to my feet, but I'm dead weight, listing, my body limp in his arms.

"Get your hands off of her," a voice booms from behind me.

He stops in his tracks, his head slowly lifting to see over my shoulder. No sooner does he do that, he's thrown backwards by the force of magic, and he lies on the grass in a lump. I crash to the ground. No one moves to help him. I swivel my head toward the arrivals storming the yard.

Their royal regalia flows behind them in the breeze, crowns strewn atop their heads. Their ethereal silks and satins brush against the dark earth, looking all the more ominous washed in crimson under the Bedlam Moon.

"Mom," I sob into the grass. She's the first to reach me and makes quick work of dismantling my cuffs. Throwing my arms around her neck, I bury my face in her gown and sob.

"Oh, baby!" she cries with me, holding me on the lawn and stroking my hair as if I were still her baby. My dad's grief-stricken faces crowd around me, and I bury my face in the familiar softness of her arms and hold on to her as tightly as I can, choking on my tears.

"He has no soul," I wail. The cavern inside my chest widens, hollow by the guilt and grief consuming me. An unfathomable void takes over my being, a sensation of regret and despair so raw it feels like my heart has turned to ashes. For the rest of his days, Jax will never rest. He won't feel Luna's beams on his skin or bask in the glory of the Bedlam Moon. He will be a mere shadow of the man I love, a spectral shade that used to be mine.

Haunted.

I should've been here to protect him. He needed me, and while he was slipping away from me forever, he was alone. He never knew the depth of my love for him, or how his presence was everything to me. The words ... millions of words I have to say to him, silent until the end. They remain trapped inside my chest, desperate to claw free, as though if only they can escape, they'd redeem him. I scream at the injustice of it all, wishing the words could break through the eternal night my soul has wandered into and save him.

I scream until my throat is raw, until my words taste like blood in my mouth. For something that is everything, I scream. I scream until my vocal cords snap and no sound comes out, until I'm hoarse; until my body aches and all I can do is close my eyes and grieve in devastating agony. As the tears run out of me, I know I will never love like this again. There is no rhythm or tapestry in this grief, no light at the end of the tunnel, only the inescapable truth of death.

My tears stain Mom's dress, and I tilt my head to the heavens, watching that crow circle above. Why does it do that? *Are you mocking me?* I want to scream. *Or are you here to save me?*

Save him?

I suck in a choked breath. Tearing away from my mother's

embrace, I lunge at my dad with a desperate plea. Finn startles and falls onto his backside while I clutch his lapel. "Dad, give me a feather. Please!"

He looks taken aback. "Please, please, please!" I shriek.

"Okay, okay. Hold on, sweetheart." He pulls us to our feet, and with a swoosh, his wings unfurl. Those huge, golden feathers have blue tips to match the color our skin glows. He plucks one from his plumage, placing the bloodied feather in my hands.

I whirl around, hunting for someone who can tell me what I need to know. Spotting the investigators huddled together, I sprint over to them. "Where is he?!" The sound of my voice is foreign to me. Its fragile, insecure tone surprises me. This feels like my brother dying all over again.

"His parents are on their way to collect his body from the morgue in Draconum now."

～

I WHIP around to my parents and beg them to take me there, praying to any deity that'll listen, hoping against all hope that it's not too late to revive him. Is it different if you don't have a soul? I'll drag him back from wherever he's gone.

After my parents glance at one another, Gideon steps forward, placing a hand on mine. In two blinks, we've sifted into a cold, harshly lit room filled with trays of glass vials and steel tools of examination. A male and female lost in their grief surround the large figure that lies on a gurney, hidden beneath a white sheet, stained crimson.

"Mr. and Mrs. Cavë." The soft, strangled noise that slips from my lips is neither a question nor a statement, but they reply as if I'd posed an inquiry. The small nod of their heads reaffirms my presence in the room, though their haunted expressions are locked away within themselves. It's obvious who they are—bereaved parents at the deathbed of their son, arms around each other for comfort, completely beside themselves in grief.

Their tear-stained clothing and flushed faces are stark in the unadorned space. Their faces are lined and contorted, and their eyes are rimmed red and swollen. Not even the company of my royal parents can pull them out of their despair.

I find my voice, clutching to my chest the one thing that can bring my mate back to life. "I'm Rose," I call, and this grabs their attention.

"His Rose?" A question written in tears on Jax's mother's face.

He told them about me. I nod, my chin wobbling under the force of my breath. "His Rose," my voice breaks.

She opens her arms to me, and I cross the distance between us, stumbling under the weight of my grief, burying my head against her shoulder. Mr. Cavë joins us, pulling her close to his chest, and then, with a voice that sounds like it's trying not to break, too. "You're his Rose. Every time we'd call, he'd talk about you."

Pulling back from our group hug, I reveal what's in my hand. Mr. Cavë gasps, and Mrs. Cavë cries out, sinking to her knees. A single quill from the most powerful fae in existence: High King Finian Drake.

"I don't know how to ever repay you for this." Mrs. Cavë reaches out a trembling hand, taking the quill.

Only some fae orders have wings, and even fewer have feathers. These can bring someone back to life, and the length of time depends on how powerful the fae is. It's why most winged fae never show their wings to anyone other than their mate, as a single feather costs a lifetime's fortune. One from a royal fae, guaranteed to give *immortality* back to the departed? You're talking generations' worth of gold and favors, not to mention a monopoly on the supply of whatever special goods that fae species trade in.

Mr. Cavë's grip on the table slips under the weight of his knees buckling. Massive, heaving sobs wrack his body, agonizing cries of anguish and disbelief roll out of his mouth, revealing a man who had lost the world, and expected nothing for it.

"I will serve you until Luna calls me home, High King Finian," his cry echoes through the chamber as a giant of a man kneels before his High King.

"It's clear you raised this man well, for our daughter loves him so.

Family of hers is a family of ours," Dad kneels, his face a mask of shock and humble gratitude at the sight before him.

Mr. Cavë raises his head, wiping the tears from his eyes. "Truly?"

Dad lifts him back to his feet and holds onto his shoulders. "Family, Mr. Cavë. Take this feather as my gift."

To give a dragon order something of such value? The gravity of it is unfathomable.

"May I?" I steel myself for pulling the sheet off, glad that my parents dimmed the lighting. Mr. Cavë gives me a nod, and I carefully remove the blood-stained cover.

I'm not prepared for the wave of grief that hits me as I stare at his lifeless body underneath. Even in death, he is handsome. Those dark curls fall over his forehead in an uncharacteristic show of vulnerability. To the world, he wore a mask. The unbreakable, infallible Jax Cavë. But to me, he shared his secrets and his heart.

And just like he said after the first night I woke in his arms, I, too, willingly gave him both my virtue and my heart. What I didn't anticipate was becoming the one woman who was completely and utterly broken after his death. Jax Cavë, you wrecked me in the best of ways.

My hand reaches up and traces the outline of his cheek before I even realize what I'm doing. Silent tears pour from my eyes as I think about how I never even got a chance to show him the magnitude of my love. It runs deep, and it runs wide. Once earned, it lasts forever, and it is infinite in its capacity. When we come out the other side of this, he'll hear it from me every day.

"I love you," I whisper as I press a kiss to his temple. "In this life and the next."

CHAPTER TWENTY-FOUR

ROSE

My parents sifted Jax's body, along with his parents, to our family home in Rift Pass on the continent of Rexuna. We hold vigil with them here in my bedroom while we wait for the feather to work. He'd been dead a while, so the process his body must go through is extensive, not to mention that of his soul.

If it works.

His mom and mine help me wrap his dressings, keeping the wounds clean, covered, and protected to help the healing along.

It's late afternoon by the time his external wounds begin to knit together and color returns to his cheeks. The air around us shifts, and the temperature rises. His larger-than-life presence fills the room, and with it comes the faint sound of something I spent many nights falling asleep to: the steady thump of his heart and the slow drag of his chest as he inhales and exhales.

Sobs rent the air around me as I realize the man I love is finally with us again. His eyes blink open and meet mine, but something about their green depths has changed. I wouldn't call it wizened. More like haunted. Where does one go when they don't have a soul? I'm afraid to ask. His gaze penetrates mine. They're still some of the most beautiful pairs of eyes I've ever seen, but there's something so deep in them now.

"I thought I'd lost you," I cry.

He makes to sit up, but his mother moves to stop him, and that's when he registers his parents. "Mom? Dad?" He looks around. "Where are we?"

"My home in Rift Pass." I take his hand in mine and bring it to my lips. "My family is downstairs. This is my room."

"The High Queen and her Kings know I'm here?"

I nod.

"High King Finian Drake gave us one of his feathers to bring you back to us." Mrs. Cavë rests her hand over ours. "You keep hold of this girl, and never let go."

Jax's lips curl into a smile. "I won't." His gaze catches mine.

After his parents have had time with their son, mine come upstairs to meet him. He can sit up now and does so when they enter the room. Jax didn't actually feel like dying again, so he had me stand next to the bed before their arrival.

My Aunt Pippa, our family's doctor, had given him a clean bill of health before she left an hour ago, though he'll need to take it easy for the next couple hours while his body heals. He might spend the next week a little under the weather.

My dads make an intimidating presence, lined up along the wall of the dark room, looking like a row of men watching a guy whisk their precious daughter away. Auguste leans back, casually using a dagger to clean his fingernails. Oz has his arm wrapped around Mom's shoulder, and little Bee is babbling on his hip. Finn looks like he might be regretting giving me a feather to save a boy I love. And surprisingly, the moodiest of all my mom's mates, Penn, actually looks pleased. He's a dragon fae. Casimir is on Mom's other side, the wolf in him always wanting to rub up against her. Grimm and Gideon, the more mischievous of the bunch, lean together conspiratorially.

"So, uh, this is Jax." I wince. "Surprise!" Mom already met him, and they saw him and me at my game, but this is my dad's first face-to-face interaction, save for Penn at the castle when we'd been attacked.

Of course, the jerks immediately assault him with a rapid-fire torrent of questions and thinly veiled threats:

- What are your intentions with my daughter?
- Are you prepared for the scrutiny you'll face as a royal?
- Are you aware the fae body has 316 bones, and I know 13,734 ways to break them?
- How big is your dragon?
- Have you ever been arrested? And don't lie to me; I already checked.
- Did you know that two of us in this room have taken a potion to detect lies? We'll know.
- I might not be able to safely suck all the blood out of your body, but if you hurt her, I will and deal with the repercussions later (Fae blood makes vampires feral).
- Did you know I'm the best tracker in this realm and the next? Wherever you run, I will find you.
- Have you begun collecting your hoard of treasure?
- I spent Rose's entire childhood teaching her thousands of ways to maim, kill, and torture a man. You just give her more surface area to work with. Keep that in mind.
- You've met Mekhi, haven't you? He'll tell me if you ever hurt her.
- Are you aware that some of us can read your mind?

I intervene when Gideon asks Jax to make him a fae promise that he'll never sleep in my bed. He's not privy to reading minds, but the other fae royals in the room glance at each other, likely already seeing every thought Jax has about that subject. He can't keep a promise like that because we sleep in the same bed just about every night, even before we were a thing. Back when it was just an innocent way for us to not feel so alone.

JAX

Dying so young isn't something one can ever prepare for. Our family has more means than most, thanks to my order's treasure hoarding tendencies, but there isn't much a family can do to mitigate death unless you get a feather from a powerful fae. We're wealthy, but not that wealthy.

So today, when I met the Luna goddess, I felt relief that I hadn't fucked up enough in my few years on this planet to go to Aggonid's Realm, where evil fae go when they die. Those of us lucky enough to end up beyond the veil with the Luna goddess avoid that fate. She'd just been discussing the implications of my not having a soul in the afterlife, but I'd been ripped from the veil before she could tell me. The resemblance between her and her son, High King Finian Drake, is uncanny. Though the king only glows when his magic regenerates, she glows all the time because she is the source of all magic.

They cancelled practice today on account of my death. After meeting Rose's family, they sifted us back to campus as soon as they opened again. They'd had it completely shut down, so no one could leave—save for the royal family and authorities—and no one could get in.

They drop us off at the cafeteria, which is surprisingly deserted. And messy, too. Full trays of food sit at every table, as though everyone got up and left in a hurry. Rose hasn't let go of my hand since I woke. I eat with my non-dominant hand, shoveling food in my mouth. Dying completely depletes you. She has one more class today, but it isn't until tonight. She'd skip out, but it's the first day of that class with the new professor, whom no one seems to know much about. Kieran is in that one, too. It's a 101 class, but it's the first time it's being taught, so there will be a mix of grades in it.

It took me longer than it probably should've to figure out why Rose was so on edge this afternoon. It's not until a notification sounds on Rose's phone with a campus-wide alert, telling students they still need to remain in their dorms because a lion shifter is still stuck in the student union building that the pieces fit back together.

Deakan, the window, and their mating bond. Rose and I run to the imposing building with its honeycomb of windows to get a closer look at the creature trying to claw its way out of the front entrance. Deakan's lion form is huge, but its size detracts from the sight of him ripping chunks out of the walls with his massive, bloodied claws, especially when he catches Rose's scent.

The last time I tried to get in between Deakan and Rose, I ended up dead, but that still doesn't ease my impulse to stand between them and defend her from an out-of-control beast. Rose's parents help campus security cordon off the area, preventing others from approaching the lion. None of the staff remain on this side of campus, and everyone is to stay in their rooms.

Worry etches Rose's brows, but she doesn't seem surprised. "You knew he was your mate, didn't you?" It goes without saying she made a conscious choice to take him as a mate. Despite feeling a stab of jealousy, I force it back into the depths of my heart, where she is safely hidden. Although it's too late to safeguard my emotions, I'll be damned if I don't do everything I can to shield her from harm.

She shakes her head. "I swear I didn't know until just before I got back to campus and was arrested."

"So, you didn't mean to mate him?"

She shakes her head. "Not intentionally, though subconsciously, I guess I did."

I nod in understanding. So, when the area is clear, I shift into my dragon form and take flight while the royals lure Deakan out of the building and into the courtyard, where it's wide open. Shifting into my beast will help take care of the last of my healing, plus I can detect the location of everyone on campus and swoop in to help Rose if the need arises.

CHAPTER TWENTY-FIVE

ROSE

Deakan's roars echo off the castle walls, sending birds scattering, though my watchful crow remains. The Bedlam Moon casts its glow on all it touches, bathing the world in its blood red color and adding to the eeriness of the campus being on lockdown. I stand at the center of the courtyard, watching the path leading to the building, waiting for—but dreading—Deakan. Will I be able to help him shift back? Or will he take me in his beast form?

I'm not sure how I feel about that.

As the enormous lion prowls into the courtyard, the ground shakes beneath his paws. He stills when he spots me, seeming to study me. I've never seen Deakan's beast before, but the sight of him calls to something deep inside me.

Home.

This creature won't hurt me because I know him, just as I know the way the moons nourish me and the way the air tastes after a summer rain. Or how the call to hunt is a call to love, and he and I can both hear it. For him, it's hearing the thunder and smelling the blood. For me, it's the whisper of the wind where it parts the clouds and the search for dappled moonlight through the trees.

He and I are one.

The ache in my heart eases with each step I take towards my mate. There is no hurry in our pursuit of each other. My hand curves into the sweat slick muscle of Deakan's foreleg and the spot above his eye, where I lay a soothing hand to calm him. His giant head bows in acknowledgement, and a soft huff puffs out of his nose.

"I've missed you," I whisper in his ear. "Let's go home."

A slow twitch of his tail sets him in motion, and the crunch of leaves beneath his paws fills the air around us. My hand rests in the fur of his neck, and his breath is warm in my face. As we make our way towards our dorms, my parents look on from the perimeter of the clearing with varying degrees of admiration and apprehension on their faces.

They've done their best to allow me to make mistakes on my own while keeping me safe and guiding me towards the realization of my potential. Even if they do try to keep admirers away, they will let me make my own choices, even if those choices are unpopular ones amongst my parents.

A melancholic roar from the sky interrupts our moment of silence, and I glance up to see a beautiful dragon soaring high above us, its magnificent tail and wings framing the moons. *Jax*. I can't wait for each of us to share a bed. To have my mates all together in my arms, together.

Approaching the dorms, curious onlookers peer out each window, watching our progress across campus. Now that winter is at our door, our evenings are cooler, though still warm. With Deakan right beside me in his giant beast form, I've managed to break a sweat. By the time we reach our building, I've realized the door isn't wide enough for his broad shoulders to fit through, so I'll need him to shift back into his fae form before we can go inside.

The wooden stairs creak under his weight, his tread slow and measured, though he could easily hop to the top step if he wanted. I drag one of the rocking chairs to a spot further down the covered porch, so he'll have room to sit next to me without a row of rockers in the way. His careful eyes watch as I take the seat and motion for him to sit next to me. My plan is to rock in the chair, but his giant head rests in my lap instead.

His gaze is so steady, like he's waiting for me to do something.

I brush my fingers through his mane, enjoying the warmth and strength beneath them. I take a deep breath before speaking in a low voice.

"You can shift back now," I whisper against his forehead. "I'm here, and we're safe."

A groan rumbles through his chest, and the baseboards bend beneath the weight of his changing form. His transformation takes minutes, as though his body is resisting what I ask of it, but his head and his heart are committed to me. I've collapsed next to him, holding him through the transition as he becomes human, and in that moment, my limbs tremble with the relief of not having to hold him up anymore.

His chest heaves and sweat clings to his forehead, and I let out a deep breath and wipe his forehead with the hem of my shirt. I'm cradling his head in my lap where I sit cross-legged on the porch. It takes him a few minutes to settle into his fae form, and when he does, his breathing evens out, he exhales, and he pulls the lower half of his face into a smile. It's like the brightness of a thousand suns.

His eyes light up, and he whispers, "You're back."

"I'm sorry, Deakan. I didn't know."

His eyes shutter just before they turn away. I cup his face, so he looks at me, and I continue. "I didn't know you were my mate until this morning, long after my heart made the decision it was yours." His eyes soften. "I'm sorry I took the choice away from you."

"You're right in one thing: I had no choice." He sits up and then reaches over, brushing his fingers against my arm. "I was a goner the moment you walked into Herbology 101. And then, when I saw your smile, I wasn't lying when I said it nearly knocked me to my knees. Whether you knew it or not, Rose, you had me then, you have me now, and you'll have me till the end."

"Oh, you two are going to make me puke."

We turn to look in the direction of the dorm entrance and find

Kieran there, with a scowl on his face. His red-rimmed eyes and hair sticking up out of place, as if he's just rolled out of bed or had a good cry, he stalks toward us in a rage.

"Jax is fucking dead, and do you two even care?"

We scramble to our feet. No wonder he's so upset with us. I reach for him, but he shrugs out of my touch and turns away, wiping at his eyes.

"He's right there." I point to the sky, where Jax still circles high overhead.

He shakes his head. "I found his fucking body, Rose!" He shoves me, and Deakan grabs him as Kieran continues shouting. "Do you know what it's like to find your best friend dead?" Spit flies from his mouth. "Do you? Have you any idea what it's like to try and wake up a dead body and feel his fucking cold, cold skin? To not be able to heal his injuries with your useless magic?! Huh? Because that's the second time I've had to do it because of a fucking Drake! The third one your family has stolen from me!" He lunges out of Deakan's arms and snaps at me with his fangs, just missing my face as he's pulled back. He was so close to biting me that a tiny drop of his venom lands on my cheek, sizzling on contact.

The pain of it disappears as memories of my brother's dead body assault me. My inhuman screams echo off the mountain as my family holds me back to keep me from seeing my twin like that. The guilt of it being my fault for his death and why Oz no longer has magic.

Pulled back to the present, my knees collapse underneath me, slamming hard onto the porch as I try to catch my breath. Hot tears pour down my cheeks as a million thoughts and emotions race through my mind.

An enraged dragon's roar pierces the sky. As he lands, the windows above us tremble, and Jax charges at the dorms in beast form before stopping in front of the stairs just as he changes into fae.

As though he'd been punched, Kieran doubles over, heaving the air out of his lungs. He stumbles down the stairs in a run and throws his arms around Jax. They embrace, but Jax pulls out of the hug and jogs up the stairs with Kieran running behind him.

"You okay, man?" Jax asks Deakan.

"Am I okay?" He brushes past me and pulls Jax into a hug. "Did you really die? What the hell happened?"

Jax glances at me briefly, and something passes between us before he returns his attention to Deakan. "It was the dumbest thing, really. I tripped and fell out of your damn window, impaling myself on the glass."

"No shit?"

∽

Students gathered in the hallways scramble into their rooms as we pass them. We're all a little worse for wear, and when we reach the landing to our floor, a shriek fills the hall, followed by the soft patter of feet.

Penelope.

She throws her hand over her mouth when she sees the four of us. When we reach her, she's trembling like a leaf—the poor thing. "What the hell happened?" she shouts. "I thought you'd been arrested for Jax's murder?!"

She's hysterical, so I usher her into our room and pull her into a hug. "Hey, it's alright."

"Did you murder Jax? What did he do?" Deakan glares at Jax, ready to fight him if it's true.

I pull away from Lopey and place my hand on Deakan's forearm while I turn back towards her. "Hey, he did nothing wrong. It was just a misunderstanding. I thought the Dean was questioning me about having sex with Theo, Jax, and Deakan, which activates my magic, which I'm not supposed to use ... so, I might've accidentally admitted to murdering three people." I grimace.

"Wait," she stops me, "you've slept with who?"

"My mates."

She grabs onto my arm. "Your who?" she squeaks.

"Surprise." I wince.

She tugs at her hair, pacing in front of us. Her steps falter, and she looks to Jax and Deakan. "Her dads are going to kill you. I can't harbor that many fugitives, Rose. Your parents actually like me—"

I cut off her panic with my hands on her shoulders. "They already know."

Lopey throws her hand to her mouth, gasping, eyes wide on Jax over my shoulder. "*That's* how you died?"

"Jesus, no." I draw her attention back to me.

"Who is Jesus?"

I inhale deeply, holding it for three counts before letting it out. "It's an earthly expression. Here, we say Aggonid's Bowels."

"Then why didn't you just say that?"

"Because I spent most of my life on Earth, Lopey," I tease. "I'll catch you up in class later, okay?"

After she leaves, I slump onto the conjoined bed, sigh, and then lean back on my elbows to look at the three men who are standing in front of me with their arms crossed over their chests.

"Why does she act like you two have committed a crime together before?" Jax raises a brow.

I giggle. "C'mon guys, Lopey's idea of committing a crime is her pretending to be my roommate so my parents wouldn't know who my real roommate was."

Jax and Deakan climb into bed, stretching out beside me. The look Kieran gives me is one of pure malice before he storms out of the room, slamming the door behind him.

"What the hell is his problem with me?" I glance from Kieran to Deakan, who seems torn between concern and amusement.

"I think he's probably jealous." Deakan's fingers trail on my neck, but as I look at him, his expression turns solemn. "He still thinks he saw you first."

Stilling, I look to Deakan, who is holding my gaze as intently as he can, as if gauging my reaction. "He did," I whisper, and he freezes. "Right before orientation. We were both late and bumped into each other. I, of course, insulted him when he hit on me."

He falls onto his back, running a hand through his hair. "Damn."

I run a hand up his chest. "No matter. You have me." I lean in to place a kiss on his cheek.

A notification pings on my phone, and I pull it out of my pocket. It's a calendar reminder about class starting in twenty minutes in the observatory at the top of the bell tower. Groaning, I slide off the end of the bed and undress. I'd helped Jax shower this afternoon after his parents left my house. Novaleigh had distracted everyone downstairs so we could make it happen without our dads throwing a fit.

I pull on my worn jeans and grab the topmost shirt in my dresser, all while the men watch with hooded eyes. "Don't give me that look," I scold. "I've got astronomy in ten minutes."

"You're making us wait until after?" Deakan sulks as he climbs out of bed and stalks in my direction. His arms encircle my waist, caging me against the wall. Without a word, he presses his lips against mine, kicking my thighs apart and lifting me. His lips blaze heat across my cheeks, then trail down to the base of my neck as his arms flex and he backs me toward the edge of the bed. His tongue laps against my throat, and his teeth close down gently on the sensitive skin beneath my ear just as my five-minute warning notification goes off.

I pull out of his hold, press a kiss to both of their cheeks, and grab my bag on the way out the door. I've got my earbuds in, blasting my favorite music for the sprint I'm going to have to make across campus to get to class on time. My feet feel like they're made of lead as I drag myself down the hall, past students just getting back to their rooms, and practically fly down four flights of stairs before I'm through the front door and running towards the bell tower.

By the time I reach it, I'm a minute late, stressed, and flustered. So, when I climb the stairs, I have to find an empty seat at the back of the room. The faint buzz of chattering students fills the ambient noise outside my headphones while I dig in my bag for my notebook and pen. The light flickers off, illuminating the observatory ceiling like a star-filled night sky and casting a blue glow.

I'm flipping through my notebook to look for a spot to take notes when someone elbows me to get my attention. I glance up to find a pretty, freckled-faced fae with a pixie cut mouthing at me and nodding her head toward the front.

"What?" I stage whisper, taking an earbud out of my ear.

"Aren't you Rose Drake?" she asks.

I sink a little further in my seat and nod; frustrated people know who I am now, thanks to Kieran, and not even the dark room can hide me.

"He's taking roll call." She inclines her head towards the front.

As I'm slipping the other earbud out of my ear and turning towards the professor, I hear an unmistakable voice call my last name.

"Drake?"

I keep my eyes on the notebook, looking down at the pen in my hand with eyes wide and listening to music like I didn't hear him.

"She's here, Professor Pyxis!" The woman next to me waves her hand to get his attention and points to me. "It's High Princess Rose Drake."

The blood rushes in my ears, and my throat constricts as my gaze raises to the front of the room. Like an ilab caught in a hunter's sights, I freeze.

CHAPTER TWENTY-SIX

THEO

My stomach drops, and my heart stutters. She's here? In my class? Rose is right there, in the back of the room, hidden by shadows. All the pieces of the puzzle fit together, and I can feel my face hardening with equal parts disbelief, anger, fear, and regret. Not for being her soul bonded mate. But for what this means to our relationship, if we're caught...

"Rose Drake." I call her name, hoping there's an explanation for this. That she's not actually a student but just observing. Maybe all new professors get a shadow until we figure out how best to teach?

Why was she in the faculty dorms, then? Is one of her other mates another professor? My mind runs through the possibilities. Jealousy rears its head in me.

Professor Sable? No.

Professor Rowan?

I kick myself for not paying better attention. I've been out of sorts since arriving on campus, all because I'd been in close proximity with my soul bonded mate.

Coach Thorn. I grind my molars, trying to remember Coach's first name. She mentioned her boyfriend Mekhi is a student ... and then there's Jax? And Brownie? Or was it Deakan?

"Present," she squeaks.

Our eyes lock, and the room narrows until it's just her and me—two people caught on an impossible, opposing path. If she weren't my soul bond, my being her professor would've been fine, as griffins don't always have romantic relationships with the god-touched they're bound to protect. But she's my whole world now, and every second that ticks by, her regret shines a spotlight on our situation.

I glance down at the list of last names on the sheet in front of me, wanting to crawl into a hole and bury myself alive. Clearing my throat, I call out the rest of the students, checking their names off as they announce themselves.

Did she know who I was? Is that why she kept who she was from me? Loosening the tie at my neck, I wipe a bead of sweat from my brow and launch into my lesson about the astronomical instruments used in ancient Bedlam and how the gods associated with astrology, the planets, and constellations were held in high regard—the most being the one they're all familiar with: Luna.

Who apparently is Rose's grandma, because she's the high princess of the fae?

Fuck.

After finishing my lecture and taking questions, I assign homework and dismiss class. Ben Vegamour, a fourth-year witch who'd asked the most questions tonight, perches himself on the back of a chair in front of Rose's seat.

"—to the Noreaster festival on Occasus if you'd like to join us. It'd be you, me, Posie Beis and her boyfriend, Felix Schooner."

"A date?" Confusion mars her features.

Ben scratches the back of his head. "Well, yeah."

"Oh, I'm mated. Spread the word." Relief loosens my shoulders.

"But doesn't your mom have a bunch of them?"

"Yeah? And?" *That's my girl.*

"How do you know I'm not one of yours?"

She stands, grabbing her bag from where it's slung on the back of her seat. "Because. I have a soul bond, and my roster is full of other mates. Sorry."

"Ms. Drake, may I have a word in my office?"

"Sure, Professor Pyxis." She smiles sweetly, brushing past Ben and toward the glass-encased room, her hips swaying with intention. It's where the panel to control the observatory is, and I can see the entire classroom from my wall-to-wall desk.

I follow, shutting the door behind us.

She crosses her legs and gracefully slides into my large, leather chair that's in front of my desk. "Professor, huh?" She grins.

Glancing out at the emptying classroom, I notice the tattooed serpent guy who'd gotten caught up with his lion friend casting a suspicious glance at us as he climbs the steps to leave. "Friend of yours?" I incline my head.

She follows my gaze and huffs. "Hardly."

After the last of them have left, I lean over her to press the button on the panel to turn the house lights off, keeping the constellations on so there's enough light to see Rose, but not enough that anyone could easily see what's going on in here before we notice them, should someone happen to pop by if they've forgotten anything.

"Did you know?" I sit on the edge of my desk, a thigh on each side of her knees.

"Did you?"

"No."

"I didn't either."

"The only thing I knew was that you were being guarded about your personal life beyond the basics. Sure, I know your hopes, your fears, your favorite foods, and what keeps you up at night. The sound you make when you walk down the hall in bare feet, and even your shoe size. The expression on your face when you're on top and I'm angled just right?" I shake my head. "But your parents? Your work? And apparently, your studies?" Leaning forward, I grip the edges of the arm rests. "Are you fucking Coach Thorn?"

"What!" she sputters. "Gods, no."

"What were you doing at the staff dorms?"

"When?"

"Go there often?" I loosen the tie at my neck even more. "After our run-in in the woods."

"That text I'd gotten was from home, and I needed Dean Fallgren to sift me there. Family emergency."

My hackles rise. "Everything alright?"

She focuses her attention on her shoes, a smile teasing the corners of her lips. "Yeah, there was a birth in the family."

Oh. Rose's admission of a birth in the family is a huge leap of faith in me and in us. Especially considering it's a royal, which poses an even bigger risk.

She tilts her head as she fixes her gaze on me. "How old are you?"

Of all the questions she could ask me, is this her first? I chuckle. "I reached maturity six years ago."

"You're young for a professor." She grins.

"Who better to teach astrology than a griffin?"

We're one of the rarest fae orders. And because griffins are connected to time and prophecy, thanks to our ability to see god-touched objects and fae, we are masters of divination, astronomy, and astrology.

"I guess I don't know much about griffins."

Gripping the rolling chair, I pull her closer to me. "What do you want to know?"

"Tell me what you want." The inflection in her tone is flirty and teasing.

"I built the Sanctuary over the summer, not realizing I'd been nesting."

"Nesting?"

"My kind does that to prepare for our mate."

"You built it for us?" Her eyes soften as she stands, wrapping her arms around my neck.

Fuck, everything feels right when she does this. "Yeah, I suppose I did," I tease.

"Why haven't I crossed your path on campus, save for that time in the dining hall and the woods?"

"I only have this one night class, and it started today."

Her lips press to mine, and I lose myself in her kiss. I hoist her off the ground, forgetting where I am until we bump into the table. Spinning her around, I lay her out on my desk, my hands and mouth exploring every part of her exposed body.

"Rose." I breathe her name, pulling back to gaze at her.

She makes to speak, but I bring my mouth to hers, muffling the sound as I kiss her again. What we're doing is risky, and if we're caught, I'd lose my job or worse. She twists her fingers in my hair, gripping me hard, and runs them down my back. My wings emerge from my back with a whoosh, cocooning us in a glow of shimmering gold. Her palms run over them as she gasps, taking in the iridescent color and thousands of tiny veins that pulse with colored light. She's seen these before, but never in the dark like this.

Tears gather in her eyes, and my wings begin to glow even brighter and pulsate stronger, in tune with the beating of her heart. Tears spill down her cheeks, and she clings to me tighter. "These are so beautiful," she whispers.

"Have yours come in yet?"

She shakes her head. "Not yet."

I pull my shirt over my head, taking care not to injure my wings. They're sturdier and larger than most fae's, but they're not invincible. I help Rose unclasp her bra and then slide her jeans and underwear down her smooth, toned legs. Her hands make quick work of undoing my belt buckle, and soon I'm kicking my slacks off and exploring her body with little nibbles.

"Now, Theo, I need you now." She arches her back.

I press her tanned thighs apart and then dip my head, breathing her in. I'm drawn to her scent, and I run my tongue along her slit, tasting her.

She smells of salt and sweet peaches, and I breathe deeply before licking along her folds. Her hands grip the hair on my scalp, urging me on as I explore with my tongue. Through our bond, I feel her pleasure as if it were my own. Her abs tighten, and her thighs press against my head as she nears completion. I spread her lips apart and lick up to her clit, sucking it into my mouth, bringing her over the edge. Her hands bury in my hair; her whole body trembles, and her pussy dribbles warm juices into my mouth.

"Please," she begs.

"Please what?"

She lifts onto her elbows, a wicked gleam in her eye. "Please, Professor."

My cock twitches, and damn if those filthy words from such a pretty mouth nearly undo me. I slide my hands under her ass, positioning her right where I need her. "Good girl." I drive into her cunt in one fast stroke.

∽

ROSE

I don't have a professor kink—I don't think—but roleplaying with Theo makes me so fucking hot. Clinging to his back, I hold on tight as he grips my thighs, driving hard and fast into me. There's a wild edge to us tonight, as the risk of being caught is high, and the dirtiness of it heightens our pleasure.

For our second round of the night, we're deep in the throes of passion and he has me bent over the desk when the door to the observatory opens and the light flickers on, illuminating the entire place. Including Theo's office.

We freeze.

Standing at the top of the steps, staring straight at where I'm bent over the desk, is Kieran, his eyes locking with mine from across the room. Heat blazes in his gaze before he thinks better of it, then it turns to fury. Using his magic, Theo flicks the lights back off, plunging us into darkness, but the damage is done.

The one person on campus who hates me the most has caught us in a compromising position. I'm not worried about what will happen to me, only about what this will mean for Theo if it gets out. We scramble to find our clothes in the dark, and by the time we exit his office, Kieran is gone.

"Is he going to be a problem?"

"He hates me," I whisper. "This is a big fucking problem."

Taking me in his arms, he holds me tight. "I won't let anything bad happen to you, Rose."

"Me? I'm not worried about me! What will happen to you?"

He rests his chin on the top of my head. "You're an adult, so I'll probably just lose my job. I don't think they send people to Bedlam Penitentiary for consensual sex with another adult. I'm not even much older than you."

"Are you sure they won't arrest you?"

He shrugs. "Pretty sure. Ask your parents?"

A hysterical giggle escapes me. "Do you want to die?"

"Not yet."

I turn in his arms so I can face him. "Not ever!"

Theo locks the observatory while I get on the phone with Jax.

"Hey, you on your way back?" In the background, I hear Deakan asking why I'm calling Jax and not him.

"Tell Deakan I don't have his number, and I need you guys to meet me at the North Woods, and for the love of the gods, don't tell Kieran."

"Everything okay?"

"No. Both of you pack a bag."

"For how long?"

I glance at Theo, and he shrugs. Turning my attention back to the phone, I tell them to pack what they need for classes and a few changes of clothes. When we hang up, Theo sifts us to the woods to wait. The call of bugs in the trees and the sound of whipples fill the air, creating an intense hush that makes it feel like we've traveled far away, though we're barely on the outskirts of campus. Tiny, biting insects find our legs and arms, and Theo uses a kind of sentry magic to drive them away.

You can't hear the sea from this deep in the woods, though it isn't far; it's just that the trees are so dense here. As we move further into the jungle, the sound of our feet stomping over leaves and branches and the sound of the debris shuffling at our feet make us feel increasingly uneasy. The hairs on the back of my neck begin to rise when suddenly, without warning, we are plunged into a dead silence.

No insects buzz. Not a single bird chirps. Theo and I glance at each other, and my hand goes to the suppression necklace at my throat. "Do you have your key?" I whisper.

"My key?" he asks as he inspects my necklace.

"The Dean gave a copy to each professor in case I need to use my magic."

"Wait, *you're* the student they wanted under lock and key?" The horrified expression on his face turns to anger. "I thought this was just a weird necklace you loved to wear!"

Ashamed, I hide my face away.

"Gods, Rose." He pulls me into his arms. "Come here." His lips brush across my temple.

Digging through his pocket, he pulls out his key ring. Among the others, there's a small, black key with a long spike at one end. He spins me around while I lift my hair, and he pushes it into the space between my neck and left shoulder blade where the necklace sits under my skin. It falls to the damp ground at my feet, and I'm half tempted to bury it or just leave it where it fell.

"This isn't right, Rose." He stoops to pick it up. "You're not putting this back on."

"They'll expel me."

"We'll get your parents involved."

I shake my head. "They already know about the necklace."

His features harden. "The school has no right to cut you off from source. Do you know what happens to Luna fae when they can't use their magic?"

"I'm weaker."

"Yeah, and do you know what else?"

"No, but during a Bedlam Moon my magic is strong enough I can use it a little bit. I'm not totally without magic right now."

"A Luna fae without their magic can be killed, Rose."

My stomach drops and I spin towards him. "What?"

"Who did you say gave you this?"

"The Dean." I reply, my voice shaking. Sure, she can be a little strict, but she's always been nice to me. "Oh, my gods." I double over, all the air expelling from my lungs. Regaining my strength, I shoot up, gripping onto Theo's collar. "You need to take me home. Now!"

"What, why?"

"She knows about Baby Bee!" I shriek. And because she sifted me home, she knows where we maintain our private residence, too. And with the missing artifact that can control us all?

"Do you know how it feels to watch you get everything you want?" An enraged voice booms from the shadows of the trees, sending shivers down my spine. We whirl around to find Kieran unfolding from the darkness, his face contorted in rage. "It wasn't enough that you took my parents from me, but you had to take my best friends, too? And now, you're cheating on them both with a *professor*?"

My throat feels like it had been stitched shut. I shake my head, trying to deny his accusation. "What are you talking about? I don't know your parents, Kieran."

A bitter laugh escapes his mouth. "Of course, you don't, your people mean nothing to your family. Prairie Fallgren and Gerard Templeton. My mother was killed in cold blood defending your traitorous family during the war. My father was so heartbroken that he ended his life shortly thereafter, and I ... was the one who found him. His body was so cold and so still, surrounded by the charred ashes of the feathers he'd plucked from his body before he killed himself."

The air escapes my lungs and tears stream down my cheeks. "Kieran," I whisper. He has every right to hate me.

Despite what he's put me through, I want to throw my arms around him. No one should have to go through so much pain and loss. But then my mind flits back to that other detail he's just spewed at me.

Fallgren.

Kieran must be her grandson. Which means Dean Fallgren must have lost her own daughter in the war. No wonder she wants revenge on my family.

The world around me spins and nausea hits me. I don't have time for apologies or comfort. Fallgren knows about Bee, and I know in that very second what she's thinking. One daughter for another.

And I can't let that happen.

Do Rose and Theo make it on time to save Baby Bee from her fate? Is Kieran helping Dean Fallgren? Is she really the one behind the threats on campus and at the castle? Or is the villain a little closer to home? Will Lopey ever stop disappearing around Eli? Will Mekhi and Rose ever mate? Are we ever going to figure out why the crow keeps showing up? Or what Bella's deal is? And which of the gods has taken an interest in Rose? **Read Arcane Scholar (Fae Academia Book 2) to find out.**

Want some of the backstory about what actually happened with Bennett on that mountain pass? Read the #1 bestselling series **Bedlam Moon Trilogy**. It follows the story of Lana and her paramours (Rose and Bennett's parents) and features tropes like found family, one bed in an inn, hidden powers, captive romance, evil cults, and a time traveling witch hellbent on making things difficult for them all.

Wondering which supernatural order you'd be in Bedlam? **Take the quiz at kathyhaan.com/quiz** and see if you're a vampire, witch, or shifter. Share your result in our brand new Facebook group, The Bedlam Fae Society.

ACKNOWLEDGMENTS

Publishing four books in 2022 wouldn't have been possible if it weren't for the army of support I have at my side. I've got so many people to thank:

You, dear reader: Someone once asked how an author feels when they're tagged in a post by a reader who just finished reading their book. I answered that I'm just as giddy as they are about my books, and you'll literally make my week. I screenshot every word of praise so I can look back on them when writing gets tough and I feel like giving up. To have people just as obsessed with the world I've created as I am? There's little else that makes me feel like I've hit the jackpot. Your reviews help other readers find stories they love.

Leo: My first born and my light. The artwork and covers wouldn't be half as good if it weren't for your insane talent. Love you more than the sun loves the moon.

The rest of my family: Thanks for helping me chase my dream of entertaining the masses. After a decade of marriage, I'm happy to have you as my ride or die, Kirk. Love you to pieces.

J: You really had your work cut out for you with this one. Thanks for helping me twist the knife.

Lori Granito: My biz bestie, I'm so freaking proud of you. Your unending support means the world to me.

Maggie Stiefvater: Your mentorship radically changed my writing, and I hope readers can see it when they read this newest book.

Others I need to thank include **Elise Kova**, **Bobby Kim**, and **Maxwell Alexander Drake**, whose business and craft mentorship have really helped me hone my skills and author acumen. **Alex Lidell**, for helping me figure out the direction I wanted this book to go. My **Blinqing fam**, who keep me entertained with endless quizzes. And **Author Cheer Squad**, for your endless support, commiseration, and memes.

ABOUT THE AUTHOR

A blood descendant of Wild Bill Hickok and a long line of artists and creators, #1 bestselling author Kathy Haan believes the secret to telling a great story is living one. The second youngest, in a massive horde of children between her parents, she did her best to gain attention and kept everyone entertained with jokes and wild stories.

She lives a life of adventure with her hunky husband, three children, and Great Pyrenees in the Midwest, United States. While this is her second series, you might've seen her work in Forbes or US News, where she's a regular contributor. Or, in Notoriety Network's 12x international award-winning documentary, #SHEROproject.

CHAPTER ONE

ARCANE SCHOLAR — FAE ACADEMIA BOOK TWO

The woods are eerily silent, as though the entire universe has ceased to take a breath. Tendrils of fear uncoil within me, snaking up from the depths of my being, threatening to throttle me. One thought consumes me.

We're the bad guys.

All it took was one moment of vulnerability—an earth-shattering accusation—and now the only world I've known seems to be unraveling before my eyes.

The scent of damp earth saturates my nostrils, making me acutely aware of my surroundings. My heart thuds against my ribcage, a wild and unsteady rhythm that echoes the pace of my thoughts. It's all so surreal—the darkness of the woods, the incessant buzzing of insects, and the oppressive stillness that envelopes everything around me.

For a moment, I feel as though I've been transported into a nightmare, a place where nothing is as it seems. Somewhere danger lurks around every corner. I pinch myself, hoping to wake up, but the sensation is all too real. I'm here, in the heart of the Witches' Woods, and I have never felt more alone.

My family's fault.

Theo's arms wrap around me, his warmth a beacon of comfort

CHAPTER ONE

amidst the chaos swallowing me whole. "I won't let anything bad happen to you, Rose," he promises, his voice like a lifeline.

But it's more than that. It's everyone. My friends, my family. If the secret gets out that we have a royal baby, the repercussions could be devastating. With such low birth rates amongst the fae—though it's on the rise—kidnapping is a very real threat, especially for a royal. And if the unhinged dean of my university gets to my family before I do, no matter how complicit we are in the events that have led to this?

I've got to stop her.

The words Kieran has just spewed toward me echo in my head, filling me with a dread I can't shake. His expression is filled with devastation and rage, the seafoam green of his eyes darkening as they bore into mine. *It wasn't enough that you took my parents from me, but you had to take my best friends, too?*

He hates me, and he has every right to. My family's actions during the war cost him everything. Now he holds the power to tear my world apart, and I'm not sure there's anything I can do to stop him.

My heart thunders in my chest as the crushing weight of our dire predicament slams into me like a crashing wave. Panic starts to ripple through my veins, consuming me with an urgent sense of dread. We need to make sure my sister, Baby Bee, is safe. We can't waste another second.

Casting Kieran one last lingering look, I see the pain etched on his face, his eyes gleaming with tears. I whisper, "I'm sorry," before turning toward my soul-bonded mate, Theo. "We need to sift to my home now," I say, my voice trembling with urgency.

Theo nods, understanding the gravity of the situation. Whispering to him, I describe my family home that's nestled at the top of a mountain pass, so he knows where to bring us. I haven't learned how to teleport yet.

With a sudden, nauseating jolt, we're enveloped by the familiar sensation of sifting, the world around us blurring as we teleport to our destination.

As we reappear, the breathtaking beauty of my family's alabaster home greets us. Nestled between two Rift Pass peaks, the bone-white walls contrast against the vibrant green of the surrounding landscape. The sound of running water echoes throughout the house, soothing despite the urgency of our situation.

My gaze is drawn to the clear floors, through which we can see the river running beneath our feet. Large silver fish with translucent fins swim past, their graceful movements mesmerizing. The breathtaking view of the Sea of Triune stretches out before us on the South side of the house, while the back side offers a snow-covered valley far below.

Before we can take in the rest of the surroundings, the weight of the truth crashes down on me. Dean Fallgren knows about Baby Bee, and she must be seeking revenge for her own loss. Kieran's mom—also Dean Fallgren's daughter—is dead.

One daughter for another.

The thought is almost too much to bear, and my breath comes in short, panicked gasps. I feel Theo's hand on my back, rubbing slow circles in an attempt to soothe me.

"We'll get through this, Rose," he whispers, strength lacing his voice, bolstering me where I have none. "Together."

His reassurance is a balm to my frayed nerves, and I cling to it, though my entire body still trembles. I feel like I'm drowning.

As we search for Baby Bee, I call out the names of my family members, my voice ringing through the silent halls of our home, shrill and so unlike my own. The house feels empty, devoid of the warmth and love that usually permeates the air. Why is it so quiet? My heart thrashes in my chest with the possibility that the dean could still be lurking somewhere, waiting for the right moment to strike.

I know we have silent alarms set up to trigger if someone without our blood sifts here. Very few people outside of the family know about this place. After the artifact went missing—the one that enables its bearer to control our family—we'd devised a spell that alerts the household when there's an intruder, but it can't be heard by those teleporting in. It casts a silencing bubble over us, so there could be a whole party going on in the next room, and we'd never hear a peep. And because I sifted here with Theo, I won't know if the alarm has been activated. It needs to be reset each time. Does this

CHAPTER ONE

mean that Dean Fallgren didn't trip it? Or that she did, and my family is hurt?

The shadows that have been lurking just beyond the edges of my world seem to be closing in, and I can't help but wonder if it's already too late. Has the darkness finally come to claim us all? As fear coils in my gut, I know one thing with chilling certainty: our lives will never be the same again.

Standing inside my family home in the mountains of Rexuna, it's more like a wilderness day spa than a castle, with a waterfall running underneath the see-through floor that spills over the side of a mountain, and white, stone-carved walls. The tranquil sound of the water offers no comfort as my pulse thunders with worry for Baby Bee.

"Mom! Dad!" I call out, the sound frantic as I search the room for any sign of my baby sister or my parents.

Theo stays close, his hand resting protectively on the small of my back as we make our way through the house. The echo of our footsteps reverberates through the spacious halls, heightening my unease.

My parents emerge from an adjoining room, their faces etched with concern. The sight of my mother and my seven fathers makes my knees buckle, and Theo supports me with an arm around my waist.

All eight pairs of eyes shift from me to Theo, their gazes narrowing with suspicion. They've never met him before, and it's only natural for them to be cautious of a stranger in their home. Do they suspect he's controlling me with the missing artifact?

"Rose, who is this?" my father, Oz, asks, his voice guarded as he holds out a cautious hand to shield Mom.

"I'll explain that in a second," I choke out. "But first, where's Baby Bee?" My voice is tinged with hysteria, causing them to pause.

Auguste takes a small step forward, his vampire eyes locked on me as his instincts kick in. He's been head of our security since long before they ever came to the fae realm. "The strength of a kingdom?"

Right. Our secret phrase, the one we came up with that'll let them know I'm not being controlled by the missing bracelet. "Lies in the bonds of family."

They each relax, approaching me with an easy familiarity.

CHAPTER ONE

"Wait!" I try to sound calm, even as my nerves threaten to shatter. "Where's Bee?"

"We got her into the safe room as soon as the alarm tripped," Gideon says, nodding toward Finn, who disappears behind them, presumably to get Bee now that they know it's safe.

My anxiety coils inside me, tightening until my chest aches like I've been punched. "I have to see her!" I cry out in desperation. Until I'm sure she's safe, every breath will be a struggle.

I tear away from my parents and race down the hallway, heading for our family's hidden entrance between the kitchen and stairwell. My fingers trace the secret rune that opens the panel, which shimmers before fading away. I lunge through it, sprinting down the stairs and across the basement floor with only one thought on my mind: I need to make sure Bee is okay.

I skid around the final corner, letting out a breathless gasp when I spot Bee in her crib. She smiles wide at me, wriggling her little body against side rails as if trying to reach me. My heart leaps with joy and my worries disappear. Bee is safe. For now.

"What's going on?" Mom calls out behind me, but I'm too focused on reaching into the crib, needing to hold her, to anchor myself to the fact she's okay.

My knees collapse beneath me, tears streaming down my face, as relief courses through me at having her safe in my arms. I press my tear-stained cheeks against hers as she babbles happily in my ear. I cradle her to my chest, trembling as I rock back and forth.

"Rose?" Finn's voice startles me, and I meet his eyes, feeling the weight of betrayal slide under my skin. "Dean Fallgren has to be the one behind it all," I gasp between sobs. "Kieran is her grandson. His parents were killed because of our war—and they hate our family as a result."

I see the moment the gravity of the situation registers on each of my parents' faces. The dean is the one who teleported me to this very house when Mom was in labor. She knows both about Baby Bee and how to get here.

We led our enemy right into our home.

CHAPTER ONE

In a broken voice, I relay what happened in the woods, and Auguste barks out rapid-fire instructions to each member of the family. Within moments, my dads fall into their roles, preparing for battle against an unforgiving foe.

Theo stands on the stairs, hesitant as he explains what he knows to Gideon, who stops in his tracks.

"And who the fuck are you?"

"Dad, this is Theo," I explain, trying to keep my voice calm. "He's—"

My words are cut off by a terrifying screech that shreds through the air like a razor blade. A chill of dread runs down my spine and I whirl around, sprinting toward the kids' bedroom in the basement where Mom's agonizing screams cascade from the walls.

"Novaleigh!" She shrieks my other little sister's name with guttural panic.

"What?!" Oz tears through the room, searching for something unknown, his fingers clawing at his hair.

"Where is Nova?" My legs buckle beneath me as I lean against the doorframe, my lungs constricting in terror. "Where is she?!"

Grimm's hands dig into my shoulders like a vice, radiating magical energy that attempts to quell my rising panic. "Where is Kieran now?" His voice rumbles with power.

"We left him in the woods, but he's probably back at the dorms now. His room is next door to mine," I explain.

Penn slams his fist against the fingerprint pad next to our cache of weapons and magic-inhibiting cuffs. "I've been waiting to get my hands on this little fucker."

"I'm coming with you." Casimir reaches for a pair of cuffs and slides them into his back pocket. "Grimm, you're with us."

"We'll search the property for Nova." Gideon turns the display on for all our security feeds, illuminating the whole room with its glow. His movements are swift and smooth, a master of his craft as his eyes rapidly scan the display, taking in every detail for any sign of movement. He barely blinks as he searches for my sister.

As my parents prepare to search and confront Kieran, a mixture of

CHAPTER ONE

dread and determination wells up inside me. We must find Novaleigh and bring her home, safely.

The tension in the room is palpable, and the gravity of the situation weighs heavily on everyone. Each of my parents' expressions is a mix of terror and resolve, but there's an unspoken understanding that we'll face this challenge head-on, as a family.

Theo watches from the stairs, clearly unsure of his role in all of this, desperate to do something but not wanting to get in the way. Our eyes meet for a moment, and I give him a small nod of gratitude for helping me get here.

With a deep breath, I gather my courage and step forward to join my family, ready to do whatever it takes to protect those I love.

We all run up the stairs, ready to scour the property as Casimir, Penn, and Grimm sift to the Bedlam Academy campus on the continent of Academia.

Mom's voice is hysterical as she calls out for Nova.

Sensing an opportunity to help, Theo's eyes meet mine again. "Rose, I can shift into my griffin form and get an aerial view of the property. I might be able to find Nova faster."

I nod, and he leads me to the deck. The wind whips around us as Theo closes his eyes, concentrating. In seconds, his body transforms into a majestic golden griffin. The sun catches on his feathered wings, casting a shimmering glow on the snow-covered ground below.

He spreads his wings wide, and with a powerful leap, takes flight, his strong wings beating against the frigid air. He soars high above the property, his keen eyes scanning the landscape below for any sign of my sister.

ALSO BY KATHY HAAN

Bedlam Moon Trilogy (Complete)

Lana sets out to find the truth about her past, and when a hot vampire begins to unravel it for her, she's caught up in the web of an evil cult, prophecies, and curses. All while falling for the King of Vampires and his royal court. This is a why choose romance.

Bedlam Moon (Bedlam Moon Trilogy Book 1)

Tales of Bedlam (Bedlam Moon Trilogy Book 2)

Wicked Bedlam (Bedlam Moon Trilogy Book 3)

Fae Academia Series (Incomplete, 9 planned)

A spin-off of the Bedlam Moon Trilogy, we follow Lana's daughter, Rose, while she attends a magical university. The summer before college is perfect until the family begins to receive threats, and Rose ends up getting into a different college from her twin brother and her boyfriend. A male roommate, his hot friends, and a sexy professor all find themselves eager to win her affection. This is a why choose romance. Books 1-3 are Rose's story, books 4-6 are Nova's, and 7-9 will be Bee's story.

Bedlam Academy (Fae Academia, Book 1)

Arcane Scholar (Fae Academia, Book 2)

Forbidden Rose (Fae Academia, Book 3)

Moonfire Academy (Fae Academia, Book 4)

Aggonid's Realm Series (Incomplete)

A Realm of Fire and Ash (Aggonid's Realm, Book 1)

A Realm of Dreams and Shadows (Aggonid's Realm, Book 2)

A Realm of Grief and Sorrow (Aggonid's Realm, Book 3)

When the commander of an elite group of phoenixes ends up dead for real, she tries to convince the fae devil there's been a huge mistake. Can she convince him to let her go before he snags her heart? This is an enemies to lovers why choose romance.

∼

Fae Gods (Incomplete)

Fae Gods (April 2023)

Fae Guardians (TBA)

They watched their charge her entire life, completely invisible to her and only intervening when necessary. When they get fed up with her miserable marriage, Jocelyn's fae god watchers decide to help. After all, no fae of royal lineage deserves to be left to wilt away on Earth. They devise a plan to reveal their true selves to her, calling themselves the Marriage Doctors. But what happens when, during the course of their live-in lessons, the infallible gods fall for their off-limits charge? This is a why choose romance.

∼

Bedlam Penitentiary (Incomplete)

Bedlam Penitentiary (TBA)

At the most ruthless prison in the fae realm, you're either at the top of the magical food chain, or you've got to form alliances with those with the most power. Because at a prison where you must expend your magic or you'll die, it's a no man's land full of dangerous criminals. This is a why choose romance.

Printed in Dunstable, United Kingdom